Interference

by

Jim Blackstone

Golden Acorn Press

Cover Art © 2010 Seth Crossman

A Golden Acorn Press Book
384 Markowitz Road
Parish, NY 13131

Copyright © 2010 by James Steimle
ISBN 978-0-9801921-3-1
First Edition November 2010

Printed in the United States of America

To Gary Barben,
my first friend in a strange, new world

Acknowledgements

Special Thanks appropriately goes to Philip K. Dick, whose run-for-your-life science fiction adventures clearly influenced this story; Officer Richard Weber, for sharing his expertise in police procedure; my editor and my publisher, whose creativity and care of fiction have helped bring you this volume; and my gorgeous wife, for her unfailing support in my Call to Art.

Chapter One

The best way to commit a crime is to have someone else do it for you.

—Milar Burton
Last Man In Prison

*B*link. *Blink.*

"Are my eyes open?"

"Just relax. And concentrate.

"But I can't see anything."

"Optical blindness is a tiny side effect."

"Oh. Oh! How could you—how dare you! Let me out."

"Still yourself. Think only a little. Push the interference away from your consciousness. Guide your wandering mind. You will see. Wait for it."

"I shouldn't have trusted you!"

"Funny thing to say, in your current state. Peace! Damien—"

"Who do you work for? Who, really?"

"Right now, I work for you. I'm working for free, I might add. Tough days to work for free. Enough of this! Be still. Now...still...better. Good. Now..."

"Now what?"

Whisper.

"Who is that? Who is here with you?"

"Damien. Do you remember the code?"

"Who—"

"Damien..."

"First—tell me. Are my eyes open?"

"Your eyes..."

Outside of one horrible little glitch, Damien Reyes had never experienced a better day in all of his memory. A perfect day! Or almost perfect. Never a happier day, not that Damien could recall, at least. It was even better than that lonely Christmas afternoon that had started the hope, the joy: the day that had abruptly sent him back to work and onto a collision course with the most beautiful woman in the world.

It wasn't hard to remember.

Remember?

Another man would charm the new girl soon enough. The thought led to panic that drove him to chitchat and then, finally to ask Caleigha Obregon to Saturday lunch and anti-grav golf at the family fun park. She'd said yes, and Damien had thought *that* had been the best day of his life.

But *this* day!

They had dated for almost six months, slowly at first, rarely. Their relationship had been chaste in the extreme. They had been saving their first kiss. For what? They never said. But the magnetism and erotic tension between them was consequently more powerful than anything that Damien had ever felt before. The time would come. And now...

Caleigha came to the rowdy Family Anti-Grav Park dressed in white shorts and sports shoes, a swaying blouse that danced from her collarbone each time she moved a millimeter. And she'd curled her hair into long, tubular ringlets. She smiled so much, Damien's eyes couldn't keep away. And she noticed. And kept smiling, seemingly flattered.

Caleigha's parents had opted for a Female 127, what some people had dubbed one of the ultimate "sporty" models. The 127 Female came with a medium-blonde hair color, which Caleigha had turned brown with the added "shadow" highlights that had become so popular in the last decade. The medical chart described the 127 XX as rugged and resilient, naturally inclined to muscular mass and enhanced bone definition for durability. They made great athletes—that was the promise. Most people called them big boned, and when the 127s didn't choose an athletic life, they tended to be overweight, sometimes masculine, and socially outcast.

But then, cloning had always been more art than science. Clones never turned out the same, not a single pair anywhere. Not only did they *look* different in the fine details, but even their genetic tendencies did not corral their freedom of thought and expression.

So Caleigha Obregon fell somewhere between the 127 XX Olympian-type and the 127 XX waddling ball of helpless cellulite and whining misery. She had a thicker chin than most women, larger cheekbones, and big brown eyes. She was curvy with a thin waist. Damien couldn't look away, even when he tried quite ardently. Why did she look so beautiful?

Caleigha glowed—of course, her makeup sparkled and literally radiated light when the sunbeams at the park hit her just right. But that wasn't what Damien was thinking. Caleigha Obregon glowed from the inside. She was an element of extraordinary power encased in a recognizable replica of some super-fit woman in the history books.

And she wasn't fat. Not at all. Or rather, she was muscular and "big boned"—yes, okay, she was that. She also had such a smoothness and softness from the rounded line of her jaw, down her arms, over her legs. She just was not inappropriately proportioned. Every move she made enticed him, and she made every move on purpose, catching him noticing her.

All through lunch in the little child-themed restaurant, Caleigha laughed. Lights flashed around them. The air smelled of cotton candy and bubble gum. He told the worst jokes—horrible jokes, only because he was so nervous. But Caleigha seemed riveted to his words. Bells and whistles from the holographic carnival games played music and cheers throughout the park.

They talked of work at CCSN. They spun visions of the future. Having studied mathematics successfully in college, Damien worked as an accountant, while Caleigha labored as an inner-office courier and administrative assistant that caught everyone's eye as she passed through the offices.

And while discussing their Utopian ideas during the anti-grav golf game—the ball zinging through space, hitting a red dragon, and then rebounding in their direction—the one bad part of the "almost perfect" day occurred.

"And in a perfect world, who shall be the President of the North American Union?" she said. Then she screamed, leaping out of the path of the pitted ball.

Damien watched her float into the air and come down again. Caleigha's hair fell and bounced on her shoulders. But his vision clouded over despite all that sunshine. "Someone better than Henry Sanchez."

"What, you don't like The Sanch?" She giggled, and the melody of her voice pulled him up from the pit of dark emotion that had nearly swallowed him whole.

Like Henry Waldorf Sanchez? Who could like that man after his invasion of the moon's Dandelion Crater? Damien's father, expatriated, had been living there. His mother had herself euthanized when she received the terrible news. No one had survived the holocaust, and—*WHY did the North American Union need to "liberate" Dandelion and bring it into the fold anyway? They were doing fine unhindered by the politics down here! And*

Mom didn't need to go and put herself to sleep—that was the President's fault just as much as it was hers! No resource could be worth that kind of war—and YES it was all about resources—it had nothing to do with freeing anyone—

Damien had felt himself seething, boiling over the top, *Don't get me started!*

It was just a little glitch, in the day.

It could have ruined everything.

But the ball missed Caleigha as she hopped to the side. She laughed, recapturing his attention. And when she bent to fix the back of her left shoe, and looked up at him, and said through her perfect lips, "That was close! Had I fallen the other way, I might have knocked you over," she might as well have said, *Damien, I have never been so happy as I am, here with you.*

Damien said, "I would have caught you."

"You would have?" She straightened into an upright arch that quickened his heart.

"Most definitely."

Caleigha took a step toward him, and it felt as if she were somehow stepping *into* him. She brightened. And her voice grew a pinch softer. "Then I wish I had fallen."

From that moment on, Caleigha walked into his comfort zone and stayed. He loved the scent of her perfume, the warmth. He could not resist the gravity of her presence. They moved about the park, but kept bumping gently into one another. They stopped one another from tripping, a dozen times or more, by reaching out and feeling an arm, a shoulder, a hip. She "borrowed" his anti grav putter, and he took hers, and they swapped again and again, and laughed, and kept laughing.

Parting was wonderful and terrible. She kissed him on the cheek and then ran away, leaving promises of Utopia tomorrow.

At home, he dropped his keys, bent down to pick them up, and stopped halfway. He rechecked his senses, then sniffed his shirt.

It was the scent of Caleigha's perfume. It wrapped him like a dream. It held him in all that wonderful memory and longing. He ran Caleigha's phone number through his head.

No. Must wait. Don't want to seem too eager. Don't want to ruin everything. Like when she mentioned the President.

The President.

Damien glowered.

Then he picked up his keys, stood, and smelled Caleigha again.

For the rest of the day, he replayed his date with Caleigha Obregon. He retired to his bed, thinking, *Yes. The best day of my life! Why can't such things last forever? Perhaps there is a way … I could go into business, making a single memory last, replay, stretch endlessly, until the client's contract runs out or the client dies. I'd make billions! Oh, the power of a single memory…* He thought of Caleigha again… Caleigha…

When he fell asleep, he slowly left the games of recall altogether.

And Damien Reyes did not wake again for eight days.

Blink-blink.

"My eyes are shut. I'm not dreaming, am I."

"No. Not dreaming. You're remembering."

"This can't be happening."

"It is, Damien. Wake up now."

"You said I wasn't dreaming… Are you still there?"

Chapter Two

We are creatures constantly bombarded by quantum effect. You fall asleep at night. By morning, you have been altered by so many unpredicted variables that your entire path has changed, your memories have changed. Your past and future have changed. You are not the person you were the night before. But as the inside observer of your life, you are completely unaware of the alterations. In fact, you are lucky that you still exist at all. You might not, come tomorrow morning. And no one would know the difference.

—Jerusha Esteves
Alternatives in Parallel Effect

The President's Primary Chief of Staff, Martin Warren, had been opposed to the trip north from the beginning. "You *know* what kind of people live up there."

"Yes," said Henry Sanchez as he chose a top hat to go with his tuxedo. "The rich and the poor. Americans! Same as everywhere else."

"Begging your pardon, Mr. President, but they aren't the same as everywhere else. And we haven't had the proper amount of time to prepare for this trip."

"Do you like this hat?" The President was a tall man with dark skin and keen opalescent eyes. He showed his well-studied grin to his political ally.

Warren said nothing.

"Too Abraham Lincoln, you think?"

Warren sighed and rubbed his temples. The PCS had a distinctive frog-like quality brought on by the extra weight he'd packed around his face and midsection for that warm and fatherly look that analysts believed would boost his ratings in the public eye.

"Stop worrying. Those who wish to kill me will go wherever I go. Right, Warren?"

"That argument is not logical enough to put yourself in harm's way."

"I'm always in harm's way!" Sanchez chuckled the wet laugh comedians just loved to mock. "I'm the President of the North American Union—the good old NAU! What are you really worried about, Warren? Retaliation from Lunar colonies? You think they have microwave cannons power-ful enough to do more than blast satellites out of their sky? Those people shouldn't have left the Union." He waved his hand, dismissing the disturb-ing images. "I have enough intelligence on this matter to help me sleep at night. Anywhere on the planet."

"Most anywhere, you mean," said Warren. "Your enemies run far and go deep. Like rats."

"Yes." The President turned and presented his bow tie to Martin Warren as if the gentleman was little more than a closet servant. He dropped his hands, lifted his chin, and waited. "Rats abound, no matter how one tries to kill them off. And yet, humankind has always survived that particular plague. Come on, Warren!" He flapped his hands at his side.

Warren started tying the tie.

"What's really bothering you? Don't want our beloved Vice President to take my place, is that it? You're not one of those men secretly opposed to having a female boss, are you?"

"It's her political party that bothers me." Warren growled. "In the old days, the President and Vice President didn't cross party lines to appease the people. They *stood* for something."

"Ha. I stand for something." Sanchez faced the mirror. "Truth! Justice! The American economy!" He laughed again, almost slobbering this time.

"I *don't* want her to become the President, okay? No secret there. But I'd serve her just as honestly and fervently as I am serving you. The North-ern States are unruly. That's my point. Since we lost the ice cap, everyone and their dog who doesn't fit into society has run north like it's a new coun-try to be populated."

"It almost is! All that land dredged up by the real estate brokers? Do you recall your history? There was a day when oil ruled the world. Now it's the land sellers and land makers and land finders…" Sanchez walked to the window and frowned at the moon. He stood there for a minute without speaking, his brow creasing.

Warren decided to try one last time. "Mr. President…"

"Go west, young man," Sanchez said in distant voice. "Go *north*, young man. Go…up… out there… young man." He turned and offered his Chief of Staff a tired grin. "It is the American way: this idea that we can all carve out a life for ourselves, for our families, regardless of our birth."

"Yes, Mr. President."

"They paid me an invitation, Warren. The first graduating class from the first true Ivy League university near the pole. How can I say no to that?"

"Say no."

"No, Warren. I'm leaving. And you will make sure that the head of the American government is going stay alive." President Henry Sanchez left the room.

Unaccompanied, Martin Warren said, "Will I?"

Chapter Three

There is no such thing as time travel. Or rather, time travel happens at all times, all around us. But we cannot travel in time in the science fictional sense. We move forward, nanosecond by nanosecond, but cannot leap into the future. We cannot go back into the past. Not exactly, anyway. Yet our memories hide in the past—and there are an infinite number of pasts. Likewise, we head towards an infinite number of different futures. Do any two of us ever realize the same timeline ahead? No, never. From the relative standpoint of ourselves, we can say that the universe takes place around each of us as individuals. Everyone else is little more than a mathematical variable.

—Gabrielle McPheresen Redfield
Before Infinity's Reach

The First Graduating Class of Philibuck University should not have been a major police event. Even then, Captain Dewitter shouldn't have called Detective Harvey Corvasce to the scene when no murder had occurred. In fact, Corvasce had plenty of other cases on his desk that required attention—especially after Mayor Brunner began his No Cold Case Initiative, the promise that every case would be solved. Corvasce had complained to Captain Dewitter just how ludicrous that initiative was, and how that initiative would likely nudge cops to file false reports, when they were on the line to becoming dirty but might not have otherwise crossed it.

Now this. A problem ready to explode.

"We need bodies," Dewitter had said. "The President himself will be here and Mayor Brunner wants all the force in action."

"So that criminals can do what they want in our absence and get away? We'll end up doubling our case load in an afternoon."

"All the force? How did my partner get out of this?"

"All that we can spare. Please don't plague me with questions to which you already know the answers."

But it wasn't the Captain's decision, and they both knew it. Federal statute mandated local law enforcement participation in times of need. "Call it job security. Get out there."

Detective Corvasce surveyed the scene like any detective might.

It was an outdoor auditorium on a beautiful northern day. The temperature was just cool enough to require a jacket capable of concealing a weapon while warm enough to allow one's head to remain uncovered. Corvasce wore a hat anyway. The hat matched his overcoat. He noticed that most of the visiting audience, including all the g-men, wore hats that hid their faces or at least their eyes from distant scrutiny.

At least no one wore ornamental masks. Masks were, of course, illegal in the President's presence. They were illegal everywhere.

There were easily as many women in suits and hats as there were men, and it didn't take long for Corvasce to spy Secret Service agents dressed in plainclothes, milling around like everyone else in anticipation of the music. They weren't talking to anybody. Just looking around, at everyone.

Atop the buildings stood the robots.

Corvasce hated robots. And these were military grade, possibly UVI-MX Heavy Armored Frogs, no doubt rushed over from Kingdom AFB across the border because the President decided at the last minute to accept some doofus administrator's invitation to the graduation. The robots looked like dirt-covered boxes with large eyes protected by a dim energy field. Dual cannons aimed like arms ready to blast everyone in the crowd. Corvasce could see the squat legs of the nearest automated stooge as it shifted position.

Robots.

Even with checks in place, robots made more mistakes than human beings—Corvasce believed this after plenty of personal experiences with ride-along automatons, regardless of the "statistics."

Every building with a line of sight around the open-air auditorium had been cleared. The police had that job, and the Secret Service did a double check, followed by multiple rechecks. Each building had a real-time scanner focused on its interior, so that the officers lucky enough to remain in the office could keep an eye out for humanoid heat signatures, listen for whispered discussions of cloaked assailants, and watch the readings on weapon sniffers.

Walking atop the buildings, agents in dark suits studied the swelling crowd. They used Type 4 MagWif Binoculars, what Corvasce and his friends in law enforcement called Gun-ocs. Anyone stupid enough to carry a firearm—even an electric—to a place where the President was visiting, would get caught.

"So why do I have to be here again?" Corvasce mumbled. "This place is already covered more thoroughly than journalists covered the destruction of India."

Through the com link attached just under the skin to the bone beneath his right temple, Captain Dewitter said, "Quit your bawling, Detective. He's here."

Corvasce straightened. A childish buzz ran up his spine and down to his fingertips, and if anybody had noticed the twitch, he would have flushed beet red. He couldn't help the sudden exhilaration: he was about to see the President of the North American Union. The boss! Corvasce suddenly wished he had come to the graduation in uniform.

The crowd was catching wind that something was happening.

The music started.

Authorities in and out of plainclothes went on alert. Some, to the detective's eye, looked terrified, others just as excited as Corvasce felt.

The buzz left him. Or so he thought, before realizing how hard his blood pump was throbbing.

Everyone stood, some on tiptoe.

And then...a bunch of school administrators and instructors entered, stage left, kicking their black robes forward and holding onto their mortarboards when the wind threatened to blow them off. Some were lucky enough to have hoods, which they held to the sides of their faces. Others were cursed with ribbons of special honor, cords, and medals. The ornaments flapped in the wind on the stage, and one mighty brain lost a soft blue sash and had to go running after it.

There was laughter. Someone caught the academic award and handed it back. There was cheering. The music continued.

The graduates entered from the rear and walked between the rows of visitors and took their seats. The intolerable waiting reminded Corvasce that he should be watching the crowd for shady figures.

But there were so many!

"Everyone looks guilty. How do I tell the undercover goons from the bad guys?" he said into his com.

The Captain didn't answer.

Corvasce changed channels and listened to the President's play by play. He was already here, evidently, and the version Corvasce received was not going to be as accurate or as thorough as the Secret Service dictation: the local cops weren't made privy to the federal channels.

A female voice—sounded like a 227 XX—spoke quietly and calmly, measuring her pace so as not to disrupt the thinking of those who might be trying to split their attention between her words and the details around them. "The President is waiting for his green from SS. Okay, he's moving now. Main Hall, Exeter Building. He's stopping. Look's like they are holding him. Some conversation going on."

The last of the graduates, standing at the end of a long line, entered the outdoor auditorium. Instead of the black gown of his fellow classmates, he wore a black hospital gown that wasn't visible to Corvasce until the kid passed. Then through the open back, his bright green boxer shorts started a peal of laughter. Standing tall and proud, the kid with the green underwear waited for the jam of people ahead of him to get seated before he could move again.

The 227 XX (was that Millie Penoza's voice? She's a 12 XX, not a 227) mentioned that it seemed the President might have been waiting for the graduates as well. Then she said that something else was going on. "He's turning around. Now, now he's facing the auditorium again. Looks like a heated argument going on." She tried to hide the amusement in her voice, but it leaked through a little. "Okay—wait a minute!—they are starting to—"

Captain Dewitter's voice engaged a channel change override and the voice of the 227 or 12 XX disappeared, even as Corvasce put a hand to the side of his head to hear her better. "All right everybody, scour the crowd. We're looking for a *male 141*, approximately six feet in height, blue eyes— prettiest blue eyes you've ever seen, so I hear. Last seen in a gray Laissez Faire jacket with four pockets on the front, black jeans, runner's shoes. This man was held at Checkpoint Three and disappeared."

"Is he wearing a hat?" Corvasce said.

The detective was watching the stage a hundred yards away. The last of the graduates took their seats and the photographers were moving into position. All eyes swiveled to the Exeter Building and the door nearest the stage.

The music shifted to the latest rock and roll presidential beat.

"Everyone's wearing a hat."

The crowd boiled over, cheering, screaming, jumping in their seats and into the aisles to get a better look.

"Not everyone," Corvasce said. He shouted into his com, though he couldn't be sure. "Foot of the stage! 141 XY! The photographers—the photographers!"

Corvasce ran hard into family guests and political rubberneckers who immediately choked the aisle. He slammed two to the ground, rammed his tall 260 pounds between the shoulders of everyone else.

He tried to keep his eyes on the suspect. Heads and hands and uplifted cameras in the way blocked his vision. On the stage, Secret Service agents touched their imbedded com links and reacted according to their training.

At the same time, Corvasce changed the channel back to Millie Penoza, just as she said, "...is coming out."

All the air and the sound in the auditorium seemed to suck away, specifically in the direction of the threshold where President Henry W. Sanchez was appearing just outside of Detective Corvasce's sight.

Then the suction of air and sound released. A bang rippled away from the President's position. The crowd gasped in shock at the first sensation, screamed at the second. People on the stage fell over. Corvasce lost his hat.

Millie Penoza said nothing.

Captain Dewitter forced a channel change.

Detective Corvasce watched his hat get trampled as he pushed against a massive tide of escaping humans shoving for the exits. He changed the channel himself. "What's happening!"

No one answered.

Corvasce worked his way to a wall so that he wasn't ejected entirely from the auditorium. When the fleeing crowd thinned enough for the detective to make headway against the throng, he ran in the direction of the President, the photographers, and the people who weren't running for their lives.

Toppled chairs had scattered in every direction. It was almost impossible not to trip.

As he shouted "Police! Let me in there!" and tried to squeeze through the onlookers, who struggled themselves to get a look at what had actually happened, Corvasce caught sight of the robots swiveling their heavy guns back and forth over the menagerie. "Pandam Police Department! Come on, people, get out of my way!"

Finally, he reached a human barrier of government agents holding force batons.

Detective Harvey Corvasce waved his pulsing blue and red badge before their faces. They still didn't let him through.

The Secret Service had not caught his suspect.

And President Henry Waldorf Sanchez had entirely imploded.

Chapter Four

Mathematicians such as Gaelin W. Ortiz and Matilda Krishnamorti have posited evidence of a grand design surrounding this limited universe. There is too much order in the chaos, so that chaos itself manifests a beautiful array from the correct perspective. If there is a grand design, then the problem (beyond the endless argument over the existence of one or more creative deities) is that the equation is so vast that the best mathematics the world has ever known are simply not yet developed enough to solve it. One thing is certain from the mathematically objective point of view: There really is no such thing as chaos, in the old-fashioned sense of the word.

Everything is happening just as it should.

—Benjamina Hurish
Correcting Visions

"*We'll try again, shall we?*"

"*Now?*"

"*If you're ready.*"

"*I don't know. I am. I think I am.*"

"*Just relax.*"

"*Relax? You actually think, after everything that has happened, that I can relax.*"

"*Sorry… but do we really know what has happened?*"

"*Just do it.*"

"*I'm not trying to argue with you.*"

"*Is it suppose to hurt like this?*"

"*Of course. Memories hurt. That's why we forget.*"

"That's not what I meant."
"Shut your eyes, if you want."
"I'll still see, won't I."
"Um ..."
"Won't I?"

A gentle pulsing sound woke Damien Reyes from an uneasy dream. There had been an explosion of some kind, and people running, and Caleigha Obregon was sitting sideways on a quilt on a grassy hill in a park. She was smiling, and her full hair lifted and fell in the wind. The collar and hem of her blue and white summer dress moved. She blinked her brown eyes at him, shimmered. And she laughed. And then Damien was running down the hill, down amidst the heavy crowds, screaming with men and women in a stormy darkness—and then his phone was ringing.

A gentle pulsing sound.

He sat up, groaned. He rubbed his face. He knuckled one eye.

"What time is it?"

The clock said, "9:51 AM."

The gentle pulsing sound continued.

"9:51?"

He rolled from the bed.

It was work. They were calling him from the office. And if Chance Bucket or Allison Chakuaina waited on the other end for him to pick up, he would be fine—mostly fine—but if Yuri Espinosa waited, sighing, drumming his fat fingertips, Damien would be nailed to the wall and possibly *fined* for his tardiness. He considered playing ill.

"Hello?"

The voice on the other end had an edge sharper than any boss he had ever known. "About time, Mr. Reyes."

"Hello?" Damien meant to say, *Who is this?* But he thought the question too forward and settled on repeating his prior inquiry.

"You will never see Caleigha Obregon again. Do you understand?"

"What? Wait. Who are you?" He waved his hand for a readout screen. A sheen of light appeared like a plate of glass fifteen inches from his nose. He touched TELEPHONE. The lights rearranged themselves in an artistic whirlwind and settled with dramatic graphics on the call's information page.

Prepaid phone: # Abraxas 98001.

Name: Unknown.

Location: The Kingdom.

Address: 7240 South 12100 West.

"If you don't do exactly what I say, Ms. Obregon will sink to the bottom of the Jordan. You have two seconds to decide."

A scream followed.

The high pitch stabbed Damien in both ears. He covered them and looked at the walls, where hidden speakers were directing privacy beams at his head. The call traveled along the beams, and for once in his life he wished he could reach up and block the sound waves from hitting him. But the science didn't work that way.

The scream abated.

Could have been Caleigha. Could have been anyone.

Damien was paralyzed. He stood at the side of the bed and felt his skin grow cold. His heart quickened. He stopped breathing.

"That will do," said the caller. "Get dressed."

Damien looked at the shaded window. Were they watching him? Polarized windows blocked outside viewers, except for when the window was set by the inside operator for two-way viewing. Only the police and the military had the technology to see into buildings. And crime lords. The tech was illegal.

"Get dressed!" The voice turned friendly and then cold and gritty. "You don't seem to understand. In about a minute and a half, you will be visited by some very unhappy police. If they reach you before you get out of the building, I will personally make sure your pretty maiden here goes under the knife? Comprende?"

"Okay-okay!"

He approached the dressing wall, which opened drawers in anticipation of his needs. He pulled on a black pair of pants—

"Faster! You only have seconds now. Move!"

He threw on a pink pullover, grabbed his midnight suede shoes—

"You want the Izod Sprinters!"

His hands released the suede, snatched the running shoes.

"Thirty seconds. Don't put them on—just take them! Go! Grab your jacket! By the front door. Twenty-three seconds! If they get you, she dies!"

Damien hit the doorframe, bounced off. He tagged the end table beside the couch and went down, knocking his chin into the white floor hard enough to cause an explosion of light in his vision.

"Up! Move it!"

One hand took the gray Laissez Faire jacket.

A camera was on the floor beside the door. "Take the camera!" said the grouch as the apartment door slid open. "You don't have ten seconds!"

Without thinking, Damien snatched up the camera.

"Turn left! Up to the roof! Move it! And go mobile!"

The white lights of the hallway turned red and began to flash. A voice-over erupted on loudspeaker, broadcasting from every apartment, every hallway, even the custodial closets. *"This a police lockdown situation. Everyone please remain calm."*

Damien's apartment door slid shut and locked. His jaw dropped. He had stopped just outside and was still standing close enough for the room to anticipate his need for the portal to remain open. His room had changed color as well—he saw that as the door shut. The red matched the pulsing lights in the hall. Then all he could see was the door. When had he *ever* had his own door shut on him?

The elevator lights began to sing of an upcoming car.

He ran away.

"Now you're too late," said the voice on the right side of his skull. "So much for your girlfriend. So long."

"I can make it!"

"If Ms. Obregon dies, it will be your fault!"

"I can get to the roof!"

"Not if the cops running up the stairs catch you first. How do you expect to get through the door?"

Damien slammed into the white portal. His body crashed to the floor. He grabbed his elbow, positive that he'd splintered the bone.

"Get up! No more communication—they are tracking you. See you on the roof, or I'll see your pretty lady breathing H20 at the bottom of the river. Adios."

Damien crawled to his feet. He touched the door. He walked in a circle, staring at the ceiling. He kicked the door. Nothing happened, it was made to hold back flames—and criminals on the run. What was he going to do? "Fire!" he shouted. "Occupant 1537! Fire!"

The building responded via direct beam communication. *"Occupant 1537 wanted by police. All privileges denied."*

"But I'm reporting a fire! Fire! Occupant 1537!"

"All privileges denied."

He kicked the door again, cradled his busted elbow.

Then he touched his personal com implant. "Building Manager."

A moment later, the super spoke with his British/Nepalese accent. "Damien, what is going on? You are sought by Peace Keepers?"

"Hundi, no time to talk! I saw a fire in the hallway just before I returned to my room and the doors locked. The building isn't doing anything! No one else saw the flames! I tried to report it, but the building said—"

"Your privileges are denied, yes I know!"

"Don't you get it, Hundi? Even if I stay in my room, the fire is going to spread! How many people are going to get hurt?"

"I'm not reading a fire..."

The elevator door made its old-fashioned *bong* sound, indicating the arrival of the maglift transport.

Damien turned and pressed his face into the door. In a much quieter voice, he said in a desperate tone, "That's my point! Since when have sensors become perfect? The fifteenth floor will burn. Nothing will stop those flames! The walls outside—"

"Caramba! I get it already!"

A single blip indicated Hundi's disconnection.

Police poured out of the elevator, stun guns raised before their white body armor.

Damien braced himself. Not for the shot in the back that would bewilder the nerves of his body, sap all his muscles of strength, and drop his limp form to quiver on the floor. He braced for the death of his dream girl.

Why is this happening?

"What are you trying to do? Damien, you shouldn't get up now."

"We're running out of time."

"We've only started."

"No. You've only started. I have to get out of here."

"Damien, you're safe here, remember. Safe."

"There isn't a place in this solar system where I am safe anymore."

"That's not true."

"Take this off. I have to go!"

"No, Damien. You have to remember. Memories seem real."

"You said they are real."

"Yes, but remembering this way makes it seem real now. Don't you see? That was then. Do you understand? Our emotions do not easily distinguish between the two time frames. Look at this screen. You are exhibiting all the symptoms of panic: quickening of breath; adrenaline; increased heart rate—even skipping a beat here and there, I see—"

"It's real."

"It was. And I know it feels real. You have to trust me."

"Trust you. Think so? How can I trust anyone anymore?"

Chapter Five

According to Yvonne Yu Lee's thesis on the Multidimensionality of Temporal Events (a paper that caused an unexpected commotion that led to her international renown and bestselling book deal), there are not only an endless number of split ("parallel and semiparallel") timelines running concurrently, there are also a similar number of timelines running non-concurrently. Stripped of Dr. Lee's mathematical arguments and colorful diction, she theorized that if one managed to slip from one of these non-concurrent timelines, one might be in the past or in the future. If this same traveler managed to jump back to the home timeline, the traveler would find himself or herself in the present age, and the only amount of time that would have transpired would have been the time it took for each trip plus the time spent in the other timeline. Which is to say, seemingly parallel universes may be further ahead or further back in time.

—Joanna Forte
Beyond Paradox And Other Delights

"Captain! The President is dead. I repeat—" But Detective Corvasce shut his mouth. Despite the stench of the imploded corpse, a smell that seemed to have spread far and wide and caught on every surface, Harvey Corvasce was busy collecting details with his fine-tuned brain. And he'd stumbled upon something seemingly peripheral to the catastrophe.

It was the shouting of the other law enforcement agents that had distracted him. They yelled at each other. Like school kids, they ran in circles talking to the air, bellowing, turning to face people who were busy facing others, everyone crying out and only few listening. They reached for light screens that wouldn't appear. They scratched the side of their faces as if there were buttons to push when there weren't any.

All the communication links were down.

The Secret Service had managed a human barricade on training alone. They had cordoned off the building's side entrance and the immediate vicinity. But the line wouldn't hold. Didn't they have any taser tape?

Someone fired a stun gun. A burly woman twisted and fell, quivering with aftershocks that would last three minutes—fewer if she was lucky.

The crowd of reporters and lookie loos dropped back.

"You'd think we were all blindfolded," said Corvasce to himself. He spun around, watched the mad exodus. Every suspect was on the move. They might have already run clear of the university. And with communications interrupted, no one was receiving the orders to lock down the campus.

Corvasce ran for the exit, memorizing everything he could as he went.

There were bodies on the ground, dropped baggage, windblown hats, trash. Huddled groups cried out for help around writhing victims. Undercover agents and uniformed men alike spoke to their dead radios. A few hammered into the building on the far side of the auditorium complex, raiding the lobby as if following suspects. But, really, everyone on the run was a suspect now.

The air stank of something like burned copper.

Above the auditorium police birds hovered in circular patterns, their heads twitching back and forth as they watched the human flotsam and jetsam. Good. But when had they received clearance to enter the zone when such surveillance and potential weapon bearers were outlawed in the President's vicinity? Before or after the implosion? The UVI-MX Frogs atop the buildings weren't shooting them down.

Corvasce redirected his attention toward the auditorium exits. He scanned for the fingered suspect—Corvasce wondered if he had even seen him at all; he could have been mistaken. The 141 XY might have been a decoy, or completely unrelated to the weighty crime.

After all, why in this day and age would anyone attack the President in person? The perp would be identified. There would be no escape. Except …had the man escaped already?

Corvasce needed a camera. With any luck, the orbiting eyes in the sky had recorded every detail and detectives far away were already scouring the data. Even better: Corvasce hoped authorities were tracking the culprit or culprits, moving on the suspects, and solving the crime. He doubted the chase into the building across the quad was little more than a run after confused innocents looking for a way out of the horror.

So why did he feel desperate for a camera? In fact, he really wanted to gather every set of automated eyes in the place.

It was all wrong. All of this. President Sanchez couldn't be dead. He couldn't be killed! Not like this. Not so quickly, publicly, invisibly.

Someone had countered the sturdy and cryptic communication systems of local law enforcement and federal agents simultaneously. Someone with a weapon that Detective Corvasce had never seen had killed the President of the North American Union before the figurehead could finish crossing a threshold into full view of the public. Could these same someones blind satellites—even secret and specially tasked satellites—crossing high above the arctic for the protection of a world leader?

If there was one thing that Harvey Corvasce had learned in his years as a detective, it was that criminals would *always* discover a way around the greatest security measures of any age—eventually.

He reached the exit without spotting a single man or woman wearing a camera. How was that possible? Cameras bounced. That was the problem. So everyone running with a camera had either snatched away the device from its hanging position above their ear or forgotten about it and unwittingly let it fall to be trampled by the fleeing masses.

Corvasce checked the ground.

Sure enough. One elongated visual recording device, the size and shape of a short fountain pen, had dropped, been kicked, and slid to the base of a raised planter. He ran for it. Picking it up, he said, "Police override delta-three-zero-lima-one, Harvey Corvasce, Detective."

"Override acknowledged," said the camera, and despite its scratched silver case and banged head, it projected a light screen. The screen vanished the moment it appeared; if Corvasce had blinked, he wouldn't have seen it at all.

"Indicate battery life," he said.

"Remaining battery life," said the female camera, "approximately 244 hours of activity."

"Light screen," Corvasce said again.

The little machine should have said, *Inoperable.* Instead, it acted as if he had given no command at all.

"Storage space?" he said, wondering if the camera had lost its voice recognition capacity. He was already looking around for another camera, one that hadn't bounced around as much as this.

"Storage. Seventy percent remaining," said the fluid voice.

"So your hearing's fine. Can you record?"

"Yes."

"Record now."

A red light switched on. Detective Corvasce turned the camera in every direction, including up, then clipped the camera over his ear.

A clawing hand snagged his shoulder.

Corvasce spun around in a neck-spike maneuver. His fingers stopped an inch from penetrating the police officer's windpipe.

"Hold on, now! You know what's going on, Detective? I can't get anyone on my—"

"We need to seal off the University!"

"Good luck. Two more minutes, everyone on campus will be press officials or too dumb to have participated in this fiasco." The cop was a young 127 XX, fit, tall, powerful, her hair an ivory color almost as white as her uniform. Terror shifted behind her eyes. "This had to be an inside job. They'll want to question every one of us. We are *all* suspects here."

He didn't have time for arguments. Evidence was getting trampled. Witnesses were running for their lives. Killers were getting away.

But the snow-headed officer's words had merit, and they shifted the direction of the wheels in his head.

How else could the President have been murdered?

How was Sanchez murdered?

"There!" said the 127 XX. "Secret Service is tagging everyone. Do you see?"

Corvasce looked out the exits. Outside the auditorium where trees still grew attached to spikes in the ground, hundreds of people scattered in every direction. Below the flag of NAU stars framed in two stripes of red and white, he saw the words written on the building: Administration.

So close? And no one's thought to make an announcement over the loudspeakers? Maybe they don't work—maybe there aren't any! It is a new institution, after all—only four years old. But ... what if there is a local broadcast system, for old fashioned emergencies? And what if all the authorities are just assuming that the system doesn't work?

He spun on his heels again. "Officer..." he smiled like an old friend, looked at the Spartan label on her breast, "Tangier." He added a twinkle to his eye. "I'm going to give you a very important job, and there isn't a moment to lose. You see that building over there?"

"Administration?"

"They must have a university-wide communications node in there."

"Yes but it's probably—"

"Get it activated. Tell everyone this is a police lock down and that no one is to leave the campus. If they have a working phone, call transit. We need to freeze all the vehicles. Are you following me?"

"Yes, but—"

"Just go!" Corvasce smiled with every word, then tugged her shoulder so hard he nearly tossed her through the exit. Officer Tangier was big, but Corvasce was an 80 XY, so he was bigger.

Before she reached the administrative building, however, the Pandam City sonic shield initiated. The initial clap of sound forced Corvasce to cover his ears and duck; the radiant hum shivered his skin. The blood drained from his face, chilling his cheeks instantly, because Corvasce not only identified the shield while others panicked in shock, but he knew about the rare threats that might actually initiate the automated defense perimeter.

So he knew he was about to die.

Chapter Six

"Perception creates a fascinating web of lies by which one rules one's personal existence," wrote Hamdu Darhea. Selective Memory studies have shown time and time again that what we think we have seen is actually a gathering of those relatively few details upon which we focused in any given moment. In that same moment, more than one hundred times as many details occurred within the easy reach of senses, especially and particularly in our direct line of sight. We remember only what we perceive in the moment of an event. As a result, we jump from one misunderstood incident to another, arranging "memories" and "experiences" that are little more than what Dr. Darhea calls a Neural Pattern of Lies. "When one looks back on this spread of misconstruction, one thinks, That's my life! Yes, my whole life. In such a case, the viewer is inevitably wrong." We are all slaves to our own confusion. When we agree on this confusion, we call it sanity and we call it science.

—Pear Dominic Utterhill
The Diverse Universe Within Humankind

"Are my eyes open?"

"They are."

"Why don't I see you?"

"What do you see, Damien?"

"My eyes are open. My eyes …"

"Damien. Why don't you want to tell me? After all we've been through. Why don't you trust me?"

"Are you sure? My eyes are open?"

"Don't they feel open to you?"
"Yes. I think. They do."
"Then why are you questioning your own senses? What do you see?"
"What do I—"

At the very moment when the police burst from the elevator car and onto the fifteenth floor, the dry sprinklers came on. Clouds of foam erased the police and all the doors along the hallway from view.

And the fire doors popped open.

Damien Reyes almost fell into the stairwell. Slick with fire-foam, his socks lost traction. He went down again. He dropped the camera. He wanted to put on the shoes he carried.

No time.

Caleigha, he thought.

And the gravelly voice in his head wasn't talking anymore.

He was up and running again, shoes in one hand, camera in the other. He had never seen that camera before. Or had his mother owned one like this, taken a picture of him with it, just before his father hugged her, stepped onto the lift, and left on the lunar shuttle? Damien could still see her scowling, weeping, hiding behind the camera as she recorded her husband's insane departure.

The thunder of police boots shook the air below him. The red flashing light throttled the stairwell at each level. Damien bumped into each swinging door at every floor. He reached the roof, found that door unlocked, and pulled it open.

A cab floated into view.

"You want me to take the cab?" he said. But his com link was connected to no one.

He moved to call it, then remembered the voice of the man who had threatened Caleigha's life. *No more communication—they are tracking you.*

He waved the floater down.

The driver looked confused. Then he nodded with a grin that split his face, as if recognizing that this was the passenger he had been summoned to pick up.

The cab settled with a hum that always managed to irritate Damien's molars. The back passenger door rolled into the roof. "The police are here?" said a comedian's voice, waiting for a punch line or a laugh.

Damien fell into the backseat. He gagged at his soiled socks.

The driver noticed them as well. He turned his beady eyes toward the door of the building from which Damien had sprinted. His gaze zipped from one flashing red light to another. A voice spoke into his cab. *"This is a police lock down situation. Everyone please remain calm."*

Damien shoved his grimy socks into his sleek, neon Sprinters. The tie-strings coiled into place.

The driver watched him, but was already pulling away from the building.

The police voice continued. *"No vehicles are authorized within the lock down zone. You may be questioned later during a follow-up investigation. Please acknowledge."*

"Acknowledged!"

"Thank you," said the automated woman. *"Have a nice day."*

"And thank you for getting me into trouble!" shouted the driver in a jazzy California accent. He eased the vehicle to a slow and steady 160 KPH. "Hello? Mr. Happy Feet? You got a destination in mind? I suppose you want to get out of here, is that it? Any direction will do?"

Damien hardly heard him. He wracked his memory to envision again the light screen that had listed the gritty caller's limited information. There had been a phone number. Abraxas *something*. It had been so easy to remember. Now it was gone. He couldn't even recall the address. But that had been in The Kingdom, the Northern Territorial State immediately east of his present location.

The Kingdom. Where the sick "pure-breds"—the pure-Bs—lived.

A shudder ran through him.

The driver's dark eyes kept staring at him from an old-fashioned automobile mirror that hung in the center of the cab on the energy glass. "Please tell me you did not just ask me to take you to The Kingdom." The driver shook his black head, and the bush of conical twirls continued to shake after his head stopped. "I don't go there! The tracks stop at the border anyway. You need a real free floater for that."

Damien was biting his lips shut. He waved a hand in the air, swatting his unintended muttering away. Then he looked through the window behind him.

The cab floated in the unseen city wavelengths that stretched laterally in eight compass directions but gave him the impression that the cab was flying like a twentieth-century airplane. He could see the traffic on the ground far below him, police Spit vehicles in the air, two Hyper-7 Dropships, other emergency vehicles and people movers all going about their midmorning business.

"Why didn't they stop the cab?" Damien was speaking to himself at first, then looked at his driver. When police vehicles clicked their sirens, floaters and ground units alike automatically pulled either to the side of the street or to building tops or sides of the towers rising above them. It was an easy way to clear traffic, an even easier way keep people from escaping via getaway car.

He thought about the voice on the phone, telling him to get dressed and get out of his apartment before the police arrived. He thought about the woman on the phone, screaming, terrified and crying out for help as if certain of her own imminent murder. He thought about the first time he saw Caleigha Obregon, how she had spotted him volunteering to take a coworker's audit duty so that she didn't have to stay late on her son's birthday—how Caleigha had beamed, impressed, when Damien was only trying to be helpful (and he hadn't had anything better to do that night anyway, so he'd felt that he'd hardly deserved the awed expression on her face). He hadn't known who Caleigha was—just someone passing through the office, dropping something off, he'd guessed—but it was her vibrant attention, the way her mouth pursed in an intense smile and her dark eyebrows lifted in surprise, that really grabbed him.

The cabby was still staring, silent, driving.

"How did we get away?" said Damien at the eyes in the mirror.

"Just lucky I guess. Lucky for you."

Damien didn't want to argue. But the man on the phone— *"If you don't do exactly what I say, Ms. Obregon will sink to the bottom of the Jordan. You have two seconds to decide"*—had directed Damien to the top of the building. Why the top of the building?

The cabby's picture ID winked at him beside the advertisements and televised news happening all over the walls: women danced on a beach to muted music while dripping beer bottles appeared and began to dance with them; headlines about the President of the North American Union spun, contributing to a growing sickness and hardening knot in Damien's stomach.

The beady eyes of the cab driver's picture blinked. The wide grin stretched toward his decorative batwing ears with flat, serrated lobes. Beneath the photograph ran the name: Arthur Putubra.

"You were waiting for me." Anger swelled in Damien's voice. "Weren't you?"

At first Putubra didn't answer. When he did, his voice had changed from the jovial foreigner who had first picked him up. Now it was a sober rehabbie's low tone. And his beady black eyes became piercing javelin points. "Man...I've been waiting for you for almost six years now."

Damien couldn't breathe.

Then he exploded. He banged the ClearCage that kept them apart. "Who are you! Where's Caleigha! What have you done!"

But Arthur Putubra was shouting back. Damien didn't catch the words until the driver was saying, "You don't remember me, my friend. That is too bad! It doesn't matter. I will honor you as you honored me!"

The cab began to slow. It dropped multiple levels.

"I have always felt it important to believe in Karma." Putubra looked over the seat and met Damien's eyes. "Do you believe in Karma?" He returned to driving, dropping the cab one level, slowing further. "It is important to believe in Karma, because regardless of your religious declaration, what you do in this social world comes back to you eventually. Yes it does. Especially when you meet your friends again. Or your enemies."

He dropped the cab once more. Damien saw a building approaching.

"How is your elbow?"

Damien saw that he was cradling it. The pain throbbed up his humerus and into his shoulder. But his worry for Caleigha had covered the sensation until now.

"I am *truly sorry* that our conversation must end this way," said Putubra.

And the floor of the cab opened up.

Damien shrieked. He grabbed for hand holds, but the walls and the doors were slick NeoPlas and might as well have been made of glass.

He still sat on the soft seat. And he pulled his dangling feet up as well, terrified that the back seat might easily disappear.

He pressed one shoe to the door, pressed his other foot against the ClearCage wall, and jammed his back into the seat, wedging his body into place.

"But I do you a favor or two."

Damien stared at the drop below him. Each intake of breath was followed by a pause of desperation. It didn't seem to Damien that he was exhaling at all. He couldn't shout or speak.

The buildings fell down, down, in angled lines to the street below him. Cars raced upwards of 250 KPH, appearing and disappearing from his vision. If Damien Reyes fell now, he'd likely never hit the ground. He'd get spattered all over the traffic between here and there first.

"You know West End?"

Damien still couldn't speak.

"My brother is a…freelance pharmacist and—he, he—specialty doctor who works above The Devil's Dante. You know the place?"

Damien's left hand, slick with perspiration, slipped. He was still on the seat, safe, but vertigo grabbed him by the head and made him feel like he was already falling. He managed a desperate screech before looking at the driver again.

"Just remember, Devil's Dante." The driver grinned his enhanced grin—good for business in his industry. "Tell him Arthur sent you. He'll know who you are. He'll fix you up, free of charge! No questions asked. And, my friend, no questions is what you will want most, eh? He-he-he."

Another car blew past, just beneath them, forcing air up Damien's pant legs, rippling the fabric like two flags, blasting him in the face.

"Oh," said the cabby, leaning over the seat again. "Congratulations, by the way. You'll be a war hero in all the history books to come! Adios."

The seat folded neatly down and into the wall. The back of the cab became a shoot of slippery material.

Damien cried out a third time. His sweating hands slipped, squeaked on the fake plastic. He managed a word: "Don't—"

And then he fell.

"And what happened after that, Damien? What happened after you fell?"

"What? What happened?"

Chapter Seven

One of the problems with the idea of traveling into the past is the repercussion of a single variable new to the scene. If a single particle that does not belong in the past bangs around and against other particles in the past, a ripple effect will continue until the future is changed. More practically, the present and future are changed when we engage any one particle in a new direction that would not have happened without our choice to begin the cascade. We never can sustain absolute control of the repercussion. No model has successfully done so. Some unforeseen consequences of intentional choice can be disastrous, especially to our design.

—Josephina Blanca
Huxley's Theorem on Catastrophe Potential

The world fell apart. Data flooded Primary Chief of Staff Martin Warren from multiple angles, and Vice President Lotti Morrison made everything worse. In a flicker of holographic light, she paced with arms crossed back and forth along the projection wall, crossing other three-dimensional Chiefs of Staff, unintentionally mimicking Warren's somber attention to data collection. He stood before a glowing table in the war room. VP Lotti Morrison only stared. "What did you just say? We are at war?"

Warren's words were a growl of derision. "Don't worry, Lotti. The people will not remember you for your confusion, but for the wise action you take in the next few days."

"How dare you speak to me that way. I'm—I'm the President of the North American Union!"

"Acting President," said Josephine Walker, Chief of Staff in charge of

Old Canada.

Of course, for all practical purposes, Lotti Morrison was correct. She was the *de facto* President, even though the assassination of President Henry Sanchez had yet to be confirmed. Too much was happening at once.

Nevertheless, she snagged everyone's attention. Even as Vice President, Lotti Morrison was the top of a small leadership pyramid with only the Primary Chief of Staff directly below her.

CS Josephine Walker covered the Canadian states; CS Tubal Seda supervised the Mexican States; CS Maxine Ojeda managed the Central American Conglomerate, including the liberated northern crown of the South American peninsula and all NAU holdings in the Caribbean; CS Delia Cordova oversaw the Pacific holdings all the way to Okinawa and Japan, which had joined the NAU for economic salvation only twenty-two years prior; and Nathaniel Osprey, Chief of Staff over Alaska, the Kingdom (technically), and the northernmost additions to the Union, bore most of the stress as everything was going wrong in his part of the country.

Acting President Lotti Morrison drilled CS Josephine Walker for putting her in her place. Lotti didn't need to make the threat; it was clear as the knives shooting from her eyes: *Yes, Acting President. And for how long? Then, how long until I replace you as Chief of Staff in charge of Old Canada?*

Josephine Walker didn't flinch.

Warren squinted. Was it a projection glitch? Josephine didn't seem concerned at all. As if she knew that the VP wouldn't be around long enough to be sworn in before the people.

Osprey spoke with aides, who did not appear in 3-D digital relief, and then raised his voice to the company. "Mr. Warren, we have received confirmation that the Chino-Rus have not declared war. Permission to engage transmission with Cardinal Lin?"

"No! We wait. If that fascist Napoleon wants me to believe that he didn't pay for the President's demise, he's going to have to use a lot more than smoothly translated diction."

The Acting President cocked her head to the left. "He speaks English. Anyway, I don't think—"

"With all due respect, we *are* at war. We just haven't identified the enemy."

"Well it seems to me—"

Warren lifted a finger. "The facts, once again? First, the President was killed in the presence of the Secret Service and a thousand recording devices. Then, a microwave blast fired from an extraterrestrial source blackened all the evidence."

"Precisely my point," said the Vice President, who sounded for the first time like the only one manifesting composure and intelligence in the D.C. war room. "We have no contact; we don't know what evidence we have anymore, how much the shields may have saved; we have no communication with anyone who *might* be at or near ground zero."

"And all we know about the Turkish Neural Shi is that all evidence of satellite control was destroyed when the earth opened up and *ate* everyone for forty-square kilometers!" said Warren.

"So we still have no idea who is behind this; no one of merit has claimed responsibility."

"It certainly wasn't the Toiletries of Bob Hope—they were first to call in, you know," said Tubal Seda.

Osprey rolled his eyes. "How can *they* joke about this? Have they *no* maturity at all?"

Speaking in support of PCS Warren, and right over the top of CS Osprey's unimportant questions, Delia Cordova stabbed a finger in the direction of the VP. "You know the Chino-Rus have been developing meteorological and geological weapons. Who else could have opened up the earth and fired volcanic spew beneath Turkish defenses? None of us is safe from that kind of attack! What if the Cardinal wanted to speak, to privately—"

"To what? Negotiate our surrender?" said Josephine Walker, waving her hands in the air. "Now that our secure footing has slipped? Forget it! We are the only country that has never descended from our position as a superpower. They fear what we can do. Let them fear!"

"Mr. Osprey," said VP Morrison.

"Yes. Yes, Madam President."

The appellation didn't make her flinch, and everyone could discern the gun in her eye. "The President of the NAU made an appearance in your territory." She pointed a finger.

Osprey's shame and rage returned, mixing red paint to the color in his cheeks. "Are you saying that I am responsible for—"

"Why didn't you attend the Philibuck graduation with our beloved leader?"

Osprey stopped with his next word caught somewhere in the back of his throat, his mouth left open and hanging loose.

The other Chiefs of Staff looked at him and waited a long time for his answer.

Chapter Eight

The Spanish Prisoner is one of the great cons of the twentieth century. Like unto this magnificent and highly successful predecessor, Marci Boliviando is the criminal mind first credited with the South American Slip. This latter entanglement enlists local law enforcement, an apparently high-profile missing person's case, and paranoia. Everything is minimized behind the caring philanderer whose sole purpose, purportedly, is to set everything straight: the "kidnapped" victim is set free, or so the real victim is led to believe; the police are led anonymously by the real victim of this crime; and the criminals are caught. The real victim in the South American Slip is he or she who is led to open his or her financial flows as bait and false promises along the way. The actual result? The real victim is arrested for fraud, is not believed by the local authorities to have been the victim of any brilliant conundrum, cannot produce even proof of the existence of the high profile missing person, and is unable to point the finger at the criminal minds purportedly behind this crime. In fact, the real victim is never quite certain what the real crime has been. And depending upon which country the South American Slip unfolds, the real victim may never even learn that his or her liquid finances have vanished, let alone how.

—Hula DeVicci, FBI Special Agent, Retired
DeVicci On Criminal Masterpieces

Life after death is a state of mind.

Detective Harvey Corvasce blinked when the alarm sounded. He blinked when the shield burst into life above his head. He blinked with the instant knowledge that on the few occasions that city shields really had been put to the test, they had never worked: all municipal power was diverted at the instant of the attack, draining the city of any hope of life after the blast, and the Federal Emergency Management Agency's precious baby didn't manage to save a single life.

Of course that had been the New Jersey catastrophe—Pandam's city shield promised to be state of the art (they all made promises with that useless phrase, and words like, "This time we mean it!" never calmed attentive and righteously paranoid members of the community).

Corvasce blinked again—one of many blinks in a spastic succession of panicked blinks—and knew that he was dead.

And then knew that he was alive.

The next life? he thought.

The shield had come and gone in a burst. The burst was just enough to stop...whatever had triggered FEMA's system. Living human beings screamed, hands over their heads as they ran into campus buildings, out of buildings—and rank or station had nothing to do with their social behavior anymore. They ran. They all knew they were dead, dying, or should be.

Corvasce looked up. This time, he couldn't open his eyes. Not at first. Had the flash occurred at night, he wondered if he would be blind now. As it happened in the day—*what* happened?—the sky rippled blue and white, a play of ions and atmosphere that the detective didn't understand. He covered the sun with his hand. He looked around again. And he knew he was alive.

Com link.

"Captain Dewitter, please acknowledge." He shifted channels. "Dispatch?" Shift. "Control." He shook his head and called person-to-person for his partner, "Ames! Do you copy?"

Nothing.

"Of course not."

Everything was fried.

"But I'm alive," he whispered. And that bothered him; that seemed distinctly wrong.

He turned and faced the crime scene once more. It was chaos piled on top of chaos. What order existed a minute ago had scattered in multiple directions. Reporters didn't feel like gathering data any longer; curious on-lookers fled as if the sky was falling (and, of course, it *had* fallen, in a sense); and the Secret Service agents vanished.

Corvasce took a step. He checked the robots atop the buildings.

Useless!

Their eyes glowed with darkness that ghosted a memory of electronic life. They would repair and reboot soon enough, then click into martial law mode, unless they received new commands from recognizable authority. But could they? After rebooting, which authority would be necessary to override the martial law protocol? Was there anyone in the city? Or would the population be forced to turn into mice and hide until the flesh and blood military arrived?

He scanned the frightened faces around him.

Did *anyone* else think about any of these things?

Of course: the invisible Secret Service!

Corvasce raced to the stage again. He tried his com link, made no connections. Then he remembered the camera that he'd picked up. The camera had also crashed, but with some luck the data he'd recorded was still there.

He looked into the sky, shuddering with the sensation that another pulse from orbit might attempt a second time to level this part of the city.

But the President's already dead? Why hit the kill site?

Isn't it obvious? said the imagined voice of Detective Alexandria Ames—the one authority that had managed to escape this failed job to protect the president—in answer to Corvasce's focused thoughts. *Ever seen anyone implode like that? New weaponry. Successful kill of one of the most protected men on the planet. This kind of thing shouldn't happen. Someone was covering his tracks.*

Someone? Unlikely.

Corvasce found a door behind the stage where a Secret Service suit had stood when everything was smelling sweet and peachy. The door was open and the stooge was gone.

"Pick a door, any door."

Corvasce saw the mess in the doorway where President Sanchez had died. He shook his head and followed his feet to the open door closest to the rear of the stage.

He didn't make it three steps into the shadows of the corridor before he felt the pins of three stun guns pierce his skin. He hit the floor with his cheek.

He saw a face before the darkness spirited him away. There was grime in the corners of the eyes. The teeth were crooked—*where in the world did anyone have crooked teeth?* And he cackled.

Chapter Nine

Variables remain undetermined until the final solution is manifest. Take any two variables, for instance. Assume that x = 2 and that Y = 3. The equation xY=n, at first glance, does not seem problematic at all. When we recognize that no mathematical equation is that simple, as Flat World mathematicians believed years ago, but that every equation includes what Robert Basie called the Indeterminant, signified by (<>), we are then forced to rewrite even the simple equation above as xY(<>)=n, and then we have a real problem. Or at least, we have a problem if our goal is to find n. In this case, n remains undetermined because a final solution cannot be manifest, not when we realize Basie's singular conclusion: the Indeterminant variable can never be accurately predicted.

—Dravidian Meyer
(<>) Unquantified: An Indeterminant Primer

"*I can't feel my arms.*"

"*Ah…you're back.*"

"*I can't—my legs; I can't feel my legs!*"

"*Don't worry. Every appendage of your body is present and accounted for. Right where you left them.*"

"*Where I left them…*"

"*Damien, where are you?*"

"*You said—you said I was right here in this—*"

"*Think, now. Here we go again. Relax…What do you see?*"

"*I can't see.*"

"*You can. You have been seeing. We still want the code.*"

"We?"

*"Yes, well, naturally! You and I, Damien. We want the code. Don't we?
You are remembering it."*

"I am remembering…I am—telling myself what I want to hear."

"Yessss."

"But I do remember. The code!"

The next few seconds scared Damien so much, his heart nearly gave way. In fact, he *wanted* to die. Just to get it over with. Because he knew it was happening anyway.

The cab was all around him. Then it wasn't there.

He kicked at the open sky beneath him, thrashed at nitrogen, oxygen, argon, carbon dioxide, hydrogen, neon, helium and other gases floating around in what he had called air—when it had mattered. Now, nothing mattered.

The cab soared away above him. He could hear the laughter of the driver. Then it was just the sound of cars, and a distant wail of sirens.

He plummeted to his death.

But he plunged for less than two seconds.

The cab had been flying forward. The cabby flushed him like an un- wanted or threatening passenger. Gravity pulled. Damien's body arched toward the brutal streets. He hit something—maybe only one second after leaving the cab. And his body pin wheeled, then flapped about like a sis- ter's rag doll chucked along pavement by cruel brothers. If shock hadn't loosened his joints, he would have snapped fibulas and forearms for certain.

Somehow he didn't. Damien came to a stop, facedown, his nose and right eye pressed hard into a gritty rooftop.

He waited a minute, then two minutes before trying to rise. He felt the black and blue spreading just beneath his skin. His bones *had to be* broken, he decided.

Then his mind shifted again to Caleigha Obregon.

He saw her.

He didn't see her.

Standing there…with the sun bright and beaming over her shoulder, her thick hair blowing on the waves of wind behind her. Damien saw her smil- ing. He heard the laugh, muted as if behind a thin wall of water: the chortle of beauty standing tall in a dream. Caleigha offered her hand. He looked at the soft curves of her fingers, the rounded nails painted pink, glistening with sparkles of sunlight. She offered…her hand.

Damien opened his eyes. The piece of gravel, rough and shaded on one side like the dark side of the moon, might have been a boulder seen through a fog. But it was real. And it was an illusion. Only a piece of gravel.

He tried to remember…when he had seen Caleigha with the sun behind her like that, in a white blouse like that, flowing in the breeze like that…

The vision had been as sharp as a memory. As real as a memory.

But it had never happened.

Damien pushed himself onto his knees. He slid to the side of a metallic box attached to the rooftop. *No broken bones*, he thought. Then he cradled his elbow again. It felt broken.

Yet his mind drifted again.

"Caleigha…" he said.

And none of this seemed real anymore.

It was as if he was living inside of someone else's memory.

But the wind touched him with the icy promise of a cold afternoon and a frosty summer evening to follow. Hide or not, if he didn't get inside and find shelter from the elements, the insomniac's sunny midnight here in the northern NAU city of Kodiak could very well kill him.

He didn't move.

Buildings, proving the capability and determination of modern mankind, stretched across the horizon. Cars raced along invisible lines overhead. Pebbles of windblown waste and detritus stabbed through his pants when he shifted again.

Slowly, Damien stood.

And he saw Caleigha.

Not here.

In a memory. Without an origin.

He shook his head, grabbed the sides.

"Caleigha!" he whispered, and he found a door and tested the lock.

Giving up at the entrance, he thought of where Caleigha might be. He replayed the voice of the call. He listened again to Arthur Putubra's sing-song messages where he sat, safe in the front of his cab.

And for a fleeting moment, he knew he couldn't save Caleigha, let alone find her. He couldn't get away from the police if they sought him—and would they listen to any story about how he'd fled arrest because of a phone call and a threatened girlfriend? He couldn't get into the building either. What now—jump off?

The door buzzed. Sound waves touched his bones. "I know who you are, and why you are standing on my roof."

He didn't move.

The lock on the door buzzed a second time.

How quaint. How old fashioned, Damien thought. Because the door was a mouth ready to open and swallow him—I knew it! Even more horrors waited behind that door. Teeth.

"Well? You coming in or not?"

"What was this then? You said you remembered the code."

"It was there."

"On the rooftop? That voice from the door? That—that glitch—"

"Caleigha. She's not a glitch."

"Well, my friend, in this case I beg to differ. The problem with memory, you see."

"I remember."

"No. No, Damien. That's the problem here! You are not remembering! You need to focus—how many times do I need to tell you that?—Damien! How much time do you think we have here?"

"Calm down, doc. You're helping me. Aren't you? What? Hello? What now? Cat got your tongue."

"My good friend. Of course!"

"So where did you go, just then? You can't walk out on me. Were you speaking to someone I don't know about? Is that—"

"I am trying my hardest to help you. But you aren't helping me. You realize that, don't you? Why else would I be so motivated—so determined to put my own life on the line? Sue me; I'm human! I got frustrated. I'm no expert."

"I thought you were the expert."

"Big fish in a small pond."

"What?"

"Old expression. Never mind. What now, Damien? Why the face?"

"Oh! Am I making a face? I can't feel anything anymore. It's good to know I can make a face!"

"You said the code was there. I didn't catch it."

"You'll see. In a second. You'll put it together and slap yourself on the forehead. Right now, I need something."

"I'll do what?"

"Just an expression. I think I'm hungry."

"It was there?"

"I just can't feel my stomach anymore…Hey. Why can't you tell me what is happening? I mean, what is really happening?"

Chapter Ten

The study of dream theory has impressed man to believe it a window to the soul. Bobbie Pratt even hypothesized, "If you could dispense with the violence and romance found inside of dreams, you would have a clear visual passageway into heaven." One thing is more certain than ever before, as the detailed chronicling and collating of hundreds of thousands of dreamers has revealed: The dreamer is seeing alternative realities.

— Kachwaina Tubaloth
Second Sight

Best not to think of disturbing things, Pandu decided. He tried to ignore that itch in his head that made him feel that Fate or Destiny or some deity or government organization controlled his movements when they needed secrets accomplished. He shared those feelings, that delusion, with no one, not even a doctor. The last thing he needed was a medical patch pumping regular doses of some mind-numbing concoction into his bloodstream and messing up his quiet career.

Pandu had never been to this side of town and certainly would have avoided coming here on a green day. He dodged the eyes of the shadow folk and the uniforms alike, and he had no clue where he was headed. The yellow day would turn into a red one when he reached his goal. Always did. That's how it worked, his craziness, his addiction. Maybe afterward he could turn around and catch a taxi home.

His daughter, Jarita, would be understanding. She had learned to live with his disappearances many times. Pandu had attempted more than once to convince her that they were a special people, that others of their kind existed. Sometimes he saw them too.

Always like lightning, their sad gazes met. They might be half a block from one another, across a busy street, one in a store window looking down, the other on the crowded promenade. The connection hummed them into a harmony that others failed to notice. They turned and met eyes; they stared. Pandu had never spoken with one like him. In fact, a part of his brain told him that to converse with similar ilk was forbidden.

He stopped, red all around him now. He touched a door with the flat of his hand. Flakes of paint scratched and stabbed at his skin. He brushed the chaff away, scanned the street to make sure no one watched, then put his pen to the wall.

He drew a round symbol. Inside the circle, he etched the number nine. Behind this object, he made a triangle appear and added shadows for effect, even though only the corner angles showed. You have to have pride in your work, he thought. He smiled.

Yet the day did not return to green, so again he felt sad. So much life to live, he thought. Jarita waiting.

Her mother had run away screaming in the middle of the night. She had sprinted into the rain, through blinding flashes of red and blue. Police swarmed the street. She fell into the arms of one of the uniforms. She looked back at the building where Pandu stared from Jarita's bedroom. Yet his wife held to her promise: she reported nothing. But she would no longer stay. "You can have our daughter. She's sick, Pandu, the way you are sick."

"Your mother did not recognize our importance," Pandu had told his daughter the following morning when she awoke. "She has gone to live with the suits and the ties and the dresses and the jeans." He held Jarita tight. His daughter did not struggle that day. She sat on the bed and wept for the loss of her mother. And as if a switch was thrown, mother lost her name. Like everyone else Pandu had ever loved, as soon as they left. I think it's just a psychological shield, he said in his mind. He would need to explain these changes to Jarita, when she grew old enough. "Your mother's a skirt now. You are not like them. I will teach you."

Pandu thought of these lies and so many more lies he had told his daughter in the years since that skirt had abandoned them. "You're special too," he said to his daughter. But Jarita never had yellow days. He never connected with her in a jolt, as he did on those rare occasions when he met others who were special. Their communion was not forbidden. Pandu loved his daughter.

The world swam in red colors again. His pen did not rise. He shook his head. Where, where, where. He scoured the torn city walls, the bars over shop windows, boards having taken the place of glass panes long ago. He scraped graffiti paint with his fingernails. Grumbling, he finally dropped his eyes, then crouched to the cement.

A different hand, a woman's if he read the penmanship right, had left a symbol in black marker on the concrete. Most of the ink had scuffed away beneath the shoes of the jeans and shorts and T-shirts. He could still see the octagonal shape behind a triangle with a number one drawn in the center. Twenty-two short lines served as an artistic shadow behind the polygons. Exactly twenty-two.

He sprinted away. Feverish and starving, he ran past an old petrol car with two flat tires in the gutter. He rushed under trees surrounded by federal warning signs: $70,000 fine and/or 10 years in Service for anyone caught damaging the foliage. He leapt over a homeless man with a broken bottle. He slipped around a corner, his soles failing him, and smacked his chin right onto the shoes of a uniform.

"Goodness, citizen! Where might you be off to in such a great hurry?" The uniform spoke without a face. He leaned forward, proffering a hand of help. "All right, then," he said when Pandu shrunk away with a moan. The uniform reached to one side of his belt and pulled the gene reader from a leatheroid pouch. "Won't mind if we scan you?" Without waiting for an answer—they never paused for him to speak, and they caught him all the time—the uniform brushed the soft edge of the silver disk over the back of Pandu's knuckles.

Pandu pulled his appendages away and nursed the skin. Any skin would do, of course; the uniform had what he needed. The gene reader did far more than ID a person. It also searched the body for intoxicants and measured chemical buildups linked to both stress and guilt, which was probably the uniform's actual interest. He stood as he reviewed Pandu's record. Uniforms always said the same thing. "My—you've been read a hundred times! But you're clean enough, so off you go."

With that, Pandu noticed the yellow day again, all around him. Yellow. He leapt to his feet and rushed away, ignoring the scrutinizing uniform who stared at his back worrying that technology might have led him astray.

By the time Pandu stopped, night had shrouded the world with darkness. The yellow tint didn't vanish while Pandu walked, knowing he was close, though he had never stood on this wharf. He dripped with hot sweat despite the fog.

Stealth ships in the bay went unnoticed by all the jackets and the coats. One could not hear the lap of water against the black hulls, for they had been shaped so that it sounded only like water lapping water. And of course, the boats could not be seen with the naked eye, especially at night.

Yet someone who saw colors and read the signs like Pandu was out there, in the dark, climbing aboard. How in the world? he thought. Just what directions had that guy received from the chaos scrawled with mathematical perfection in the red zones? Pandu wished he could ask. The man sensed his presence. Pandu squinted across the black waters, and the man stared back at Pandu on the concrete pier. Pandu did not see him, but electricity seemed to sizzle recognition up his spine, transferring data, making him aware of the secret vehicles. Affirmation. Confirmation. Acknowledgement. Yet Pandu's only clear and conscious thought was, That man swam all the way out there?

Please don't make me do the same! Pandu asked the wind.

Time passed, and Pandu waited though he did not know why. Then he found a wooden pylon left over from the old days, preserved with some kind of sealant, rising from the waters and etched by years and years of troubled children. With his pen, Pandu scribed a triangle there, offset by a box with the number nine written in the center. He had not even noticed the red before he moved. His legs throbbed after standing for so long at the water's edge. Then he waited some more and felt himself slip in and out of dream.

When everything turned green, he flagged a taxi and headed homeward. He found Jarita slouched in a chair with a bowl of popcorn on her lap. She watched swimsuits and baseball caps on the wall. Ashamed, she switched the program off and offered her father some food. "You've been running in the rain?"

He peeled off his coat and dropped it on the closet floor. "How can you sit there staring at them all night?" He waved his hand where the wall now showed a beach and a yellow sun over a green sea. The image moved, but no Hawaiian shirts appeared. "I hope you ate something healthy."

Still sweating, he washed himself in the kitchen sink, thought about a shower, then grabbed a pad and started doodling. She came over and hung on his shoulder, peering at the interconnecting circles he drew over and over on the screen. "What does that mean?"

"We're not supposed to know."

"You sure it means anything?" she said, hitching up her sweat bottoms.

Pandu looked at her face, suddenly fearful that her features might have vanished. She grinned, as polite and loving as ever. "Well," he said, "this might be only practice. I'm exercising my hand."

"Practice for what?"

"Work," he said. "On yellow days. You know."

"But you're an architect. You don't use your hands. All the CAD systems are eye-sensitive and follow your voice."

They had been over this before. The last time she went to her room crying. It was months ago. Her courage and mounting late-adolescent impropriety reminded him of his youth, which terrified him. He hadn't been fourteen before noticing the green days. At fifteen, the days turned yellow once in a while, and he had to start walking. He remembered the first sign he saw, spray-painted in the corner of a billboard: the circle and the triangle. He nearly went crazy as the year passed, yellow days became red without warning, and his parents lost their faces. They turned him loose. They called him emancipated. They said he should be happy.

Pandu decided against another contentious discussion with his daughter. He made coffee and sipped. Facing the black window, he imagined the sea and the stealth ships and the special man on board. The guy would likely drown tonight, he thought. He wondered why he thought that, why he felt so sure. Then he added, Will I drown some day?

Jarita stood against the kitchen island behind him. "What would you say if I told you I followed you tonight?"

He burned his tongue on the coffee. "Is this because I tell you not to date the shirts?"

"You dated the skirts, Dad. You got married and had me. How else will I have children? I don't want to be a drone mother. I couldn't bear to have children and have them taken away from me."

"But you like the shirts. You watch them on the VR when I'm away. You think I don't know? You think I don't love you, Jarita? I know what is best for us."

She turned to leave, stopping in the hall. "Maybe I did tag along behind you. To see what it's like. Walking for forever and a day." She left him and shut her bedroom door. Twenty years old and still she had not had a yellow day. They could come, though. Yes.

They would light the way for her, and Jarita would keep her face.

Chapter Eleven

The pea game works in stages. A pea is hidden beneath one of three shells. The audience sees this. The showman shuffles the shells. The shells are set into a neat little line again. One member of the audience points at the shell where he thinks the pea is hidden. The showman lifts the shell to show that the choice has been made correctly. Voila, the pea! Then the dealer slides the shells more quickly, moving hands without moving shells, moving shells incongruous with the moving hands. Even moving the pea from one shell to another. When the shells are lined up neatly the second time, the audience is certain—or mostly certain—where the pea hides. The dealer knows where the audience thinks the pea hides. And the pea...well, where is the pea? Until the dealer lifts the shell, the pea only exists in the form of mathematical possibility. It is beneath all three shells; it isn't under any of the shells at all. For these are Schrödinger's Shells now. And the pea has crossed the universe.

—Tii Flanders
The Cosmic Pea

The police academy had been tough—no doubt about it. All a part of the job. Harvey Corvasce had been subjected to tear gas, nerve agent 106, and stun needles before—just to know how it would feel, so that it wouldn't be so much a shock to the system during a crisis situation.

But it was still a shock, and when Corvasce woke up, he felt certain that the needles were still protruding through the cloth of his jacket and stabbing his arm, his hipbone, and his left side.

The room smelled of tangy mold and rotting marsupial excrement. Fractured light scattered shapes over the dark walls and ceilings. Voices spoke in half-whispers, echoed from this oddly gothic setting. Far away issued a sound of metal drilling into concrete or stone.

Corvasce moved with subtle care. If he had been taken prisoner by his assailants, he didn't want them to know he'd grown conscious. Was he bound? He pulled his right wrist from his beltline. No, not bound.

He checked for needles, sliding his hand slowly and quietly, no more quickly across his hip than an inchworm might proceed.

Nothing. Only the ghosts of stingers remained, to haunt his nerves.

He cracked one eye.

Across a roughly hewn hall, the likes of which Corvasce had never seen, one man in a disguise of filth took another suddenly by the neck and spoke in a threatening whisper that hit the walls with guttural sounds that didn't sound much like English by the time the words reached the detective's ears.

The victim jerked his head towards Corvasce. He swatted his assailant's hand aside and pointed. Then the assailant crossed the littered floor, in bounding motions that made Corvasce recoil, eyes wide, even as the footfalls splashed through puddles, spraying putrid water into his face.

"He's awake," said a voice, thick with sticky fluids.

No reason to hide now. Corvasce righted himself.

A woman with knotted hair to her elbows strode toward him with a fiber blaster aimed with shaky determination at his chest. Fiber blasters—those were nasty, and outlawed, war weapons developed in India fifty years ago. The detective swallowed. Now, he'd never felt a hundred fibers pierce him at once, but this too he had learned about in basic training. His instructor at the academy had snickered when he'd said, "*You'll wish* you were dead: It's like someone whipping a cactus over your skin. Only, the fibrous spines go deeper, stabbing through your nerves and rubbing against them each time you move. And just try to pull out a thousand of those silicon spikes; you can't hardly even see them."

The woman fit no recognizable genetic profile. Could *that* be a disguise? She rubbed her nose, spreading a sheen of greasy fluid over the back of one holey glove. "Don't expect the rescue party anytime soon. Your GPS signal is blocked by," she twirled a finger in the air to finish her sentence.

He looked at the coarse ceiling. Then she fetched his attention again by sliding the black nozzle a little closer to his face. "*This* will hurt."

Corvasce raised a hand of submission. He opened his mouth to utter a brave, *I know*, while his mind screamed, *Please don't!* The resulting guttural hiss from the back of his throat brought a smile to the woman's broken face.

"Who do you work for?"

"Pandam PD."

"I can read your badge, Sherlock. What I want to know is *which side* are ya on?"

Corvasce had no idea how to answer the question. He felt his mouth drying up. "If I said your side, you still going to shoot me?"

"Depends. If you're that easily bought, can we really trust you?"

He didn't bother to answer that. She was right. If he had no integrity, he'd turn on them as soon as he was out of danger. But as a man of conviction, he could only pretend to work with them instead of against them. She had to already know all this.

Yet the woman had a steely look in her silvery eyes, as if she sought that very conviction in him. To use him? he wondered. Or to find permission to shoot him and watch him writhe until he fainted beneath the pain?

She tilted her head to the right, measuring Corvasce for something he could not determine—level of danger, perhaps?

Then she stowed her pistol within a coat that fell past her knees. "All right, big boy. Up you go. Do me a favor, will you? Don't try anything. My 'friends' here"—she used her gloved fingers to throw quotation marks around the word *friends*—"won't have misgivings about cutting us both to pieces if you try to grab me or my piece." She bounced her frazzled eyebrows. "All for 'the cause', you understand."

"I don't," said Corvasce, groaning as he slowly came to his feet. "But my father always said, *Prudence is wise*."

"Knew a girl name Prudence once. Anyway, you'd never find your way out of here alive."

He blinked when she turned her back on him. He hadn't really expected her to—to what?—test him this way. It was a test, wasn't it? What about all that talk regarding whose side you are on?

She drew a torch from her coat and shined the beam ahead of her. "So you had a father? Dog!"

The other gentlemen with broken teeth and wiry whiskers laughed at him silently as he passed from the one hole in the wall to a second corridor, tighter, and—he realized with the raise of an eyebrow—*not* built of stone at all but lined with hemalite, the old synthetic stucco sealant invented to imitate stone while actually proving to be more malleable and secure.

He didn't ask questions. Not even after they had long wandered alone in the musty and muggy walkways. He'd learn more by following, he decided. And if these thugs were behind the assassination of the President, he had to see and hear all he could.

Twenty minutes of travel gave him more information that he could handle. Each time the woman opened her mouth to say nothing meaningful, Corvasce filled another page of facts in his head:

Outside of NeoGothic cathedrals and theme parks, builders rarely used hemalite indoors anymore. Even in the first days of NeoGothic revival, hemalite wasn't used to this degree. Nor were the other squalid and gritty materials that had long since degraded and fallen to rust around him—rust! Ladders, hemalite concrete drains, catwalks promising to fall when the next person crossed. A nightmare maze made for man-sized rats.

They were climbing. Level upon disused level.

"You're French Canadian," Corvasce said.

She scowled at him, then followed a slope running with water that stank of dinoflagellates. She lost her footing. Corvasce caught her.

He felt the gun under her coat. They were making their own noise now, echoes through the endless and crowded nothingness, without any other human being in sight. Corvasce seriously doubted that her armaments or training included anything that could keep him from overpowering her now.

He let go.

"Thank you!" Her eyes stood wide with shock and sincerity. "A dog, and a gentleman as well." She sniffed the wetness of the air, considering some other option. Then she continued her upward course.

Corvasce chose again to bide his time. "May I…ask where we are heading?"

She breathed heavily, then laughed. "Oh. You'll know soon enough." She laughed again until it became clear that the moisture he was hearing in her chest meant that her body was fighting some kind of illness, the sort of illness easily managed when a doctor was involved. But she had no doctor. Who didn't have a government-assigned physician?

At some point, Corvasce decided that he should have been marking distances more carefully. He had been noting what might have been termed as landmarks along the way: turns, barred passages, changes in direction, water flows, heat ducts—that seemed odd. No windows whatsoever.

He took another chance: "So you're not going to kill me?"

"What purpose would that serve?" She guffawed and faced him. Then she drew herself up, albeit painfully, into something close to a fine lady's posture. "Don't let this fabulous female exterior distract you." With a wave of a showman's hand, she indicated her shabby attire. Then she slumped back into herself. "I don't do nothin' without a reason." Turning to continue on her way, she added, "And I bet you'll wish I'd just as well killed you, soon enough."

Corvasce ran his attention in every direction that might serve as an escape when the time came. He could still overpower her. Or thought he could.

Rotting organic matter flowed beneath a metal grate over which they crossed. It smelled like sewage, but where in the world did sewage flow freely in this day and age? It was a health risk eliminated long ago when the NatureRebreathers had been invented. He had to be wrong. Or he couldn't be in the NAU anymore.

They climbed a staircase that led to a ladder. She pulled out her pistol, pointed it at him, pointed it at the door up the tube in the ceiling. "This is where we say *au revoir.*"

He swallowed, then squinted at her. "Your French Canadian is slipping. The accent's fake. Isn't it."

She grinned her web of crooked teeth.

The gun jerked in her hand. "I'd hate to waste the ammo."

He followed the motion, grabbing the highest rung of the ladder first, in the case he had to pull himself upward double-time while she shot at him anyway.

She didn't fire.

He reached the hatch in the darkness above him. His hand found the icy curve of what felt like a metal handle. A pull and a push—how incredibly manual!—and the door unsealed. It sprang upward of its own accord.

Corvasce hadn't climbed any higher before his eyes blew wide, and he gasped at the horrors around him.

Chapter Twelve

No one believes anymore in Krishnamorti's Crossover Effect. Why is that? Who is to say that the theorems of Yvonne Yu Lee, regarding the Multidimensionality of Temporal Events, aren't true? In fact, who is to say that we are not sliding from one parallel universe to another every day, or—consider this!—every nanosecond. Would we even know if we shifted from one reality to another, to another, to another again? Could we perceive these crossovers, even if we wanted to? We are talking here about the very nature of reality itself. If reality is perceived by each of us individually, based upon the data that streams through various media, into our individual consciousnesses, then why would we be aware of any shift at all? The Krishnamorti about whom I write may only be the Krishnamorti of whom I am, at this instant, cognizant. The mathematical possibilities posited in his theories may include a singular variable that he did not recognize: our own inability to see the big picture because we, the viewers, move too quickly from one reality to the next.

—Jerusha Esteves
Alternatives in Parallel Effect

"I have a concern …"
Hush.
"Did you hear me? I am talking, aren't I? You hear me talking? I hear me talking. Am I talking?"
"What is it?"
"You hear me talking."

"What is your concern, Damien."

"I don't…I don't feel so well. You said I wouldn't feel anything."

"I meant that relatively. Are you in pain?"

"You sound like you already know the answer to that."

"Well, I should. I'm your doctor, aren't I? Right now, I mean? Shouldn't I know that you're in pain? We aren't living in barbaric times, when doctors didn't know that their patients were in pain."

"There was such a time?"

"Is that your concern? You don't feel so well? Let it go, Damien. You are the one who wanted us to hurry. I'm trying to help."

"Well…as I go along…sometimes I wonder."

Sigh. Sigh. "About what?"

"About you! About this! I mean—"

"Your memories…"

"Well, yes! I'm remembering things. But it's not right! I don't feel right!"

"It hasn't exactly been the best time of your life, has it. Look, Damien, we're tapping where no man should be allowed to tap. Know what I'm saying? We are opening memories and exploring them as if experiencing them for the first time. Which is good. Which is what you wanted. I think I understand why."

"Well then tell me!"

"Because you are being dishonest with me, Damien. You are being dishonest with yourself."

"I don't think—"

"You are experiencing a normal and logical lag in linear brain connectivity. Experiencing something once, like feeling a handful of snow for the first time, and then experiencing the very same 'first time' feeling of a handful of snow…that just can't be easy for the mind to handle. Is it your first time, or isn't it? The brain was not engineered for that sort of clash. A computer would say, Ah! I am feeling snow for the first time. And then, if you told a computer that it is registering the same event 'for the first time', it couldn't agree with you. It could only agree if it retained no memory or could not access that memory of the previous 'first time' and therefore thought that this was the first time."

"I have no idea what you're talking about. I was saying—"

"Of course you don't understand. Because the brain retains every memory you ever had! The way we're are poking around and replaying events, it's no wonder that your systems are crashing. Except they aren't. The human brain is phenomenal. We can duplicate so very many of its processes.

Computers can exceed the human brain! And yet, there is still something there…that Indeterminant quality Robert Basie discovered."

"Please stop. I don't get anything that you're saying. I'm an accountant. I'm not a scientist."

"Look at it this way. Your memories weren't intended to be replayed, not this way. Your brain thinks you are experiencing these memories over again for the first time."

Hmmm. *"Well…that doesn't explain what you said about being dishonest."*

"You haven't wanted to see the truth. You don't want to remember the truth now."

"I have reason to hesitate."

"You have apprehension—I can read that right here, right on these hormonal registers. Damien, I'm talking about something else. You don't want to remember what you know. And you don't want to tell me. Why is that?"

"I never said that."

"But I know it. And your needs will give us power to break through this wall. I suggest you consider what it is that you are trying to hide from yourself. It's more than the code, I think. You indicated that the code was obvious."

"It will become clear."

"But isn't that the whole reason we are here? Right now? Here, like this?"

"The code…is just the beginning. And I was just starting to get it…the code…"

Flashing green lights strobed along the top of the dark hallway in the ornamental fashion of the geeks twenty years back. They were so proud to be different, though they were in no way the strange animal eaters of the previous century, nor the hyper-intelligent social outcasts paid impressively for their aptitude and capabilities at the dawn of the Internet Age. Damien's father had proclaimed himself one of the last real geeks. He told Damien that this sort of pretty techno-toy did not a true geek make.

It was the panic on the roof that made him think of his father, though. Not the lights. He just hadn't realized it. Those terrible nightmares…

In the nightmares, he saw the attack on Dandelion from his father's point of view. He'd once asked a friend at work about it, and the friend had said something about race memory, but that hadn't made any sense to Damien because Damien hadn't been at the Lunar colony during President Sanchez's invasion. Damien hadn't been on the Moon at all. In fact, he'd never left the Earth in his life. And before his mother had paid good doctors to put her to sleep (at the taxpayer's expense, of course—decreasing the surplus population, and all that), she had made him promise to never leave the planet like his father. *"Don't follow in his footsteps. I used to believe. Leave it alone. Just don't. Please."*

…in the nightmares…the black sky was speckled with stars—not a cloud in the Lunar heavens over Dandelion. Peace-lovers sleeping everywhere. Crickets chirping. *Why crickets? Doesn't make sense! Or digital, mimicking Earth? Or just a cockamamie bit of gibberish fabricated by a troubled mind to indicate that the attack happened at night?* And the ridge on the east side of the crater. Then…military AdMarks (Advance Mark Defense Units, which was the polite and politically correct term that replaced the previous Automatic Stage-one Reconnaissance and Assassin Condors, ASRACs) flew without warning into sight and then out again, "going camouflage" against the white rock down the side of the ridge.

Then, death. Everywhere. Everyone. As wave after wave poured into those sections not deemed military. Those were obliterated by the AdMarks.

And then, his father's ghost. A memory. That never happened.

Damien!

Why the peaceful smile on his face?

There's something you need to remember for me. In the case I don't.

But in the dream, he's not hovering like in the memory, sitting there beside the levitating baby mobile looking down the sides of the crib at the infant too young to be sucking his thumb.

In the dream, he's bleeding to death on the top of one of the rises. He watched the brutal attack. He knows they're looking for him. For *him* in particular, though they don't know his name. Not here. And Marcus Reyes, Damien's father, turns his eyes up to the Earth that has been up there in that black and starry sky all along.

Damien.

"Why are you stopping?" said an amused voice from the walls. Was it a direct communication beam or an open broadcast? Direct beam most likely. The hollow echo Damien heard was just another wanna-be-geek special effect, like the lava lamp walls that lit and began to undulate as soon as he went through the door at the end of the first hall. Just like the quaint scent of winter firewood letting smoke into a clean sky of mountain air. Toys and more toys. "Stunning," said the voice. "Isn't it!" A laugh. "Keep going. Never fear. Your *salvation* is drawing near!"

The laughter echoing through his bones seemed something out of a nightmare. It was the sound of a loved one, happy and yet partially demented. Someone a family member could not easily get rid of.

The hall widened until three doors presented themselves in the swirling orange light. Damien realized that he must have passed others that were masked by geek technology.

"Ah!" said the voice. "Pick a door, any d—not that one! You don't want to go that way, trust me. And you'd better hurry. We don't have much time."

Damien backed away from the third door. He began losing control over his muscles, and he wondered if the cold sensation on his face meant that he might soon be passing out. He considered retreating.

But where could he go? Back to the roof?

He saw himself jumping from the top of the building—just to get it over with!—as if he had done it before; as if he would do it again.

Then he heard Caleigha's high timber resonating somewhere in the walls of his memory.

"Is she alive?" Even Damien's throat quivered. "Is Caleigha alive? I *need* to know."

"Who?"

"Is—" Damien bit his top lip. "Which door leads to the elevator? I need to get out of here. I need to find—"

Laughter again.

Damien reached for the third door. The panel slid open, even as his host shouted, "No!"

Yet another ornamental corridor raced downward, arching to the right.

Three open archways manifested themselves along the right wall as he sprinted. They appeared as if they were meant to appear at that exact moment. Damien stopped and studied the ceiling ridge above each portal. Of course! They appeared as if by magic behind flat holoscreens that mimicked the wall itself. He passed through the first doorway—

—and nearly head butted a grinning fellow who stood boldly in his path.

Damien cried out.

"Hi! How're you doing?" The stranger fit the voice from the halls. Actually, he wasn't standing boldly at all; he was leaning against the inside wall, almost reclining there. His shoulders filled out a white shirt and made him look like a serious jut of the wall itself. The shirt hung open, dark curls of chest hair prominently displayed, and enormous collars pointed in the direction of what certainly must have been enormous biceps. He grinned widely, in spite of getting caught.

"Don't freak. Come in. We don't have much time. You know how thorough the police are. I will never underestimate them. Best to overestimate!

Follow me."

Damien held still. "I want to see Caleigha."

"You want the pain in your elbow to stop. No? I did a scan and read your health index already, my friend." He spoke softly, and his last words grew hard to discern.

Damien found himself walking, gently easing himself into the suite.

The room broke into one cell after another, all tight, all filled with colorful pieces of junk.

"My name, if that is what you are thinking, is of no importance, but as I must call you something and you must call me something, I shall be... Husk!" He chuckled once more, without facing Damien this time. "As in husky—the brave dogs that ran wild and tame in these parts back when the cold dominated the northern parts of Planet Earth."

Damien watched him prepare a solution and an adhesive.

"If we lived in those barbaric American days, I would sink a needle into your arm to stop the pain."

"I'm fine." Damien thought of the cabby's friend in West End.

"You're on fire! You just don't feel it much, do you. I think your mind is not quite with us."

"Where's Caleigha." Damien spotted a brass candle with the light piece on top doused. The inward curves running from the wide base could serve as the fine handle to a hammer, or a dull ax, if he lifted it and swung the metal candle upside down. He thought about reaching for it. His muscles quivered.

"Please. Stop asking me that. Anyway, I was talking about needles. Hollow pins. Isn't that frightening?"

Damien had never been a violent man. Confrontation just wasn't a part of his natural repertoire. Hooking up with Caleigha had been a miracle, a pure impossibility that had happened only because of her ability to cross the line that Damien had ached to cross.

Could Damien defend himself with a spontaneous weapon, though? If he had to? He asked himself. He looked from the pretend doctor to the shiny brass tower and back again. He moved his hand, just a little.

After all, he knew what a solution and a small bandage meant: epidermal drugs. Potent pore osmosis. Which in this case could mean anything.

Help the pain in his elbow? Sure.

Knock him out? Of course!

Kill him?

Why, though? Why would "Husk" do such a thing? And how would he get rid of the body.

Husk turned around, grinning, holding the mini-adhesive bandage in his left hand. "I'm not that kind of doctor."

For a moment, no one moved. Husk's grin didn't flicker away. Damien didn't blink.

It's a choice, Damien thought. *He's giving me a choice. He might have well said, "Do you want to see her again, that girl you keep speaking about?"* Husk didn't seem to know Caleigha; he acted like he didn't know her. Yet the glimmer in his eye made it clear to Damien that Husk knew something.

Finally Husk said, "Trust me?" He lifted the bandage on his finger half an inch.

Damien chewed the inside of his cheek.

Inside his head, he heard his father's voice speaking from a time in his youth that Damien couldn't possibly remember. *"Trust me?"*

Then, slowly, Damien lifted his shattered elbow.

And the amateur doctor smiled, laughing again.

"Why are we stopping?"

"Damien…"

"Wait. I know we've stopped. Tell me why we've stopped!"

"Damien, I'm tired. I'm exhausted! I haven't slept. And you're sleeping all the time! I have to sleep."

"I'm not sleeping! How can you say that I'm sleeping?"

"Are your eyes open?"

Sniff. "I…You said that my eyes were open. I can't see. I haven't been able to see. I can't smell anything, either. The more I think about it…but … we're talking."

"We are communicating. Yes, we are. Damien. Do you really think we could do all this…and keep you conscious?"

"You're going to leave me. You're leaving me, aren't you. You got the code from my memory of my father."

"No, Damien. I didn't understand that. Did you?"

"No."

"You don't sound too convincing."

"I'm not lying to you."

"Damien. We've been through that already… "

"It will clear. You will see. I feel it."

"Are you saying you have it? Or that you don't have the code yet in your own mind."

"I know where it is. I know I'm gaining access. And I feel…what I said

before. The code is just the beginning."

Shuffle. Whisper.

"You're leaving."

"I'll be back. I won't go far. I never do."

"Never? Wait. How long? How long's it been? Since we started? I don't have a clear...memory of the passage of time. That must have something to do with going into my head like this, right? Reliving other...timelines? When did we start? I was...just wondering. Because...like I said. I can't even...I can't even hardly remember starting this. I'm not sure where I...um. Hello? You're going, then? And I'm asleep, you say? Can I...can I sleep, then? I mean, can I? I feel like...I'm always waiting for you. Or I'm not here. Here here. Do you know what I am saying? I'm...I am...I'm alone, aren't I. I'm alone. You've left me. Alone."

Chapter Thirteen

Liars can only be trusted to do one thing: they begin with the truth, lest they be caught in their lies. The truth acts as a foundation of trust. The liar confirms the trust by playing upon the victim's knowledge of the foundational data. Then the liar is ready to take the first step, which might be gradual or intentionally shocking. Rarely will the liar jump somewhere in between. The liar hugs close to the foundation, or 'shares' the unbelievable as proof of their secret intimacy. Often, the more powerful of the two lies does the best at capturing the prey. If the victim feels that the liar has gone out on a limb to reveal some amazing piece of forbidden fruit, some bit of 'knowledge' that seems to put the liar in jeopardy, the victim is more apt to believe and then to play into the liar's hands again and again. The victims of liars always long for the intimacy that the liar provides, no matter the humiliating cost that often comes later.

—Jennifer Corazon,
Trusting Humankind Through Psycho-social Understanding

Martin Warren did not like to look at Tubal Seda. Their names were vastly different, but they were both 22 XY type males, and Chief of Staff Seda never bothered to counter the balding process. What was worse than that, CS Seda was over ten years younger than Martin Warren, so the Primary Chief of Staff had a perfect view of what he might have looked like at sixty-eight years of age without physical augmentation.

Tubal Seda had come to Washington directly. "I know you don't want to hear this. I wanted to tell you personally."

"Mr. Seda," said Warren with a growl of anger and hidden fear, "I have seen that look on your face before. What have you done?"

"I made contact with the Chino-Rus."

"We made a decision!" They were barks more than words. Warren stopped pouring the alcohol and slammed the base of the glass into the counter. "*We* decided!" Then he became a different person, smiling suddenly and growing soft and friendly. "Does Lotti know?"

"You want to know if I gained her permission secretly, is that it?"

"I'm wondering if you think there will be no consequences to your actions."

Tubal Seda held very still. He had a cigarillo between his fingers, and the healthful smoke ran up past the length of his tweed blazer, past his white collar, and past his face in an almost perfectly straight ribbon. "You knew what they would say. *You* didn't get them involved, because *you* knew what they would say!"

Warren laughed. "You're sounding like a conspiracy theorist. Now answer my question. Were you directed by the Vice President to contact the Chino-Rus?"

"No."

"Was the VP aware of your covert actions?"

"Not at all."

Warren cocked his head. He poured the drink he had promised the Chief of Staff from Mexico City and crossed the room, handing it to him in the rippling light of the aquarium that filled one wall. Dangerous fish swam those waters, and Warren gazed at them as he spoke.

"You didn't speak with Cardinal Lin, I gather. An aide?"

Seda shook his head. "I have a connection."

"Ah. Okay. I see." Warren's voice powered up again. "And how long do you intend to manage affairs in this country without the leaders with whom you are sworn to work? I could have you arrested and tried for treason!"

"If that were the case, Mr. Warren, I wouldn't have come here to the capital, now would I? I asked *you* a question. I answered your question. Quid pro quo."

"I think you feel you have more cards than you were dealt."

"I think you know a lot more about the assassination than you are letting on. And that suspicion with all my evidence, that sealed file, has been sent to Acting President Lotti Morrison."

A bluff? Martin Warren listened with his mouth shut.

"Of course, Mr. Warren, the file will only go visual when the key is sent. And that key will be sent in forty-one hours."

After waiting for more, Warren lifted his chin and said, "Forty-one. *Unless*, Chief of Staff Seda?"

"Unless nothing, PCS Warren." Seda crossed the room and set his drink on the counter where Warren had slammed the glass earlier. He turned and put on his most serious public face. "I am a patriot. I *believe* in the freedom of our mighty country. Its unity! Its possibilities for all! I will live and die to protect it."

"And to get another term of office. Lotti can dismiss you as easily as the next President in line."

"Of course!" But Tubal Seda did not look in the least bit perturbed. And that was when he left, without another word.

Like he was *asking* to be assassinated himself.

Chapter Fourteen

The injustices with which man has treated himself might be likened to a body intent on consuming itself. The Praying Mantis has been known to do this: without food, it will begin to consume its own arm. But a man could never survive self-cannibalism. Yet this is precisely the history of our world. Instead of caring for one another, humans have spent lifetimes attempting to kill each other, just to have enough of the necessities of life. All for one purpose, really: To live in peace. The solution lies in defining what, exactly, is enough? Humankind is not ready for the answer. So in the meantime, beware the peaceful man with a gun in one hand.

—Tara Ashman
The Unaffordability of Peace

The world had become a stretch of frozen badlands. Death reached in every direction as far as Detective Corvasce could see, which wasn't far under the black night. He thought he discerned low clouds in the sky, but it was difficult to be sure. There wasn't a twinkle of light anywhere. And the wind was blowing.

The cold chilled a thin layer of ice over his cheeks. His nose stung. He looked at the sky again, at the blanket of clouds that kept the temperature just above unbearable.

But it was still death out there. The tip of his nose slowly became a foreign growth, an unnerving cancer, a part of him and yet steadily detaching from his skull. The tips of his ears began to shriek with pain.

I can't go out there.

He looked down the ladder beneath his feet.

The darkness stared back.

Not even a glimmer of his guide's flashlight.

He examined the broken road outside again, just below the level of his chin. A ruin of faintly familiar buildings lingered at the macadam's edge. The decaying architecture was old-style: crosshatch windows with the panes long shattered, short "Eskimo style" doorways that stepped down into entrances like airlocks designed for low temperature zones—the doors were ajar and even missing in some cases. Fallen eaves left skeletal remains of frames where they had hung above entrances and window fronts.

Corvasce climbed back down the ladder.

The night was suddenly worse here, but without the wind chill the cold was hardly noticeable. He looked for his guide.

She had left him. In his mind, Corvasce could hear her laughing again, a dragging cackle now a distant echo. In the thick blackness hiding walls, tunnels, catwalks, and drops into putridity, he wondered if he might really be hearing the witch.

She was right, after all. Leaving him alone like this was almost worse than getting shot.

Almost.

He reached for his penlight. It was missing. In fact, everything had vanished from his pockets, including his Frost & Fire gum. Only the badge remained.

He brushed at the wall for a railing of some kind. He spread his fingers into the underground night. He took a step down the inclined concrete.

Shouldn't my eyes get used to the dark?

Corvasce paused, waited. He stepped forward and could hear the uneasiness of his breathing, the sound he might make with a knife wedged between two of his ribs.

"Hey! Hey, lady! Come back here!"

His voice echoed, and in echoing away from him tried to sound controlled and tough, tried to sound for all the world like the imperturbable cop, when in fact he felt like wetting his pants.

"Where'd you go? Huh? You hiding? Or you just..." *gone.*

He wasn't acclimating to the lack of light. It really was pitch black down here. And the air felt a whole lot colder than he remembered it the first time.

Oh, of course. The hatch in the old road above him stood ajar. Heat escaped up the shoot while frigid air sank into the recesses where his foes explored an endless night. His heart pounded like the heart of a frightened child.

The ice-encrusted fingernails of a corpse scratched at his left ear. He recoiled. Instead of screaming, Corvasce swallowed and held his breath. Then he reached up slowly, and his hand discovered the sharp tips of some bent wire hanging from the wall close to the ceiling.

He swore.

Then the psychological volcano inside him burst. "Come back here! Whose side are you on, huh? Yeah, I thought so! You don't know what you *had!*"

Corvasce knew he couldn't stay down here. His unblinking eyes were useless. His ears tried to pick up the distant and uncertain blend of sound waves, but they proved incapable of acting like the sonar equipment of yesteryear or even the special hearing of blind folk trained from youth to walk like bats among humankind.

His mind didn't help at all. His deductive reasoning skills scrambled as images of silent hoodlums breathed slowly in the dark, watched him with night vision gear and snickered at one another. They didn't even seem human, in his imagination; these crossbred "pure-B's" living the lives of moles or serpents in an inhuman underground world—what civilized rules would they deign follow, if any, and why would they bother? Morlocks.

Yet he leaned on his deductive reasoning. It was a matter of habit now.

The woman knew right where she had been leading him with a confidence bordering on indifference. She had had a captive at her back and never bothered once to second guess her path. She'd just kept on walking and walking, and after letting him up the ladder, she'd turned and headed for home.

Corvasce had heard about street rats like these living in the tunnels beneath the old cities of the continental United States. They were here, in the maze, and Corvasce could wander in the dark until he died of starvation.

He buttoned up his overcoat and headed backwards until his heels clicked into the base of the metal ladder.

Above him, light seeped down and carried the hints of an icy breeze in a scent of old earth and burnt timber.

I have no choice.

Corvasce had no idea of his location. He had no clue how long he had been out of commission. That sure as heck didn't look like Pandam City up there, and he couldn't be sure of any communication possibilities.

For a few seconds, Harvey Corvasce wondered what it would feel like to die of exposure...

Then he reached the top of the ladder, felt the grit of the frozen road dig into the palm of his right hand, then his left, and heaved himself onto the street.

He didn't make it halfway out of the hole before a grind of metal on metal swiveled a heavy shadow up and around. Red laser crosshairs painted his chest in a brilliantly sharp glow.

The robot took one massive step out of the darkness of a wall. The foot broke the concrete of an archaic sidewalk, spitting bits of man-made stone across the road. A dilapidated growl issued from the machine's loudspeaker. *"You are in—innnn—no man's land. Identifa-a-a-a-i—or be eradicated."*

The robot twisted, took a second step, and dragged his other leg without lighting any of its frontal bulbs. The giant walking box slid rather than stepped onto the road.

It looked half destroyed. It looked forgotten. But the turrets under its right shoulder spun and relocked into position as Corvasce dropped one knee onto the road and held still.

The heavy guns looked like they would work just fine.

"Idennnntify or be e-e-e-e-e-e..."

Chapter Fifteen

Free fall. That's what this is. We are all in a constant state of plummeting, abyss-bound entities dropping endlessly into a hole that is the universe. Not only do we face the icy grip of death, our planet is forever dropping into the sun, missing it, dropping again, missing again, and dropping again to fall one day into its doom. Our solar system likewise cascades in a brilliant display of light against darkness toward the center of the galaxy, into the promise of a crushing blackness. Our galaxy drops endlessly toward nowhere, like so many other galaxies—all of them, in fact! And in the end, cold oblivion awaits us, in endless free fall.

—Widowood Walker
Lithium Revelations

"*All right. I feel better. A little, anyway.*"

"*Don't you ever leave me like that again! You said I was asleep! I wasn't dreaming! I couldn't rest—I didn't—I COULDN'T EVEN DAYDREAM!*"

"*Not to worry, Damien. Did you think?*"

"*What?*"

"*Did you remember things? That's the great thing about your current position—*"

"*What if they had found me while you were gone? You can't leave me!*"

"*I told you: I needed to rest. You are resting. You've been resting.*"

"*All night—was it night?—all night long, I sat here listening—*"

"*And what did you hear, Damien?*"

"*I heard... it was... like crackling sounds. Like bugs with little feet running all over the hard floor.*"

"Damien. Don't you remember? I'm standing on a plush carpet. I'm surrounded by thick nap!"

"You're laughing at me."

"No. Yes. With you, maybe."

"Bugs on the walls then. Creeping. Climbing everywhere... You're laughing again."

"Just listen to yourself. Think about it, Damien! Were your ears always so good that in the night, before you got to sleep, you heard bugs... walking?"

"I... well. Crackling sounds then. Like electricity, maybe."

"Maybe..."

"What are you... what are you doing now?"

"Continuing. You don't want to quit now, do you? When we are so close? You said we were close."

"You sound like you don't believe me."

"Don't hold back this time, Damien. Relax. Dream... even if you think you can't dream. Where were we? Ah... yes. You were getting your elbow fixed."

"Right. Or at least, I thought that was the plan."

Damien woke up the next day. Or at least it felt like the following day. Time seemed to be getting away from him. And he was certain that the pain reliever that Husk gave him shouldn't have put him to sleep.

There was a woman singing in the shower. The bathroom door—well, there was no bathroom door. Just another arched doorway wide enough to push a couch through. But there was a woman humming in the shower. Unless Husk's musical voice was powerfully female. He heard the water splashing, running, rushing, slapping the glass door as she moved. He heard the woman's beautiful vibrato echoing out of the top of the shower stall, between the bathroom walls, and out the arched doorway.

Damien could see the doorway. Husk had placed him on a wide bed in what must have been the master suite. A liquid mirror undulated magically along the wall, awaiting an image to capture. Dressers were closed up in walls—he saw the doors and could only imagine the type of NeoGeek "helpful furniture" units that stood on the other side.

He might have recognized the voice earlier, but he felt straps on his ankles beneath the sheet. When he tried to reach toward the tight sensation of a strap cutting gently into the skin, his wrist locked to the bed. Both wrists. Husk had tied him down.

Then he recognized the voice.

Was it wishful thinking? A drug induced hallucination? Was it a happy dream inside this sudden nightmare?

The singing stopped. The woman told the shower to cease. The glass door made a peaceful whooshing sound as it slid into the wall and squeegeed off the water on the way. Damien couldn't see it, but saw it all in his head. A moment later, the woman walked into the room as carefree as if the suite were her own. Maybe it was.

She wore a plush neon-pink towel darted tightly under her arms. She patted her long hair into a powerful rope inside a second towel of the same color. She approached without a pause, stopping at last at the wall where a dresser waited some seven feet from the bed.

Damien couldn't breathe.

She wore a slight grin of amusement. Reading his thoughts? And she said, "I thought you were awake."

Damien trembled. He couldn't keep quiet. The woman opened the wall, and a dresser that gave the illusion of being made out of liquid and electricity stepped out and handed her a brush. As she started brushing her dark hair, never taking her amused eyes off of him, Damien's mouth opened and he spoke in half whisper and half plea: "Caleigha!"

She laughed. It was the kind of laugh that he remembered. And she continued to brush her hair in long, slow strokes until it began to steadily bunch up again into full curls, thick and reaching. She leaned to the right as she brushed, letting her hair drip all over the carpet as it hung almost to the curve of her hips.

But there was something wrong, even in her kindness, even in her openness.

Damien's smile quivered. Tears played in the corners of his eyes.

"If that's not a man in love, then I've never seen one before. Poor boy."

He didn't mean to, but the word slipped again from his mouth. "Caleigha."

"I get it," she said, swinging her hair over to the other shoulder and brushing vigorously. Big curls leapt into existence. "You've known someone who looked like me before. Even my hair color, huh?" She frowned. "Why so sad?"

But it *was* her. It *was* Caleigha. Not just another 127 XX. Damien felt this impossibility in his gut. Why would she lie to him?

She wouldn't.

"You lost her, didn't you. You *really* loved her." She stared at him in long contemplation for what seemed a year.

Damien couldn't speak.

The woman took her clothes from the dresser.

"Please!" said Husk from the doorway. He wore a different shirt, a blue muslin button-up with an even wider collar than he'd had the previous day. A gold chain sparkled with inset lights around his neck. "Let the 'poor boy' sleep!"

"I didn't wake him," said the woman in the towel. She headed for the doorway.

As she passed beneath the bowed ceiling that led into the next room, Damien couldn't stop himself. "Caleigha!"

She froze, holding her towel up with one hand, holding her clothes in the other. She looked at Damien with clear familiarity in her eyes. She faced the next room just as quickly and gazed at the floor in thought.

Then without a word or another glance of recognition—*and it had been recognition!*—she left Husk and Damien alone.

"Don't get distracted, Damien."
"Who's there!"
"Just me. The question is, who is here with me? That you, Damien?"
"You're mocking me now. You think this torture is fun, don't you."
"Oh, you have no idea."

Chapter Sixteen

Most beginning historians remain ignorant of the fascinating details that prove that the End of the World has approached and occurred many times over the years. Depending upon which cultural record one examines, one might find the End of the World at the end of the reign of the dinosaurs, at the fall of biblical giants, with the destruction of the Mayan men of wood, with the consequences of Messiah Simon Bar Jonah, Y2K and its decade-late economic depression, or the cataclysmic and totally unexpected fall of Europa into Jupiter's stormy atmosphere. Signs? Perhaps. The world ends all the time, and it is certain to again.

—Father Boadecia Vatilla,
A Doomsday Book: For Today, Tomorrow, and Whatever Follows

Warren found the letter inside his satchel as he prepared to leave for the day, sending all of his internal alarms into a high and silent scream.

Who could have slipped the fauxpaper note into his bag without him becoming aware? How was it possible when PCS Warren never let the bag out of his sight. Even when it sat in disuse beside a two-hundred-year-old spruce banzai tree, the leatherette case was largely out of reach around the far side of his desk from the entrance to his office.

Warren realized right away that he shouldn't have touched it. How many leaders across the centuries had been murdered by poisoned paper or cloth? Of course, any concentrated form of poison should have been detected by White House security sniffers in the walls. But that didn't change the fact that someone had somehow bypassed his personal and natural self-preservation defenses and slipped him this note.

The slightly yellowed page sat on his desk, open because he had opened it, but curling back in on itself because he had dropped it at the thought of poisons. He looked at his fingertips. He awaited...something...a tingling perhaps, a numbness. And he almost thought he felt it there. But it was only his imagination.

Nevertheless, he groaned up from his chair and crossed the room in strides unbecoming a person of his age and rank. From a cabinet, he withdrew a curved device with a concave fan of bristles on one end that looked a bit like a comb. He placed his thumb on a pad and a green light responded.

He swept the room with the hand-held sniffer, swinging it from left to right. It made a slight humming sound, but raised no alarm. He waved the sniffer over the paper, and when nothing different happened, he swept the paper with the bristles to guarantee contact.

It could be a new product, he thought. *Viral. Biological. The molecules of the paper itself—*

But no. *This is paranoia*, said the voice of his belovedly estranged wife. *Get a hold of yourself! Or give yourself a good slap in the face—that's what you need. Call me. You know how much I love to serve you.*

He set down the sniffer and listened to the nearly non-existent hum disappear slowly as it powered down. And he picked up the paper.

He would send it to Analysis, or rather Security would do that for him. And they would see his fingerprints and read his biosigns, and they would snigger about it—no doubt—and frown and send him a message reminding him about typical safety protocol. Politicians should be smarter than this.

He held the paper and read the words anyway.

Messier Warren,

By all means, be afraid. Fear has done more to change the world than all the hope and benefits that life has to offer.

You seem to have lost something. Can you figure out what it is? Before it's too late?

I bet you like to be the one holding all the cards when you sit at the gaming table. This time, unfortunately for you, you don't know what game we are playing. Do you?

Sincerely,
Your Private Nightmare

Warren crushed the paper in his hands.

The damage hardly mattered. He couldn't actually give this to security. The insinuations alone would drum up too many questions. People would need to investigate in areas where they shouldn't be looking right now.

He flattened out the paper, folded it along its original crease lines, and then tucked it back into his bag.

Calling up a light screen, he dialed a number without a name or address attached.

The call replied with a voice twisting with so many accents at once, Warren could never tell which the man was trying most to imitate. "Bartlebee at your service, Gov."

"You know they make software that will disguise your voice, if that's what you're after."

"Don't know what you're talking about. I was born this way, Gov. I'm a veritable smorgasbord of endless possibilities!"

"That's why I'm calling."

"Another threat? Don't the government have regular avenues for such—"

"Don't waste my time, Bartlebee. I need another rat."

"A rat! Last time you needed a mole, I recall. The time before that, a worm. Seems I'm running a zoo of lesser creatures these days!"

"Do you want the job or not?"

"Well—"

"Because I can take my untraceable tax-dollars elsewhere."

"Have I ever disappointed? What you need is connections, I know. I've got endless connections. Mine is a government under the government. Private industry. As if those tax dollars are really untraceable." He laughed a choking cigarette laugh.

"We'll use the last drop. Take a look over this letter. I want the source. I want it eliminated from the game."

There was a pause. "Just like that? Don't care to know who you're dealing with first? The name of your, your letter writer?"

"Just do it."

"Oh, I will. I always do." Bartlebee had dropped his ridiculous accents, which left him with something like a southern drawl with a twist of Latino music. "But let me get this straight from the horse's mouth: You want me to handle the matter, no matter who it is."

"Are you deaf?" Warren felt just about ready to pop. He saw his reflection in a mirror shaped like a rose. His face darkened with blazing red.

"Just do it."

Bartlebee's happy accent menagerie returned. "Always do—"

And then the voice cut off. A sweet computer voice played in his ears as the light screen detailed a security breach in his call. "Your call is being interrupted by...Vice President Lotti Morrison."

Her face appeared beside a government address. She leaned towards him. "Martin Warren. It appears that we have important matters of state to discuss. Wouldn't you agree?"

Warren's reflection went pale.

Chapter Seventeen

Each man and woman will be pushed into the black. The black is the place where every cadet realizes how much pressure he or she can take, where he or she will break. The black is a real place inside the cadet's mind, and it must be comprehended. Without coming face to face with the black inside each of us, we are not in a position to combat those evils necessary as a peacekeeper of the people.

—Department of Justice,
Police Academy Primary Training

The massive security automaton swiveled the barrels of its gun again. There had to be something wrong with the barrels. The antipersonnel systems must have detected a systems malfunction. Then it settled on a barrel and kept Harvey Corvasce red lit, ready for what the robot called "eradication." As if the detective was a rat and the automated soldier in charge of pest control.

Maybe that's what the broken machine thought.

It tried a third time to speak with a damaged colloquial unit. *"Eye-e-e-e-e-e—"*

Corvasce knew what it was trying to say. With his hands raised high in the air, he deemed it prudent to identify himself, even if his speech triggered the robot's firing mechanism. "Pandam PD! Detective Harvey Winchester Corvasce!"

The robot didn't seem to hear a word, or ignored every one.

"Override delta-three-zero-lima-one, Harvey Corvasce, Detective!"

Nothing.

Corvasce suddenly realized he needed to speak computer language. There was only one way he could pull off such a miracle. He needed to transmit from his badge. "Hold for badge number!" But was there time?

When the robot continued its attempt to talk, Corvasce felt more than his skin chill in the darkness. *"Eye-e-e-e-dentify yourself or be-e-e-e-e-eradicated!"*

Great! The frigin box's mics are busted!

"Pandam PD! Hold for badge number! I'm going for my badge! Hold for badge number!" Corvasce lowered one hand toward the inside of his coat where the elaborate shield hung on the inside pocket.

"Don't move!"

The robot didn't wait for the detective's reaction. It opened fire.

The heavy guns clicked wildly.

But that was all.

So ...

Corvasce ran.

He fell almost as soon as he took his feet. His right foot slipped beneath his left, and he went down, smacking his hands into the ground to stop the fall and save his face. Icy gravel broke the skin.

The robot called again. *"Don't mo-o-o-ove! Halt! You are in-n-n-n-no man's land! Identify yourself or be eradica-a-a-ted."* Wheels whirled, grinding old metal until the joints squeaked in painful, high piercing sounds like android screams. But these were no screams, even though the machine ought to have screamed—if it had feelings. It was trying to move again. It had every reason to be discouraged. The gun wasn't necessarily empty— the beast should know if its arms had been depleted—but the barrels, like the rest of the stumbling contraption, didn't look wholesome enough to fire successfully.

And that's what Corvasce was counting on: that the armored security unit wouldn't get a second chance to pull the trigger.

He scrambled up again and sprinted in a vector that required the robot to swivel more and more if it was going to paint this human target red a second time.

Thunder hit the ground in one powerful thud. The robot swiveled, ground the upper part of its body into the base until it squealed in a jam. Then it pulled out of its stuck position and moved its mobile leg. The second leg lifted, crunching down on itself.

Corvasce thought it amazing that the monster could balance at all. Not that he paid much attention. Just as he reached the side of the nearest building, the automaton shouted, *"Halt or you willl-l-l-l-l-l ..."*

When it couldn't finish the word, the thing just opened fire again.

This time, the gun worked. Shots blew fist-sized holes through the wall of the buildings so quickly, the gun cut a dotted line up and down, right behind Corvasce.

The detective threw his hands in the air as he ran. He heard himself cry out, but didn't register the sounds until after he'd stopped. He sprinted in an arch that took him across the street again.

He ran to the fallen walls on the robot's side, counting once more on the fact that the deadly machine would have difficulty tracking him due to its agony in swiveling all the way to its right.

A second later, the robot let loose a third time. It tore a ceiling from its moorings and brought a second floor down hard upon the first.

"Halt! You will be eradicated!"

It hadn't gained a lock on Corvasce. And he ran between the buildings as his man-made assailant strategically blew away the concrete overhead.

Huge chunks of rubble rained around the detective. He howled when a piece of crust the size of his leg caught his hand in the fall. Then he dove, certain that the sound of his tumbling gave away his position.

But the darn thing's deaf! he thought in the seconds that passed. It had not responded to his override command or his verbal attempt to announce himself as a peace officer.

The firing continued—no lead, no explosives, no electricity, just molecular compression composites powerful enough to rip a man into little bits from three hundred yards without the slightest problem—but the line of fire continued in the direction Corvasce would have taken had he stayed on his feet.

Of course. The automaton had projected the detective's egress and did its best to take him down.

Which meant that he had to move, or the robot would reckon the likelihood that he'd fallen in the rain of rubble and then check for life signs, heat signatures—unless the machine was also partly blind.

Corvasce scrambled without thought of noise but with much thought of all the possibilities regarding the machine's ability to see. He climbed through a broken wall and crossed a room opened to the brutal cold of nature and covered with debris.

He twisted his ankle, just a bit, catching himself. And he kept running.

He put his hand down to steady himself as he crossed a pile of what might have been wood, but what most likely had been DuraChalk wall remains, and his hand splashed into frigid water that made him hiss. A rotten smell filled the room as if he'd broken open a nasty egg. The cuff of his sleeve was drenched. He tripped again. As he continued, he splashed his foot into more rank liquid. But a moment later, he was out of that room and continuing in an angled direction away from the robot.

"You can't ever escape those things," a trainer had once told him of military units similar to UVI-MX Heavy Armored Frogs. *"People think they can, but they really can't. Those buggers are faster than they look. They can always find you. That's why they are so effective against the enemy."* The words had not been a problem to Harvey Corvasce in the academy: he never expected to be on the receiving end of an automated assault machine. Times change. He was not going to take any chances.

Yet he also didn't want to freeze to death.

What had the thing been anyway?

Besides discarded? Old war junk? It obviously thought martial law was in effect, at least for the area. The machine kept saying, 'No man's land.' What machines said such a thing? Where in the NAU was there a no man's land?

Detective Corvasce hadn't recognized the model. He wondered if it was foreign, a leftover of one of the secret wars that paranoid people said were always happening around the world, just beyond the sight of the happily ignorant public.

Maybe it was just really old. It sounded like it. It acted like it. The darn thing might have been sitting in the rubble, out of commission, for a couple of decades or more before the nanites got some of the basics working again. Then how long had the thing been trying to heal.

But wait a minute! If that were true, then where on the freaking planet am I?

The robot had spoken in English.

Now it was speaking in thumps and slides, echoes that shook the earth and caused walls to disintegrate around him.

Thump. Slide. Squeak.

Thump. Thump. Slide. Thump.

Corvasce's jaw began to shiver. His lower teeth banged against the uppers.

Thump.

He stopped on the far side of the building when he saw the pile of wire mesh and the walls leaning precariously in his direction. With that giant walking around, he was lucky that those walls hadn't fallen and smashed him when he couldn't see them. The darkness was worse here. But the robot probably didn't see light and dark the way he did. Who knew what visual arrays it had at its disposal?

Thump.

Sand rained down into Corvasce's hair.

Thump. Slide.

Gravel crunched as the detective began a slow retreat. He couldn't go back. But he didn't dare climb through the mesh of old wire—welcome to my webbing...

Thump. The sound of a brick being pulverized beneath an angry grinding foot.

Thump. Slide. *Screech*. Thump.

It was closer now. Corvasce could feel its proximity in each metallic footfall.

Thump!

The walls shook. The water splashed in unseen puddles all over the room.

Thump!

Corvasce crept in a new direction, away from where he thought the ten-ton automaton might be.

Thump!

But it was getting impossible to see. It was dark. Inside this crumbling building, it was darker. He climbed what must have been a second floor fallen and inclining into the first.

Thump!

His feet lost traction. He slid back to where he started, just another chunk in the entropic mess.

Thump!

A tremendous crash ripped through the building. The arms of the robot swiveled into the room. The walls came down even more. The guns took aim for the last time.

And Corvasce was pinned.

Chapter Eighteen

All the world is a stage. Or perhaps more accurately, all the world is a drawing board, or a piece of paper, or figment of the imagination filled with that which we prefer to call reality. It is not the mind that is a tabula rasa, but the world around us. For years, mathematicians and scientists the world over have written observations in what we once called Mathematical Expressions. What we failed to recognize for many years was how very much observation played a part in the reality we were trying to record. The truth, which we now must concede, is that mathematics are the reality, and what we have called reality all along is no more than our perceptions of our observations of the mathematical reality all around us. Numbers are real. Everything else is a matter of interpretation.

—The Linear Brotherhood,
Book of Lies

"*We're doing better. We're on the right track now, I see.*"

"*I'm glad you feel so confident. How much longer…*"

"*That depends on you.*"

"*Are you speaking with your mouth full.*"

Laughter. "Does that matter?"

"*I'm hungry.*"

"*You're not hungry. Trust me. I'm the doctor. I can see everything from this vantage point.*"

"*But not the past?*"

"*I'm not interested in the past, Damien. Surely you've figured that out. It's the future that interests me.*"

"*And I'm the key. You think I have it in me?*"

"I've never doubted it. I think you're looking for something else, something you're not telling me. You know it as well as I. You're just holding back. You're always keeping secrets. I wonder... if poor memories are really a matter of subconscious secret keeping. Every scrap of memory is encoded within the brain, you know that don't you?"

"I just want to get this over with. Before it's too late."

"Sure you do. Okay. Here we go. I have faith in you, Damien. Please don't let me down again."

"Look who's laughing now."

He struggled to concentrate as Husk spoke his jovial and soothing words. The effort proved so difficult, Damien Reyes ultimately decided that he must have hallucinated. That couldn't have been Caleigha a few moments ago. But that last look she gave him when he'd called her name, that face of recognition...

No. He had to be drugged. Or at least still kicking his way out of a doped state.

She's still in the other room. Dressing.

"What did you say?"

Husk ran through lines of nothing once again—blah, blah, blah. Chatter important to no one, relevant to nothing.

And Damien felt himself dreaming again of his father:

His dad was floating to the front of the classroom after a parent-teacher conference. Damien couldn't have been older than the fifth grade. The teacher had left the room and Damien's father stepped up to the white IntelliBoard and grinned like a mischievous instructor. *"It's like magic, Damien!"* he said, picking up the LightWrite pen from the silver shelf beneath the board. *"You remember? It's simple, really."*

And Marcus Reyes wrote the code on the board:

$\{w(@\$)\}\text{-}f = Mna$

It had been magic, all right. Almost as soon as he finished the handsome scrawl, Damien's father turned the point of the pen around and wiped the board clean with a flourish.

Then...he said the alien word. *"Wasurenasai."*

A door shut in Damien's young mind.

And Damien was back in Husk's room, strapped to the bed, trying to listen to his captor and getting none of the one-way conversation to enter his brain.

"It's simple, really."

"What did you say?"

Husk chuckled a little and pushed his black hair behind one ear. "Come. Do you want to go for a little ride?"

Damien nodded as Husk undid the restraints.

"Your arm...should be...better than new." He uttered his evil friend laugh, a sort of Dr. Frankenstein chortle no doubt mimicked from the recent Virtual out of Hollywood. "Assuming Sienna didn't hinder the final stages of the healing process. I would have rather you slept another five or six hours, just for the finishing touches. Try it out. Just don't whack the elbow on anything else until morning, okay? Go on, try it out."

Sitting up carefully, and getting ready to sprint off the other side of the bed (if it was the only way he could get away), Damien curled his arm. Then he rotated it in the air.

No pain. None whatsoever. The arm didn't even feel as tired as the rest of his body.

"Huh?" said Husk with pride gushing from his face. "Did I say better or didn't I?"

Damien grabbed the elbow slowly, gave it a gentle squeeze. Then he moaned. "Ah, it hurts so bad!"

Husk's smile dropped into a limp frown, his eyes wide with surprise. "What?"

Damien wormed a grin onto his face. "Just kidding. You're right. It's much better." As he lowered the arm, he saw his fingers shaking. He wasn't going to bluff his way to freedom. Then, he'd never been very good at subterfuge of any kind.

She's still in the next room. She might come back.

Husk saw Damien's eyes glide to the doorway through which the female 127 had passed. He turned his head and looked, then looked back at him. "You ready to go? Then let's go! Shall we?" After helping Damien from the bed and onto shaking feet, he smacked him on the backside in a playful pat.

And the nudge almost knocked Damien over. "Why am I...so..."

"Dizzy?"

"Not dizzy?"

"Good. The problem with nanite surgery that, um, goes 'unregistered' is that the anesthesia tends to be a little—what's the word?—rough, around the edges, you know? Sluggish. It comes on, it goes away."

"Nanites?"

"Surgery, yeah. Don't worry. They've already cleaned out of your system. But the issue of telling your nerve endings not to report anything back to the brain…well, that's complicated, you know? Easy to damage things. They have doctors whose entire responsibility has to do with anesthetics. Anesthesiologists. But you probably know that. Anyway—"

"To fix an elbow? What did you do to me?" Damien's knees were quivering now, as if he was about to take his first step in years.

"—well, I'm not an anesthesiologist! All right?" Husk was shouting, but he was also smiling, almost laughing. Damien wondered if he was on a little Happy Powder himself, a little self-prescribed medication. "But I am a good doctor. Am I not?"

"Why aren't we in a hospital?"

"We are in a hospital! My hospital. You see, a doctor's hospital is where his white coat rests. Ha, ha, ha!"

They were walking, albeit slowly. A scent of chamomile and rose oil wafted across the room. It may have always been there. Diagonal lines of vibrant colors raced down the walls, giving him a start until he realized they were decorations reacting to their presence. The lines swam upward into a portrait of Damien's face. Husk barked at the wall, "Not now!" The colors exploded into fireworks, one color at a time, leaving purple stars against a cloudy sky.

"Nice house," said Damien.

"Thank you!"

"Where are we going, then?" *Away*, he thought, though he didn't think it very hard. He wanted to find Caleigha, and all he had was a fragment of an address and a threatening voice. And the woman in the other room.

She can't be Caleigha. She's just another genetic type, who happened to choose Caleigha's hair color and…and nail color.

A memory of Caleigha's nails sparkled pink, glistening with sunlight, as they touched his arm…

SO WHAT if the woman in the other room chose the very same kind of nail polish? They are genetic matches! Maybe something in their genes prodded them both toward the same choices. It could happen!

He wanted to see Caleigha. He wanted to save her, if she needed to be saved. And right now…he didn't know for sure. Intuition crowded his mind with confusing possibilities. Like, "How long was I out?"

"Does that matter? We'll just go for a little ride, is all. I think the fresh air and the city lights will do you good."

You're not trying to get me out of the building until Caleigha, or whatever her name is, has departed, are you? Sienna. Yes, I think you said that was her name.

Damien didn't need to ask the question. He couldn't speak anyway, his heart ran at high speed as they walked into the room into which the woman had slipped.

And she was right there, fully dressed now. The towel was on the bar between the main room and the kitchen. She wore a pink Flappin shirt split up the small of her back and flapped open, gray culottes exposing her calves—clothes that showed no regard to the deep northern weather. Sienna had her back to them, and the thick curls of her hair fanned and then duck tailed down her back to the part in her shirt. She spoke into a hand device of some kind—some other NeoGeek toy, no doubt. And she closed the doors over the device and turned just then.

"Are we ready?" Husk said.

Damien felt Husk's guarding hand taking the recently healed elbow.

"I'm not going, if that's what you mean." Sienna crossed the room, stepping into the recessed floor and walking barefooted through the high nap of cream-colored carpeting.

Damien peeled his eyes away from her and looked at Husk.

Husk looked at him and shrugged. "She's not coming. See you later, honey."

"The car's downstairs." She sat in one of the couches, and the pillows shifted to meet her preferences. When they reached the front door to the cushy pad, Damien spied back at her. Sienna had placed a Virtual bud against her forehead and shut her eyes. She sipped from an orange slushy drink in an iced-over glass, set it on the table beside the couch, and snuggled into Hi-Fi delirium.

"Who are you?" Damien whispered. He asked the question in Caleigha's direction, but Husk answered, which was fine because he did sort of mean both of them.

Husk was rubbing the back of Damien's neck. "I'm your new best friend, Damien Reyes. But first things first. You afraid of the big bad wolf? Stay real close to me, and you'll probably live to see the sun rise!"

"Did you get it that time?"

"Did I—of course I got it that time! What I didn't understand was the alien word. It sounds like something...can you tell me more about it? Consciously I mean?"

"No. I can't. Really. But I think my father said it..."

"As a part of the code? I see..."

"Do you think that my father...programmed me?"

"Definitely. I think that is perfectly clear."

"But how, exactly?"

"Oh, there are so many ways. The programming of the human mind has been going on for centuries. Mesmerism, I think they called it. Hypnotism, they dubbed it later. There are so many ways. Brain washing."

"Neural plugs? I heard about them doing that, in Chino-Rus territories."

"That's speculation, but certainly not impossible. You 'heard about them' in the movies, didn't you?"

"Well …"

"That's science fiction, Damien. According to the medical journals, neural plugs are exceedingly dangerous. The brain is just—"

"Wait a minute. 'Exceedingly dangerous?' What about what we're doing?"

"Anyway, I think it is clear that he programmed the code into you from a very young age."

"You didn't answer my question."

"That's because I'm your friend, Damien. Of course what we're doing is dangerous. I told you that. You wanted to do it. Right? All forms of medical exploration and learning are dangerous, at first. Until they are deemed to no longer be dangerous, because they get to be understood. It's okay, Damien."

"So… my father hypnotized me."

"Something like that. Thus the alien word, I think."

"When you mean alien—"

"Enough with the science fiction, my friend. I don't mean 'out of this world' alien. Nor did you, I gather. Just foreign. Just something you wouldn't likely encounter between hypnotist and subject."

"But… the crib…"

"Oh, that's easily explained. Your father started programming you before you were born. The secret you're after… it starts with your own DNA."

Chapter Nineteen

They say that the future of espionage is dead. Are these lies upon lies? Can our science and modern police force be so enhanced as to put spies out of work? Or are we, the public, so naïve that we are easily led into false senses of security? What if enemy states already own and control the NAU? In a future age, would we even know when our leaders became puppets?

—Kris Parkhill,
The Obsession for Clarity

In the office, Pandu noticed a green triangle with two mirrored lines squiggling down the center. The image flashed only once over his work, and he did not understand the meaning. He never did. Shirts came to him with questions about previous accounts. He answered without looking into their faces. They went away. With both hands gripping his pen against his chest, he flicked his eyes across the view screen, gave commands, watched the air ducts appear in his drawings. He did not forget the symbol. The day might turn yellow at any moment.

Only twice had he left work without a legal excuse. Once he told the head suit he felt ill. After that, the building EMT scanned him and reported elevated serotonin levels, but no disease. So he told the suit he just had to go home—he just had to. The lies did not make the suit happy. Pandu did not go home. He walked, and he drew, and he read symbols. He was never fully conscious of their meaning. When the day turned green, he returned to the office and reported that he felt better. The suit had no smile, for he had no mouth. There was no point in explaining anything to the suit. Perhaps someday Pandu could retire as a bum on the beach. Might it be wonderful to drown in those Hawaiian waves? But he had to think of Jarita.

After work, she met him in the lobby. "Come with me. I have something to show you." She hooked her arm around his. She glowed. She glanced at the empty faces of sweatshirts, jumpsuits, and sweaters. She smiled at them, as if they shared her excitement.

Outside of the Lupine Café, she held him beside a lamppost. "Before we go in, I must explain to you, so you don't freak on me."

"Let's go home, Jarita. I am tired." It was still a green day. What did that symbol mean? Why had he seen it? He stared across the street at a uniform on horseback. "Do you see him? Is he staring at us, Jarita?"

"Please don't try and change the subject." Her fingernails were digging into his forearms. "This is important to me. I think you will like him. He's inside."

"Who?"

"Ed. You will notice what I noticed. He is special. He is like us."

"I don't feel anything." Pandu pulled away and bumped his head into the concrete pole. He grabbed his forehead. He saw the red blood on his fingers. The green day remained.

"He has a face, father. Come look at Ed." She tugged at his jacket. "I've told him about you. He also sees the signs you write and read. He says he has blue days."

"That's just an old expression. My grandmother used to say it. She didn't believe me. Her face—"

"Dad! Come sit down with us. Ed is waiting. You will see he is special! And we are getting married."

Numbing—his lips alive with vibration, his cheeks buzzing, his lashes unable to stay up, his eyes focusing on the grit of powdered concrete at their feet—Pandu let her drag him into the café. He smelled coffee and chocolate and raspberry pastries. With his fingers, he caught the word, "Marriage," as it escaped his mouth.

She balanced him into a chair. He blinked at a man's hands on the polished stone tabletop. For so many years, he had protected Jarita. He kept her home, schooled her with the Interactive when he was at work. He denied her college, promising Distance Learning when he could afford to further her education. He had even shut off the VR, but—clever girl—Jarita had figured out how to restore the projections. And they had not argued over that sin. She was just a young girl, he had tried to tell himself. Just a young girl.

"Look at him, Dad," said Jarita after the introductions.

Ed waited. Pandu knew what he would see: no hair, no ears, no true head at all, but a mist of color, a movement of human scent, a truancy of physical existence.

So instead, he raised his eyes ever so slowly. He looked at his beloved daughter. And he screamed.

Chapter Twenty

Game theory posits all the logical possibilities a player may take in any given game. The developers of gov.com years ago attempted to apply high-level game theory to human political design, with disastrous results that well might have wiped out the human race. Machines have their place, as well as their limits. Humankind has its place, and right or wrong, humans have decided it a moral imperative to keep machine minds in their subservient positions. If Robert Basie's Theory of Indeterminance has any truth to it at all, one might suggest that it is only a matter of time before the creations of man take over anyway. Unless, of course, there really is an over-seeing deity in control of the Indeterminant variable.

—Liddy Comptrolor
Social Scientist's Almanac

"The robot hovered over Corvasce for two seconds. The wall continued to crumble around the machine's boxy polygons and the rounded barrels of its low-slung arms. The ceiling crackled and fell on one side, casting particleboard, braces, and DuraChalk dust behind the detective.

In the demolition, the detective's legs were buried by debris. He felt cut somewhere, bruised severely. He would have prayed that the bones weren't broken, had he time to think of anything beyond the pulse weapons of the monster above him.

The robot brought the guns around. Its upper body casing squeaked under the strain of movement. *"Ha-a-a-a-a-lt!"*

Just as the red laser crosshairs lit and rolled through the swift clouds of dust, landing at last upon the detective's chest, Corvasce succeeded in his last play for life.

From his coat, he pulled his badge. It was the only thing the rats had not stolen from his pockets. (But why?) The sheild came to life with flashing red and blue lights and repeated signals of identification.

The flashing lights lit the war unit's numbered chassis and body armor.

The robot stopped. It froze as if suddenly out of power. Even the laser switched off, so that the only light in the remnants of this room emanated from the red-red-blue-blue-red-red-blue-blue from the badge held like a real shield at arm's length.

Thick dust wafted over Corvasce's face. Panting, he broke into a throttling choke that curled his body and caused him to lower the flickering wallet.

In a panic that stopped his breath altogether, he hefted the badge between himself and the robot.

But the security unit had not moved. It showed no signs of life whatsoever. Suddenly, it had become a part of the wall, a decorative memorial to the war of someone's father.

Nevertheless, the ceiling continued to make crackling and slipping sounds as the archaic structure bent without the wall's supports.

Then the robot returned to life. He spoke, but Corvasce didn't understand the fractured message: *"Wa-a-a-a-ar-r-r-r—"* The guns swiveled up. Compound bursts tore away chunks of wall and breaking ceiling.

Corvasce figured it out. And he got out of the way, crawling straight past the machine that struggled to save him from the danger of falling debris. He stumbled again in the alleyway, and accidentally slapped the badge into an asphalt path.

The badge stopped flashing.

The robot backed into the alley, allowing the remainder of the building to crumble in on itself. Then it followed Corvasce as quickly as its heavy feet could carry it.

Thump. Tear. Thump. Slid. Thump. Scream. Thump.

On the cold street again, Corvasce examined the badge. It still wouldn't flash. He touched his communication. "Dispatch, acknowledge!"

He didn't even hear a crackle of static in the implant.

"Control, please respond! Officer in distress!"

Nothing.

He changed channels. "Ames!"

Again, not a peep.

He tried a general channel. "Officer in distress! Please acknowledge! Can anyone hear me!"

If anyone could, none replied.

And then the robot stopped behind him.

Corvasce felt his insides grow as cold as his skin and the icy breeze around him. He turned slowly, wondering if the metal beast would give him the dramatic experience of at least seeing the red crosshairs on his body one last time.

Unlikely.

When he somehow managed to turn all the way around and face the war machine, he found it once again disengaged, silent, dark, waiting.

Corvasce stood there, growing colder and colder in the wind. He didn't move for close to a minute, fearful that suddenly flight would trigger an automated response similar to shoot first and ask questions later.

The guns hung at rest, pointed level with the road.

"Great," said the detective. "I get it now. You recognize me as an officer of the law, is that right?"

The robot remained a quiet statue. If a bird were to land on it now, the thing wouldn't likely budge an inch.

"And you're deaf." He turned around, scanning the street for any other signs of life that might have awakened during his attempted escape. Of course, who would show their heads with this mad dog running around. "Super."

He considered his badge again. If he thought he could pull it off, Corvasce might have tried to open up the robot in search of a communication device.

No man's land?

But with the lights in his badge no longer working, he didn't think that kind of tinkering would be a safe idea.

Yet the machine might prove useful. Especially if he was in some sort of war zone.

But how could that be? And where?

He faced the robot again and waved a hand for it to follow. "Okay, let's head out!" He shouted, as if that might help, though he doubted it. Acting with authority, though…that was probably a good idea. So long as the sentinel remembered who it was or who he was with. With any luck, the code for "Detective" transmitted clearly and his rank would be of worth.

Corvasce started to walk.

The robot righted itself, squealed as it turned on the street, and began to follow him.

Bang! Slide. Thump. Grind. Thump.

The detective's heart thundered with the realization that the machine behind him would go nutty again and paint his back with red light immediately prior to blowing him up. He kept walking anyway. He glanced carefully once or twice over his shoulder. Both times, the robot looked complacent, obedient—though it was hard to tell, as it had no head and no androgynous features beyond the upper torso, lower torso, heavy legs, and guns hanging like arms from the box of its shoulders.

Corvasce tightened his coat around him, drawing up the collar and buttoning it so that only his nose and the tips of his years and the top of his head protruded from the soft fabric. Still, the collar didn't seem to help, and he started to wonder how warm the robot might be. It had to be warm, his gut told him. But his gut also told him most vehemently not to try and touch it.

"Nice doggy," he said, wrapping his arms around himself. His breath went before him as he walked, and he drove his frozen nose and cheekbones through the cloud before it could dissipate.

They walked for a few miles, before Corvasce began to wonder why the sentinel behind him didn't acknowledge a territorial limit. He thought it had to be some sort of security guard, which would have received such orders. Yet, his metal mutt was old, rebuilt from the inside to varying degrees. Maybe it couldn't recall anything but the simplest of its last orders.

Or maybe it had been waiting there for some other purpose.

Corvasce thought of the woman who had put him up there on the road. How she had laughed at him. And how she had asked him what side he was on. The NAU wasn't at war.

As far as he knew.

But someone had killed President Sanchez in a public place, in front of cameras, in front of the world. Corvasce had no idea how much time had passed—he'd been out of commission long enough for his captors to transport him to some underground maze beneath a 'no man's land.' Hadn't the president just been killed this last morning? Or was it a day ago, now? Or had it been days since the catastrophe?

Well, he thought, *so long as the mutt doesn't shoot me in the back and remembers who I am, he may end up protecting me from...whoever's out there.*

They kept walking. They didn't see anyone. Yet the detective felt that someone was watching him. Someone somewhere.

And then, finally, he saw a light.

He had walked for so long, stamping his feet, trying to keep warm, that he had started to look at the shorter buildings around him and in the yards and fields that stretched away from him, seeking a shelter for the remainder of the night. He wasn't thinking straight. Everything looked warn and destroyed. Smashed. A real no man's land between two warring political bodies.

More than a mile off the main road, a window flickered with yellow light. Were it not burning so brightly, Corvasce might not have noticed it at all. His animal instincts took over, so he might have been wrong, but he would have sworn in that frigid instant that the flickering glow came from a fire. A real fire. With heat.

Chapter Twenty-One

Energy is everywhere and has long been suspected of degrees of intelligence that we are only scarcely aware of. So-called empty space was proven to be quite full so many decades ago, the point hardly seems worth noting. Many decades before that, Oppenheimer and other scientists figured out how to release the energy from a single atom, causing a chain reaction that killed hundreds and opened a door of threats and fear that would last forever in the story-books. What we are only now beginning to discover in the theories of sentient energy is that some energy is distinctly good and some decisively evil. Good and evil, of course, are relative positions. So depending on which position one takes, there is energy that exists that may be personally aimed to harm that individual. Some energy will consciously help a person. Compasel Wright, therefore has suggested that he or she who can tap that energy, communicate with it, "may have power to do things heretofore seen as magical."

—Umbar Brecht,
Uncovering Celestial Symbiosis

"*S*it still."

"*Sit? Am I—am I up?*"

"*Can you tell, Damien? Hold still for just a second. I have to…attach this…*"

"*This what!*"

"*Mojo-bob…*"

"*What's—you're joking with me.*"

"*If I named all the devices I am currently using, Damien, you'd be lost on the second word. Now, you do your part, and I'll do mine. Can you feel* this?"

"Are you—are you doing something? Am I sitting up? I don't feel anything. I can't see anything."

"Curious…"

"Why are we stopping?"

"We're not."

"I can hear us… are we going somewhere? Are you whispering to—to someone else again?"

"Just relax. We're taking a short precautionary trip."

"Turn it off! Get me out! Turn it off! Right now—they're here, aren't they! Wake me out of this—this blindness—I feel like I'm not even connected to the planet anymore!"

"Stop."

"You're whispering again."

"Yes, but I'm whispering to you now. Do you want to live?"

"How can you ask me that?"

"I need you to do two things right now. Listening?"

"Get me out of—"

"Damien, if you aren't quiet, I'll have to pull the speaker, which will essentially cut off your verbal—"

"My verbal what? What is happening?"

"—Stop, Damien. You have to… No, I don't think that would be a good—"

"What wouldn't be a good idea—You're whispering to someone else again!—Who is there with you? Is that—is that who I think it is?"

"Just listen!"

"I can hardly hear you now! Stop whispering! I can't tell when you're talking to me or to—"

"That is because we are in real danger right now, and we have to move, and you have to be quiet! Okay? That's the first thing: don't make anymore sounds or I'll have to—"

"To… UNPLUG THE SPEAKER? Are you saying that—"

"Yes. You are no longer using your mouth. You are communicating directly from your brain so that your mouth is no longer necessary. Now, the only—"

"Slow down! You're talking too fast!"

"—reason I haven't switched off the speaker yet is to make sure that you are still with us, all right?"

"No! It's not all right! Wake me up!"

"There's no time. QUIET! They're coming. They're here! But the *machine's still working. There might be time! You have to keep going! I'll stay with you."*

"GET ME OUT OF HERE! WAKE ME UP! GET THIS STUFF OFF OF ME! HURRY—hurry! Hey! Hello? Hey. Can you hear me? Can... anyone hear..."

Crackle...

"All right. Okay. Concentrate. I'll concentrate. Try to relax. Remember... what happened next... and get that key... I know where it is. I can almost... almost taste it..."

Why aren't you running?

The thought that Husk had injected nanites into Damien's body for a little elbow repair work made him wonder how many other computer-controlled intelligences that the NeoGeek could have put into him.

But that's not it. You're holding onto something, aren't you.

When the elevator doors parted, the street level of the building looked no different from any other office building in the northern City of Kodiak. A gorgeous android with sparkling gold hair and retro silver skin acted as the front desk clerk; Vivaldi played quietly through sound beams that touched everyone crossing the lobby; a gaggle of teenagers bantered about their attire, then left through the clear front doors and into the party lights of the new state holiday festivities.

Husk and Damien rounded a fountain of illuminated water. Husk kept bumping into his side and hanging onto his elbow.

Damien couldn't take it anymore. Not that he wanted to spring away.

But why aren't you running?

He looked down at Husk's hand and worked up as much quiet anger as he could, shoving the fire into his tone. "Afraid I'll make a break for it?"

"Not at all! I understand the police are seeking you in great earnest, my friend. But this only works if you are very close to me." From his pants pocket, Husk slipped a device that looked oddly like a manual stapler. Then he made it disappear into the pocket again.

"Really?" Damien said, adding sarcasm to his tone. "Wow!" He wiped his brow. "Well—whew!—now I understand." But he was shaking.

The police are after you.

A little good angel appeared invisibly on Damien's shoulder and told him that he should turn himself in.

Yes, yes. But what about that reason you aren't running? Can you be truthful with yourself? Can you?

Husk laughed, pure conspiracy. "Anyway, I can't lend you mine. We need to get one for you. Otherwise the authorities will track you down in a matter of seconds."

"I don't—"

"Of course you wouldn't understand. Did I say the police were after you? I think I did." They went through the double doors and walked down a sidewalk lined with DuraTrees— *"All the perfect size and shape of a real tree for only half the price, and they don't get bigger as the years go by!"* — and ducked under the orange and green streamer lights playing Disney music for the shoppers walking the other way.

"You said they were."

"And of course you look like any other nanika nanika XY —"

"141."

"Right!" Husk put an arm around him, as if they were real buddies. "The field generated by the object in my pocket dampens your implants. You are a nonentity, according to sensors that might try to read you. Actually, that's not true. If you were a nonentity, all the alarms would go off, right? And the police would be called. Because only bad guys wear black hats."

"What?"

"Never mind. Anyway. The cops can't ID you by your face, even if they have you narrowed down to a male 141. There are too many! This thing scrambles your coded ID so that sensors just think it's a familiar computer glitch, a false positive—there are so many glitches going on, that: well, thus the phrase, right? Glitch happens!" He laughed again, 'shaking the moon' as it hung in the chilly sky above them. "Here we go."

He opened the door to a standard triangle car with one seat up front and four in the back.

"Where to, boss?" said a little kid behind the wheel.

Damien gasped. At first glance, the kid looked no older than six. He even had a speech impediment that made *"Where too, boss?"* sound more like *"Wa ta, bass?"* Then he saw the crack of intelligence in the little face as it grinned a wry smile.

Husk hurriedly did introductions as he shut the door and slid across the half-moon seat and squished up against Damien. "Damien, Shorts; Shorts, Damien." Then he added, "Take us uptown, for starters. I need to get my friend here a widget."

With his arm leaning over the back seat, the kid said, "Shorts?"

Husk leaned forward. "We're speaking in code." He bounced his eyebrows like the world's worst undercover spy.

"Whatever!" *What-eba.*

Shorts spun around, and Damien understood. He was a stunt. His parents, for whatever devilish reason, had decided when he reached the age of six to retard his growth. That kind of alteration to a body type had to be predetermined, during the post-conception process. But here he was now, "Shorts," and he might have been fifty or eighty, but he looked six, and he'd look six forever. Or until his time to check out of this life. Damien had seen very few stunts in his life: maybe two, in all his years. And the speech impediment? That had to be well practiced. Practiced to a degree that the kid — the stunted man — probably couldn't speak normally now if he wanted to. Unless he was mimicking someone else.

The car jolted into the traffic. The autos up and down the road registered the movement, projected the stunt's vector, and made way. A few of the other drivers honked their horns anyway, just to let Shorts know their unkind feelings toward him.

Shorts shouted at the window — a pointless, old-fashioned practice that Damien had only seen in historical Virtuals.

Husk was smiling at him again, like he was thinking about giving Damien a big wet kiss on the cheek.

Damien pressed himself into the far wall of the car.

"Ah, oh," Stunt said, checking out a flashing screen on his dashboard. He punched a button — literally punched it, with the center knuckle of his right hand — and the ceiling slid apart, leaving only a sheet of NuGlass between the passing universe of flying vehicles above.

"What is it?"

A squad of police bumble bees converged slowly, black and yellow lights flashing.

"Company."

The sirens began to sound. And all the cars — all of them — automatically pulled over to the side and locked their passengers in.

"Hello? Did you... did you pull me out? I'm not in the memory. I've left it. Hey! HEY! Are you—"

Crackle. Snap. Crackle.

"You there? Where you go? Can you hear me?"

Crack.

"Bugs again. And I'm alone again. Alone with my thoughts? Except, I can't replay my own memories! DID YOU HEAR ME? You have to—flip the switch, or something! Rest the thing-um-a-bob! Reattach the mojo-meter or whatever that was!"

Crackle.

"Can you hear me now?"

Snip.

"Why… do I have the feeling… that someone… is dissecting me… while I'm unconscious?"

Crack. Crackle.

"Hey…"

Chapter Twenty-Two

Imagine a box without a lid, a base, or any sides. Imagine a circle without a circumference. Imagine a triangle without points. Imagine Time. Now you finally see clearly.

—Adolain Mongoli
At Its Best

Jarita did not come home with him. Pandu slept in the house alone that night. He wondered about his daughter. Her name would soon leave him, as his wife's name had evaporated. Of course, he would still remember her name if ever it was mentioned at work, or if she called. But she wouldn't phone. Nor would his daughter return. She knew he would see only a blouse and tights and heels. She recognized better than her mother what Pandu experienced.

When the yellow world arrived, it woke him from dreams he wanted to forget. He had been running blind through architectural plans like those glowing lines on his work screen. Sitting up in the bed, he watched the door radiate with sunbeams despite the late hour. He dressed with speed, then exited the building without locking his front door.

Across town, he paid the cab and waited for the car to fly away from him. Then he began to pace, though he couldn't understand why. Fourteen long steps one way, fifteen back, sixteen around again, seventeen—was he just killing time? If so... why? This had never happened before tonight.

"You look like a man who could use some help," said a uniform who appeared out of nowhere. He didn't bother to ask for permission. Whipping out his gene reader, the uniform did a swipe, pondered the results, then said, "I'm gonna call this in."

"Why?" Pandu said. He started to sweat. "Is there-there something wrong? I'm just out for a walk."

"You live on the East Side. Long walk."

"But is there something wrong?" Pandu tapped the gene reader. He wanted to see the small screen. Not that he would have been able to decipher the images, but no cop had ever detained him.

The world was still yellow. He needed to walk. His feet turned to go. He held himself still. He started pacing again.

"Where do you think you are going?" said the uniform.

"Nowhere," Pandu shouted to the distance. He spun around, walked past the cop. He couldn't stop the perspiration. "I told you! I'm just walking!"

"Hold still," said the uniform. "You're making me nauseous." He tapped his com link. Nothing happened. He tried again.

Pandu turned around. The sweat stung his eyes. The world stayed yellow. Where were the signs? What did he need to write? Where was he supposed to go? He almost screamed against the madness.

The uniform caught him by the shoulder.

"I'm committing a crime?" Pandu's volume increased with his words. He shrugged free and continued to pace, twenty-two steps now, twenty-one the next time, then twenty, back and forth in front of the uniform. "I can't walk on this street outside these—these industrial buildings?" He only scanned his environment for a moment to figure out where he might be. Even then, he wasn't really sure. He had directed the cab in the same way he walked and ran on the yellow days: *left, straight, keep going, right here, wait, go forward again, now right, and follow the curve…*

He heard the uniform try to contact dispatch again and fail.

"What does the gene reader say, Uniform? Am I crazy? Paranoid? Demented? What did you *read?*"

"You're fine," the uniform said. He watched Pandu pace back and forth. "You may go." He didn't seem to mean it.

Then Pandu understood the reason for the uniform's lack of sincerity. Pandu turned around, paced eighteen steps, turned, paced seventeen, turned, paced sixteen steps—Pandu wasn't going anywhere!

The uniform watched, swearing blasphemies from the back of his throat. He studied the gene reader again. Disbelieving the results, he brushed the device across the side of Pandu's neck on another pass. "What are you doing?" Pandu whispered. But the uniform again said nothing for a time, mumbled, reading no problems.

Twelve steps, turn; eleven steps turn; ten steps, turn.

Pandu curled his fingers into his hair and pulled, but not hard enough to dislodge the roots. He gritted his teeth when he faced away from the uniform, held his breath, all to stifle a scream. "I'm missing it! I'm missing it! I'm missing it!" he said and searched the ground for signs, the buildings for the smallest etch, even the uniform twice as he passed the cop. Sanity did not reappear.

He walked three steps, then two steps, then turned...

"One step," he said. He moved his foot forward, ground it into the concrete. "Turn. One step." He started to cry. "Turn. One... step. Turn."

Three overcoats appeared behind the uniform. One ran a gene reader over his own wrist and showed his personal results to the cop for identification. The uniform backed away, started to whistle a happy tune, and followed the sidewalk to nowhere. The second coat kept his hands in his pockets and watched the dark buildings. The third flashed a device in Pandu's eyes.

At last, the world turned red. He stopped.

"Download," said the third overcoat. He kept the red disk in front of Pandu's eyes.

Images began to burst through his head at high speed: circles, squares, triangles, lines, dots, dashes, a string of measurements with meaning, colors as cues, and deep-set instructions so that he could focus, so that he could act, so that he would not be paralyzed by fear or confusion. Pandu felt the agonizing drawn-out sensation of excessive vomiting, only his stomach did not purge: his brain seemed to empty of important information that he could not process. He saw his daughter for an instant. Then he envisioned the man, who was like him, climbing aboard the stealth ship in the bay and then sending confirmation through the darkness and the fog and the red color. Then came a jolt of memory Pandu did not recognize: that same man, now facedown in the water, his task finished, his life over, and all his precious memories therefore eradicated.

Pandu could not blink. He tried. "Who are you?" he said, his voice a wheeze.

"Counterintelligence," said the coat and the hat without lowering his hand. "Don't worry Mr. Pandu. You are serving your country anyway. And just like you don't remember working for them, you won't remember what we are doing here...in the morning."

Chapter Twenty-Three

Truth is, of course, relative to any given situation. Jackson Hilt once noted that truth is even relative between one delusion and another, reminding us that delusions are socially defined: a delusion in one country may seem perfectly acceptable logic in another, depending on the cultural and historical background of the people. "Make no mistake about it," he said in his seminal paper Our Dream Within The Dream, "we all live in our individual delusions." What we see as acceptable truths are based entirely on our belief systems. Our lives, being defined by our experience and therefore by our personal beliefs, are always delusions to someone with slightly different beliefs. Our lives follow absolute truth, if we define 'absolute truth' from our individual perspectives. Regardless of one's beliefs, truths also become relative to the defining characteristics of any given situation. Whatever situation in which one finds oneself, facts will redefine truth into new forms. So the question is this: What is true? The answer is clear: Everything, depending upon the variables surrounding the observer.

—Abi Shimai
AnyYear's Zen Master Almanac

"I resent the accusation!" Osprey's image flickered.

"I'm not saying that you had anything to do with the murder of the President—"

"But you're not defending me—I've been in politics long enough to understand your defensive, tactical maneuver. You're thinking it! Everyone's thinking it. It's being reported on the news! The people are talking impeachment—replacement!—prison! Firing squad!"

"Just your enemies, Nathaniel. All politicians have enemies; that's just a part of the game. No hard feelings. Other parties hope that your failure to attend the Philibuck graduation ceremony was an intentional move."

"—I told you it was intentional! Henry Sanchez and I stood at odd on funding issues. I was showing the people I represent that I wouldn't change my schedule just because a president, who didn't respect our fiscal concerns, was coming to town!"

PCS Martin Warren sighed, sat, and wiped his brow with a handkerchief handmade by, well, by the widow of the late President. "Calm down. We have plenty of other problems right now."

"I don't! Lotti Morrison thinks that I'm an integral key to the problem!"

"The Vice President is scared, that's all. And she should be. Consider: The President is dead; if the Chino-Rus are not behind it, we don't know who is; we can't speak with them freely as yet—and that is foolishness, in my view; and are geological weapons in use? Was that an instance of geothermal warfare in Turkey? We just don't know yet. And now, who is next in line for possible assassination? VP Morrison? The Secret Service is running without sleep right now." Warren stopped talking.

The image of the Chief of Staff of the Northern States flickered, though the motion had nothing to do with transmissions. Osprey stared at something in his own far-away office. He held a couple fingers to his bottom lip. He shook.

"Martin...my—my wife left me this afternoon. Jerit took our little girl and went to her sister's place in Kutuk. She says—she says she doesn't trust me."

Martin Warren played stoic by holding perfectly still and shutting his eyes. "I didn't know you had offspring."

Nathaniel Osprey seemed to be speaking to himself, emotion clouding his memory that he was conferencing with the Primary Chief of Staff of the NAU. "She thinks the talk is true. That I had something to do with the President's—obliteration."

"Nathaniel."

His circular eyes found Warren again. "Tell me, Martin. Would you quit your job...to save your marriage? Do you love your wife that much—does Pat mean to you what she does to me? Huh?"

Warren straightened in his chair. He wondered if Osprey knew that Pat had taken a legal love partner. She had argued that it was better for his career if they didn't get divorced, that it was 'legal,' but her decision had effectively separated them and ruined their marriage more than a year ago. "This issue is bigger than a single man's marriage."

But Warren's image must have vanished again in the swell of Osprey's depression. Osprey seemed to be speaking to the wall again. "I love her, Martin. I never wanted to scare her. I fear that I've hurt her! By—what?—doing my job? Martin!"

"Stop it, Nathaniel!" Warren jumped. "Do you want to give your enemies something to grab hold of, something that they can really use to get you replaced with their own, sad candidates?"

"I don't know if I care anymore!"

"Take something!" Warren gasped a long and flourishing sigh—all for dramatic show, really. "Think!" He needed to get this train back on track before Osprey crashed and ruined everything. "Will Jerit love you or trust you any more if you run from your responsibilities? You need to prove your consistency. Prove to her that you are worth trusting, Nathaniel. Don't be wishy-washy!"

Resolve brushed over Osprey's projected image. "Yes. Yes! Yes. Of course."

Warren said his next words like slow hammer blows. "Solve. Your. Problem."

"Yes. Yes-yes. I know...who to call."

PCS Warren cocked his head to one side. "Just don't do anything illegal."

For the first time during the call, Nathaniel Osprey smiled. A crazy light lit somewhere in the Chief's eyes. "Since when would a politician do something illegal?" Then his projected image vanished.

* * *

For the next two hours, Warren brooded over a virtual chessboard, reconsidering his position. He hadn't commanded any piece forward for close to ten minutes. The chessboard didn't mind. But Warren did.

There she stands, he thought, looking at the queen ghosting on one side. Her dress blew in a virtual wind. Her squinting eyes considered him considering her. *Lotti Morrison? Yes, I know you. I know what you're really after.*

Warren looked at a bishop. *The pious Nathaniel Osprey, I presume?*

He looked at the other pieces, each ready to make a move against him. *Delia Cordova of the Pacific Islands? Tubal Seda? Maxine Ojeda? Josephine Walker? And all the rest of you? I know what you really want. But you won't kill me. Not me. I'm too important at present. You need the secrets that I have. You won't say it openly, will you? But in private...a cutting blade from behind? A threat? I only wonder if you really think me ignorant of your unshared hope.*

Warren placed a call to the Secret Service.

"Dodger," said a hard and careful voice. Clearly the man knew the source of the call; he always answered this way. After all, the Primary Chief of Staff couldn't be calling for a report, when regular reports were being issued by the SS—so it could be a chew-out session, just so that the politician could tell the population he had done so. Special Agent In Charge Raul Dodger had every reason to maintain his angry Spartan composure.

"Dodger. I have a new lead for your team to follow."

The Agent in Charge said nothing for a moment, which made Martin Warren unexpectedly gleeful.

Then Dodger's voice came through, still rough, though slightly befuddled. Almost untrusting. "You do?"

"Indeed. It seems that Cardinal Lin has been sighted somewhere in the North American Union. Do you want to hear more?"

Chapter Twenty-Four

Darkness is only an absence of light. Light is the crowd of social particles that we prefer. All the world is a stage. And if all the world is a stage, then there is no need to be frightened. So what if everyone's watching you. You are looking back at them. How often do you see clearly? Answer: We see through a glass darkly. Because there is little light on this stage.
— Blandish Duncan,
Actor's Paradise: The Philosophy of Young Dr. Rosa Abrahim

How did it look? Frightening, probably. But that was her problem. The old woman appeared when the door opened, a yellow rectangle of warm light in all the chilling darkness. Corvasce barely made out her expression: a woman spotting a banshee with hollows for eyes just outside her door.

But that's not how it must have looked. Certainly just as frightening. Perhaps more so: a tall stranger with a walking tank behind his left shoulder.

"Who goes there!" she said. In English.

Almost as quickly, a red cross in a circle appeared on her stomach, and the robot hummed another attempt at speech. The attempt failed, grinding sounds upon itself.

"Detective Corvasce, Pandam PD!" He said, conscious that he very well might have sentenced the old lady to death by bringing the mech to her front door. With his dark badge held in the air, he strode forward, doing his best to put himself between her and the heavy guns behind him.

The robot flared with excited noise that no longer made sense. No doubt it was trying to warn him, and hopefully it wouldn't assume the woman a viable threat and eliminate her. *Can you see how old she is, ya dumb bag*

111

of lug nuts?

He saw wrinkles. He saw the gray in her face and in her hair. If she was any genetic type at all, he didn't recognize her.

She took a step back.

He hid the excitement in his body language from the metal beast as much as he could, hoping that metal monster wouldn't perceive any of the stress he felt.

You might just as easily shoot me in the back!

"The old junk heap back there is deaf and hardly running. But its composite weaponry seems capable enough to do us both in. Take my hand. If we look like allies, it'll back off."

"You don't look like you really believe that," she said, grit in her aged voice.

"I've had a hard time communicating with the mutt."

"You don't look like police. Why should I believe you? Is that a real badge."

"Real. Busted."

"Pandam City?"

"Yes."

"Then maybe you can tell me what happened."

"What happened?"

"It's freezing out here. Come inside before you catch your death." She scanned him up and down with her eyes. "Look about halfway there already." She took his proffered hand.

Corvasce didn't see any red laser light, though it could have been on his back, for all he knew. Or somewhere on a roof support beam, if the war machine thought he could kill the woman in an avalanche of timber and—what was that? Mud? He looked over his shoulder.

The big dog had turned to stone, or cooling metal, once again.

"It won't follow you, will it?" She trembled.

"I sure hope not."

They went inside, and Corvasce shut the door himself, slowly, watchfully.

The robot didn't move.

"I heard the boom. People are talking. No one knows for sure what's going on, but some say they saw a dome appear for a moment and then disappear just about as quickly. I don't know…"

The old woman walked about as gracefully as the mechanical beast, shuffling just a bit more daintily. She led the way into a main room. Two doors sealed this room off from others.

112

The house couldn't be more than 500 square feet. The hot air almost hurt. All the walls appeared to be constructed from timber and earth—how barbaric. A closed hearth jutted toward the center of the room. Vents on the sides allowed heat from the fire to pour out of an oven with a glass front. Beyond the glass, Corvasce noticed hooks and metal pins fixed into the brick walls. The construction appeared to be efficient, spreading both heat and light through the room.

"Why in the world are you all the way out here?" She sat in a large chair cushioned with hairy pillows and blankets—was that real wool? She indicated the second chair.

Corvasce sank among the blankets and pillows of this seat, wrapping himself quickly in their warmth. There was a garden smell, an animal scent, sweat on the air, spices of some kind, a faint smell of something like bread and maybe a little over-aged fruit. The walls were covered with the skins of animals that must have been as big as bears—not that he had seen any. Shelves of food storage ran toward one of the doors. Other shelves held brittle paper books that might have easily been a hundred years old or more: the covers had cracked away, the corners of pages were eaten by time, and the combination possibly added to the taste of dust and age all around him. He didn't care. It was warm. Almost sweltering, which was far better than what he had experienced outside. The tips of his toes, though, didn't seem inclined to shift from their suffering state. He buried his fingers under his arms.

"More to the point, I suppose: Why are you out here in the middle of the night? The equinox has passed us by. The winter will be here soon. You don't want to be out there in the winter, not even with your metal pet." She watched him shiver until he forced himself to stop. "I take it you're not here on official business."

"Lady…"

"The name is Manda. But you may call me Mrs. Guth." She paused. When he didn't continue, she rolled her eyes away from the gruffness in her voice as if reproaching herself for her rude behavior. "I'm only awake because the Sandman came and stole my sleep. He does that, you know. No, I suppose you don't know. When you are young, the Sandman brings you the gifts of drowsiness and dream. You are all babies upon whom he leaves his blessings. You have no idea of the price, though, do you? Of course not. When you are like me…" She stared into the fire, talking to herself, as if this was her normal practice here in the house through long nights.

Corvasce waited.

Manda looked at him with her droopy eyes. "…when you are old, he comes. Years of payments all unpaid. That's when you pay for the bliss of youth. And you try to catch up. Sure, during the day, you try. Sometimes you can't do much else. Sit. Lay back. Remember. Dream a little, or think you dream. Wake an hour later. Rested? No. Still tired. Still cursed by the Sandman. For you know that night fast approaches, even through the longest of days. And the Sandman will be at your door. He'll slip in through the cracks. He'll wake you after bedtime and stand there grinning like death, but less kindly. And he takes the rest of the sleep you needed that night." She pinched at the air before her face. "And he runs out of the house, laughing to himself. And you know you'll see him the next night."

Corvasce just needed to get warm. Let her talk. He could do what needed to be done as soon as the strange itching feeling left the toes he busily wiggled inside his service boots.

Manda laid her head in one corner of the chair. "Do you ever wonder," she said, with the firelight flashing yellow and orange over her eyes again, "what it will be like…when both of them come at night from their vastly different shores? Or are they brothers? Will Death drive off the Sandman, claiming me as his own, in that day? Or will the Sandman make a bargain! Steal my sleep one last time. Make me sit up through the longest night of the year…the winter solstice…until the sun rises at last. And then…never return. I'll think he's come back…but it will be Death at my door then. Death, in cahoots with the Sandman."

Corvasce matched her frown with his own.

She rocked her head in his direction, and smiled.

"Where am I?" he said slowly, hoping against hope that she wouldn't say, *Neverland!*

Drawing two breaths, she kept the smile on her face. "Why, child, you know where you are."

"I was kidnapped."

She scowled. "Well that can't be right."

"Nevertheless."

Slowly, she sat up in the chair. "You are in grave danger, here. If you really are who you say you are."

He listened to the wind blowing into the house, threatening to push it over.

"Robot or no robot." She cackled, low and slow. "You are far outside of your jurisdiction."

The wind rattled the pane of glass.

"Liable to become prey to the Seekers."

Corvasce tensed. He spoke slowly, eyes touching the other doors in the tiny house. "Where am I?"

"I'm amazed a detective like you can't figure that out!" She sat back again, and said with a long breathy sigh, "You are on the edge...of the Kingdom."

Chapter Twenty-Five

Yoshi Harwood, Living Buddha, said, "In the field is a flower. In the flower is the bee. On the bee is the flower, the pollen. In the pollen is the bee, or that which the bee needs. In the needs of the bee are the molecules of the flower. In the flower are the atoms linked to the bee. In the bee are the quanta of the flower and the bee. In the quanta is the universe, in which we find the galaxy, in which we find the planet, with the field, and the bee or the flower, both, all the same, all connected, because it's all the same. You are the flower. I am the bee. And I am the pollen. And you are the molecules ….." Despite his popular vote, Harwood was shot and killed—rejoining the mixing universe—on his birthday.

—Candice Sheori
The Mixing Universe

"I heard that…"
"Ah! You are cognizant."
"What?"
"You are thinking. You are sentient. You are aware."
"Who… who's there."
"Damien Reyes."
"No. I'm Damien Reyes."
"Of course you are. I was addressing you."
"But where's—"
"Where is… whom? Hummm?"
"—the other doctor. Where is he?"
"Are you crying, Mr. Reyes? My, this is fascinating! I must contact some of my associates. You won't go anywhere now, if I leave you for a

moment?"

Sniff.

"I didn't think so. I shall return in a little while."

"Where would I go?"

"Astonishing! That you would ask such a question! Good day to you, Mr. Reyes."

Damien had always thought that police bumblebees were enormous. And the name was appropriate, because they sure didn't look remotely able to hang in the air the way they floated about the triangular automobile this very instant.

Shorts looked over the back seat at Damien as if suddenly aware of the sort of cargo he carried.

Husk lifted a hand to calm him down. "Just wait for it, my friend." He squished closer to Damien and clapped a hand on the ID scrambler in his pocket.

"You think that's really going to work? If they picked up his tag somehow, they'll guess you're jamming their read and search every building and vehicle manually." Shorts looked like a kid, but he clearly knew what he was doing. Even if it was almost impossible for Damien to understand what he was saying with such a bad speech impediment—it had to exist intentionally; that's the part that got Damien the most. At least he wasn't being driven around by a fool.

"Well if you have a better idea, my friend, I'd love to hear it." Husk glanced at Damien, and his nervousness stood out like electricity in a dark room.

Shorts nodded, staring at their special passenger. "Mousse."

And he might as well have been a prophet. Damien watched the black and yellows drop slowly into the vicinity, eighteen in all. Officers in full armor stepped onto the street. Other cars continued to land.

Meanwhile, all civilian vehicles were stuck to the side of the road or the side of the buildings above their heads.

A woman with a black goatee and a long detective's coat appeared from an unmarked police vehicle. She stared at the floaters pinned to the buildings above her like bugs on a radiator. She pointed up at them and shouted orders. Armored officers ran to their trunks.

Hornets sprang from the backs of their cars: swarms of the glistening metal seekers took the air, swam in a complex mathematical pattern like fist-sized tadpoles with swishing tails. They flashed little red and blue police lights in unison and made their way to the nearest of the floating cars.

Loud-mouthed irritants shouted from nearby autos.

The woman barked other orders and spun a finger in the air.

A moment later, a pleasant female voice spoke from the radio. *"This is a police lockdown situation. Everyone please remain calm."*

Shorts threw a green and white disk into the back seat. Husk caught it deftly, and pressed the center button. White foam filled his palm. "Come here, big boy." He squished the foam between his hands and started rubbing Damien's hair up into wavy spikes.

"You think this is going to keep the police from identifying me?" Damien said, laughing through a peculiar mixture of joy and terror: glee that this insanity might end at last, that the police would sort everything out; fear that he might never see Caleigha again (*Fear that he had already seen her again, that something else very strange was going on, that Caleigha was in on it, but that maybe she hadn't been in a position to tell him the truth—NO, NO, NO! THAT'S MORE INSANE THAN THIS!*)

"If they don't scan us," said Husk, working quickly. "Those hornets up there? That's all they can do. People are lazy—once you figure that out, the rest gets easier. The police will trust the hornets to find you, if you're here, which they are probably unsure of."

"How did they locate him anyway if you've had him near a scrambler all this time?" said Shorts with harsh suspicion in his little eyes. "Someone tipped them off! It's the only possibility. Somebody called the fuzz. Somebody talked."

"Peace, Shorts. Stop it, will you?" said Husk with an intentionally relaxed smile. Then he resumed his conversation with Damien. "If an officer looks at you, he'll see someone matching the description of the man they are after."

"What—"

"Criminals are idiots. That's why they are always getting caught." He finished, sat back, then pressed close to Damien again and held his hand like a boyfriend. "Try to look natural—not ambivalent about what's going on. Curious, instead. Interested and concerned. Hopeful that the cops will get their man!"

"But you're criminals."

Husk grinned to the point of showing off his beautiful teeth and healthy gums. "We are patriots, Damien. A far cry from criminals."

Shorts moaned in the front seat and repositioned himself so that he could see the officers checking out the cars in front of them. He had to lift himself a bit to see clearly. Damien wondered how he managed to see around the steering wheel at all. But then, he hardly needed to use it. The car no doubt steered itself.

"No. Criminals are stupid. They are always so close to getting caught that they go overboard with their disguises. But come on! In this day and age? How do you make a male 141 like yourself look like someone else? First you dye your hair. Then you throw on beard or something, like that fashionable lady running the show out there. Then you change your ears, you change your nose, you change your eyebrows—usually criminals will do things so sudden and over the top to look differently, like go for the death nostrils look, that that's what cops look for. They never expect their prey to look normal, because criminals tend to look guilty. Just do what I said."

"It's not going to help." Shorts pointed a short finger. "Take a look."

The armored storm troopers approached each car in wary gatherings of three. One androgynous figure with no face carried a pulse rifle raised against a padded shoulder and aimed at the driver. A second black-clad figured carried an electric riot stick extended to the full seven feet of its possible length. The last carried a handgun in a most peculiar way: he, or she, held the pistol in the right hand while keeping the cocked right forearm level with the ground and parallel to the car. The forearm acted as a table upon which another gun sat without a muzzle. The officer held this second heavy and uncomfortable device with the left hand and tapped buttons with a thumb.

"Those, dudes, are P10 Weasels—the latest in deep-scan sensors."

Husk didn't reply. He sat quietly for so long, Damien couldn't help but speak through his mixed emotions. "So the mousse won't help?" He almost laughed at these so-called patriots, these "smart" criminals.

Husk must have noticed the glow in his face. For the first time, he grew sincerely dark. "Do you know why they are after you?"

Shorts interrupted. "The question should be, do you really think they won't shoot us on the way to the station?"

Through nervousness, the laugh escaped Damien in spite of his desire to keep quiet.

Shorts dropped his brow. "I'm not kidding."

Damien looked at Husk.

Husk brightened a little, if for no other reason than he thought he was starting to get through. "You are wanted for the assassination of NAU President, Henry W. Sanchez."

Blink.
Sniff.
"I am...I am still here..."

Crackle.
"And I am alone…"

Chapter Twenty-Six

Psychologists came to favor masks for one primary reason: an individual can act as himself or herself without thought of the social cost. If, therefore, a mask turns a man into Don Juan, it is because the man really is an insatiable romantic inside. If the mask turns a woman into a mass murderer, then the killer was already there. Some psychologists, after these studies, believed that masks should be outlawed rather than promoted. Yet most concluded that the inner clash was the real problem. And that it would be best to get the dirty members of society to expose themselves, so that they might get the help that they need and become new people. This is the real origin of Dr. Jeshua Kniter's famous statement, "The mask makes the man." In the end, they were outlawed anyway.

— Barbara Hernandez
Peace Beneath The Face You Wear

Corvasce stared hard at the old woman. With her soft eyes and sagging eyelids, she stared back, just as seriously. He thought about running for the door. Surely the robot outside would target any threat to a police officer, if the decrepit war machine still remembered who he was.

If it didn't, then the robot might just as easy rip the house to pieces to get at him again. His race through the old buildings on the cold road in the dark was too recent for him to take any such possibilities for granted.

Beside the fireplace, just an arm's reach away, six black iron pokers with nasty hooks and points stood in an ornamental holder covered in ash. They wouldn't hold up well against guns. But they were better than bare hands. Especially cold hands. And his fingers were still cold, despite how deeply he dug them into his armpits.

He blew into his fists, slowly, one hand at a time, as if unafraid of the Seekers that Manda Guth had warned him against. His eyes checked the doors again.

The two doors, like the front portal he had shut himself when he had entered the house, bore latch doorknobs with aged remnants of ornamental brass color that lingered, flaking, in a few places. If any of the doors opened, he thought hastily, he'd see one of the latches twist downward first, turning toward the wiry hairs carpeting the floor.

But then, the flickering of the fire made the handles look like they were moving a half an inch up and down all the time. None of the shadows in the room held still.

"Is there anyone else in the house?"

She smiled a little, and shut her eyes. "The Sandman's gone, if that's what you're wondering. If you mean someone else? I have lived alone in this house since my husband died of old age just after his fifty-first birthday."

"Fifty-one?" Corvasce thought about the things he had read regarding the Kingdom. So many virtual vids had been made about these backwater naturalists, so many novels, stories, lies, how could he tell what was true and what was the imagination of creative minds?

According to the history, a few Amish families were among the first to lead the charge into the new wilderness in the Northwest, the man-made lands that no one wanted. The last vestiges of Native American tribes, starting with the Hopi and other anti-city groups, likewise laid claim to the borderless lands. There was a big Hollywood Virtual about warring sects, that made a ton of money a decade ago—Corvasce remembered that. Mormons vs. Mountain Men, he recalled, but did either of those groups really exist in the Kingdom? Did any of them? Or were they all wild folk living off the land? If they believed in survival of the fittest, then maybe only the strongest and most barbaric endured here. Or maybe the peace-loving stories were true, and the Kingdom was swarming with hippies who really were making the world a better place.

But the old woman had answered that question already, hadn't she? She had warned the detective that he was in danger. That the Seekers would get him. Question was, were there any already in the house? Was she one of them?

She hardly seemed a viable threat. If her husband died at fifty-one "of old age," then the constitution and medical resources of real people in the Kingdom had to be next to nothing compared to everywhere else in the NAU.

And if he really was on the edge of the Kingdom, then he couldn't be too far away from the Kingdom Air Force Base. Kingdom AFB had been built on the border in the early days, when there had been problems. Or rather, when the skinheads had started to persecute the Kingdom folk who lived in the border towns. Corvasce suspected that the military base was really situated there, "on federal land," just to make sure that nothing bad ever brewed to life inside the Kingdom.

He thought for a moment about the ruined town from which he had escaped, and the old military unit that had come to life in order to defend the "no man's land" there. He *harrumphed* to himself as he looked into the embers. Maybe there was a lot about Kingdom history that never made it into the modern record that children had been learning in school for the last half a century.

And it was when he'd made the sound that he realized that the warmth of the spice-scented house was getting to him, washing over him like a spell that was putting him to sleep.

He was almost dreaming.

So he sat upright. He took a deep breath.

"Ah!" said old Manda in one long sigh. "He comes to bless you now." She nodded. "You just wait...Ol' Sandman is a thief and a liar. In the end, I think he is a kind of devil, a fallen angel, who..."

She continued, speaking more and more softly. Possibly falling asleep herself.

Corvasce slowly leaned forward, reached, and took a poker from the side of the brickwork.

He sat back, and just held it.

Manda laughed a little, but didn't say anything.

Not even when he fell asleep.

Chapter Twenty-Seven

Albert Einstein spent a great deal of time discussing the fact that light travels at its own speed. Dusty Meyer expounded in no less than seventeen books that time, likewise, travels at its own speed. To say that the speed of light is a constant and that the speed of time is a constant causes no clash. Yet when we theorize that a particle moving faster than the speed of light moves backward in time, we are identifying a quantifiable vector that disagrees with Meyer's Law of Temporal Direction. For a particle to move against a constant stream of time, that particle would have to be in a state of irrefutable motion. Meyer proved that a particle in perfect physical stasis was nonetheless racing forward at 1 TC (Time Constant). His conclusion that -1 TC equals Einstein's faster-than-light into-the-past time travel cannot even be clarified by Basie's Indeterminant, even when the math works out every time. This incongruence has led some theorists—Tritia Rowan, Delia Finart, and Echart Rorigues, to name a few—to posit the unproven idea that if time travel were possible, the traveling particle would literally exit this existence altogether and exist somewhere else until it returned again. If this shocking idea were true, then we are talking about something far beyond the old theories of multiple realities, multiple universes, and multiple timelines. We are talking about something like heaven. Or hell. We are talking about opening a door, stepping outside, shutting the door, and then coming into the house through the door again wherever we please, or perhaps entering through the window, or the attic breezeway.

—Sister Buddy Olivett, Ph.D.
Yesteryear Approaching

"*...yes, I see that the machine is still running.*"

"Is it not astounding? Is it not brilliant?"

"But he does not respond? Are you sure that he spoke to you?"

"Mr. Reyes. Damien..."

"I would like to believe you."

"But—"

"It is all very amazing, yes, what I can see here. But I still have no clue what to make of it. Even if Mr. Reyes did speak to you, Doctor, or rather even if you heard his voice, how can you be sure—"

"This is not a matter of fact versus opinion! I have the recordings—"

"Which you know are not enough to prove anything at all."

"—I will... wait. Where are you going?"

"I am a busy man, just as you are. This—this!—is theoretical at best. You know that. My friend, don't waste your time chasing after angels and demons. Trust in the science that you know! The police don't even know what they are looking for."

"Please. Come back!"

"When you have something stronger to go on than that monstrosity!"

Click.

Growl. Sigh. "Damien Reyes. I know you can hear me. I know you are keeping silent on purpose. All of these... these readouts. I can read them!"

"Sounds like someone isn't very happy with me."

"Ah!"

"And why would that be? I seem to be your prisoner—more like a pet in a cage, I gather. And you seem to like that."

"And you would make a mockery of me before the head of my department?"

"What department? Who are you?"

"That doesn't matter."

"Are you crying, professor?"

Hiss. "Why did you call me that?"

"Does it bother you?"

Growl. "No, Damien. You are the greatest thing that has ever fallen into my hands, do you realize that? And you are going to make me great, memorable, unforgettable! Or—"

"Or what? I don't seem to have anything to lose at this moment."

"Au contraire! By what I see here, you are quite frightened of losing everything. And you can't escape into the past, you know; dive into your memories to get away. Your mind is open for me to view! Watch what happens when I do this!"

"I didn't *kill the President!* What sort of talk is —"

Husk put a hand on Damien's arm. "It hardly matters, my friend. What matters is that they think you killed the President." He jerked his head in the direction of the cops scanning the cars in front of them.

Across the street, a rich man in a floatable caddie that had happened to be driving at road level when the bumblebees hit their sirens, shouted through a loudspeaker at the officers. His windows had rolled shut and locked, as his car pulled automatically to the side of the road. He spoke about how much his time was worth, how he would be suing the City of Kodiak and each of them by name. But his case wouldn't be helped by the fact that the use of the sort of loudspeaker he had, not to mention its installation, was illegal. Three men in black approached him, scanned his car quickly, and moved on just to get away from the noise. Damien thought it odd that none of them stopped to write him a ticket.

It made him really wonder. "Is the President honestly dead?"

Shorts snickered in the front seat.

And the three black-armored solider cops on the road just ahead of them moved to the last car before the triangular that Shorts was driving.

The officer with the rifle tapped on the window twice with the tip of the barrel. Damien couldn't see their mouths, due to the night-colored face-plates, but by the nods of their heads they were talking to the driver, projecting their voices into the car's sound system directly.

The scanning officer passed the P10 Weasel slowly along the length of the sleek blue Toyota Sliver. When he finished, he nodded once to the storm trooper with the extended baton.

And they turned toward Shorts, Husk and Damien.

They took a few steps before they reached the front of the vehicle.

That's when an explosion overhead rained dead or dying police hornets all over Shorts's car.

The stunted man cried out the loudest, though they all shrieked in surprise.

Some of the police officers were hit directly. Their armor easily deflected the shrapnel from above.

The woman with the goatee and detective's coat pointed up four floors to the side of the building across the street. Damien heard her shouting orders but couldn't make out the words.

Through the triangular's sunroof, where one fried hornet lay on its side with its pulse stinger exposed and partially snapped off, Damien could see the floating car with smoke pouring out the side window.

Glass rained down next. It bounced off the street like snow that would never freeze. And that's when Damien spotted the man jumping from the top of the floater and into the building through the hole he had made in the glass. It was just a glance.

The cops had evidently seen enough.

Half of the black-clad crowd rushed the building's entrance. The rest made for the black and yellow bumblebees.

A moment later, bumblebees roared into the air to the fourth floor. Others flew around the side of the building and out of view. Still others made for the roof.

"See?" Husk said. "Criminals are dumb."

Power returned to the dashboard. "We're out of here," said Shorts, and he pulled into the traffic quickly enough to head the way.

No one with a badge noticed them.

Damien watched through the rear window anyway, certain that the stunt's careless desire to escape so quickly would red-flag their car.

"Don't worry," Husk said, scooting over a little. "They think they have their man. Or almost have him."

"But who was he?" Damien said, fearful—by the thing they'd said—that the cops would shoot first and ask questions after they noticed their blunder. Big oops.

"A criminal!" Shorts said, laughing quickly.

"Bob Hope. Who knows."

"Who?"

"You never heard of the Toiletries of Bob Hope? Well, it could have been a real thug paranoid that his time had come. Had some serious gunpowder up there, didn't he!"

Shorts laughed a little more, in his baby laugh.

* * *

Shorts slapped his music player and classical electric guitar riffs serenaded them for hours. At the top of his voice, Husk sang along. They stopped at a drive-thru for food, left the city and passed into West End.

This is it, Damien thought.

But he received no answered.

They kept driving, passed through the city and reached Pandam before the sun came up. They made one stop uncomfortably close to the capital building. Damien asked Shorts what it was about, after Husk left them sitting alone in the music and the sunrise. Shorts told him to mind his own business. *Mine-you-own-bidness.*

So Damien did. He worried. He pined. He thought of somehow waving down one of the police cars and turning himself in. He thought about Arthur Putubra's friend who was supposed to fix him up. He thought about the voice that had awakened him and sent him into a panic racing him away from the cops.

Before he knew it, they were pointed homeward.

Husk smiled a lot. Shorts shared secret looks with him through the mirror.

Damien asked no questions. He thought of Caleigha, and hid his tears against the window.

Prior to leaving the City of Pandam, they made another stop for food. They used the McDonald's restrooms—Husk stood too close for comfort, at all times and in all places—and when they got back into the car, Shorts shook his head in communication.

With a sigh, Husk said, "Well then!"

As their stunted driver pulled again into traffic and drove southeast through West End on his return trip to Kodiak, Damien finally thought of Sienna and caught Husk's eyes. "Short trip, huh?"

Through his joy, Husk beamed. "Uh, huh! Just a jaunt."

* * *

Returning to heavy traffic zones, Shorts took them across Kodiak to a building with Corinthian pillars and a wide bed of steps leading to a single set of double doors.

Damien blinked rapidly. "The *court house?*"

"Where's the best place to hide your illegal firearms?" Husk said in answer.

Shorts killed the engine. "In the cop's house!"

"All right! All right. Damien Reyes, I think you and I got off on the wrong foot—as they used to say."

"You think so." Crackle. Snap. Snip.

"Tit for tat?"

"Huh?"

"Ask me anything. I'll answer your questions. I may even be able to help you."

"I know when I'm being lied to."

"I know even better! I see all, before me here. I feel like a god talking to my first-made man in my little, pretty garden. But ... I digress, don't I?

Forgive me. My name is Winthrop Rothgar, Dr. Rothgar."

"Okay, doc. You know my name. Nice to meet you. Where am I?"

"In a holding cell, of sorts. You have been apprehended by the police. When they brought me in, I saw that you weren't—you weren't quite with us. Completely unaware of the... arrest, I take it?"

"Well. Yes."

"Ah. Now, Damien. I think we can work together, you and I."

"Think so?"

"Oh, my, yes!"

"And why is that?"

"I told you. I'm playing god here, aren't I? In a sense?"

"You said that..."

"Damien, what do you want? No, don't laugh. I'm not whispering for my own good here. Let me hear it, from your own... your own lips, so to speak. What do you really want?"

"What do I want? Like you'd let me go."

"Is that all? You only wish to be released? Small price to pay, I think."

"You... you do?"

"Oh, my, yes! But the legal authorities would know almost instantly, wouldn't they? So... let me ask again... What would you have me give you, if you had me playing god?"

"I don't... I don't understand why you would ask me that."

"Well, then think about it for a little while, Mr. Reyes. Because I think you do know why. Deep down, I think you know very well why I would give you... anything!"

Chapter Twenty-Eight

If the key to Law is command of the English language, then the key to politics is command of words and their various meanings. Specifically, if a leader says "I will come!" she may be giving an affirmative answer to a question, but that affirmative answer may not be restricted to the timeframe of the inquirer. She may tell him later that she will come, when she has yet to do so, even if a long time has passed. And she may never come at all, if her term has ended. At such a time, she is freed from her obligations, and this is understood by all parties. Therefore, she who commands the meanings of the words being used is best suited for public office, because she can tell everyone what they want to hear, mean it, and still do what is, in the end, in her opinion, best for her constituents.

— Avi Dartmouth
Light Things and Government

PCS Martin Warren fiddled with his fingers behind his back as he stood to one side of Vice President Lotti Morrison as she stepped to the podium for a long overdue public address. "My fellow Americans," she said with a peaceful grin. As if nothing untoward had happened at all.

Then she turned serious before the cameras. "By now, the whole world is aware of the pain we are enduring as fellow citizens. We mourn a tragedy, a terrible loss, that will set the name of Henry Waldorf Sanchez beside those great leaders of yesterday who died in the service of our country. I mourn *with* you. President Sanchez and I did not always see eye to eye, but we provided you good people, mothers, fathers, husbands, wives, children everywhere, all of you, with the balance that our separate nations and united states promised from the beginning."

Every word had been prepared by her press secretary, Davie-Tasia Wilson of the short pleated skirts—she worked hard for Lottie, but was also known as an active womanist, who like other womanists believed that women should use their feminine wiles to dominate men. Davie stood with her calves lifted and her eyelashes glittering and her white lace gloves clasped on the side of the stage, and as always she winked when she caught Warren spying her, even for a second. If it wasn't for freedom of speech and expression cases upheld by the Supreme Court of the NAU, womanists like Davie-Tasia would never get away with such overtly sexual attitudes at work. In the old days, it would have been deemed a form of harassment. But now sexual harassment was more clearly defined upon documented specifics.

Lotti Morrison continued with her sad and bonding platitudes until she reached the point at which the presentation was to take a more human approach. She lifted a glowing paper and read the words. "The funeral for President Sanchez will be at 3:00 PM, today, Eastern Daylight Savings Time, at an undisclosed location. Everyone is welcome to attend."

Warren held back from rolling his eyes. Undisclosed location? The President's body was no more! The funeral was to be entirely virtual, a partly interactive holographic vid accessible to all, untraceable for security reasons, even though it wouldn't matter if the stream were traced anyway as it wasn't remotely real. By the people, for the people. Warren thought it sad that politics had become such a show. But then, maybe it always had been.

From the corner of his eyes, he looked in Davie-Tasia's direction again. She pretended not to notice; perhaps she didn't. Perhaps she expected that men would always gawk at her. Either way, she licked her glossy lips, and they sparkled as they changed color from deep red into soft pink.

As soon as the Vice President finished, she said, "I have one minute for questions." One minute had become the standard in any crisis situation. And no matter her soft touch, this was still a crisis. She jabbed a finger in the air. "Mr. Tate."

The reporter from *The Yucatan Live* stood politely. "Madam Vice President, why haven't the press been allowed access to information regarding the investigation into the President's murder?"

Concise, thought Warren with a nod. *Well put. A well-chosen question.*

VP Lotti Morrison leaned over the pulpit as if spilling the beans to Edwardo Tate alone. "Many voices have claimed responsibility. Many other activists from various countries, including our own, have attempted to use this vile crime as a tool against their individual enemies, providing inaccurate evidence and in other ways pointing the finger in directions that have proven repeatedly to be inaccurate."

Was that a dodge? Of course. She can't very well say that we are going to war until we know for sure who is to blame.

"Mr. Havesham."

An intentionally old-looking man stood with a bend in his spine. "Why aren't you letting the press in on your findings?"

Same question, Warren said to himself. He checked his watch. *One minute's all you get, America, remember.*

"The momentum of the investigation has necessitated safety protocols that require us to keep the press at bay."

Warren's eyes went wide. He quickly hid his surprise.

But Davie-Tasia noticed. He saw the corner of her mouth turn up in a little smile. As if she had, once again, planned everything that the Vice President was saying.

Maybe she had. *Time Magazine* had once predicted that Davie-Tasia Wilson would silently become one of the most powerful people in the nation's background. The note had been made in a headline to an article entitled "Womanists in Washington." And Martin Warren had not taken the journalist's idea lightly.

Which was why he let her think that he was interested in how she looked.

The VP's words caused a murmur among the members of the press seated in the little hall. They only had seconds now.

Lotti Morrison lifted her chin. "The reason will be obvious in the days to come. If the public believed the strategic lies that have led police repeatedly down wrong avenues of investigation, retaliatory and vigilante actions would necessitate that police slow the current momentum of current investigations in order to keep the peace."

Bare seconds left.

Henriettita Javanovich stood without being recognized. "Is it true that Pandam City is under martial law?"

Time.

The Vice President stared her down. "That's all we have for today." She left the podium directly, heading straight for her press secretary. And she looked suddenly furious.

Martin Warren squinted to see through the milling crowds.

The press were all on their feet now, shouting questions at him or anyone else on the little stage who might answer.

But Warren was trying to read Davie-Tasia's shimmering neon-blue lips. By her sagging shoulders and by the way she had her head thrust forward on that long neck of hers, Davie-Tasia seemed to Warren to be speaking hurriedly and defensively.

Lotti didn't want to hear a word of it. She actually lifted her hand and stuck it a centimeter from Davie-Tasia's face. She marched away, and Davie-Tasia's little skirt bounced in a way that made her look childlike and pouty as she chased after her leader.

"What's the problem?" Doogie White Hawk said at Warren's side. He stared at the skirt until it disappeared around a turn among the blue curtains lining the walls. "The boss angry that no one asked her a question that began with, 'As the new leader of this country…' ?"

Warren shrugged with a little laugh. "Maybe." And when his number-one aide left the stage, Warren added, "Maybe something even better!"

Chapter Twenty-Nine

Once upon a time, a man asked the question, "If a tree falls in the forest and no one is there to hear it, does it make a sound?" To answer the question, we dream. In dreaming, we wander forests where trees fall—and fall up-ward. Reality exists: realities where we are not who we are, where the laws of physics say we may fly, where the laws of morality relinquish their holds to allow genocide, plague, death, bloodshed, and devastation. In the end, we still wonder the same question. "A tree fell in the forest. Did it make a sound?" And we answer that question, "I don't know. I wasn't paying attention."

—Anonymous,
The Sweaty Bottom: An Invitation to The Toiletries of Bob Hope

In a panic, Corvasce spun in green fields of tall grass that stretched as far as the mountains beneath a low southern sun and as far as the dark gray barren hills to the north. There wasn't a hint of civilization anywhere. No houses. No roads. No—

He opened his eyes. The light from the window and warmth from the fire cooked the skin on his cheeks. He pushed out from beneath a heavy blanket. His coat held him down as his limbs struggled to wake. He sat up, eyes wide and heart pounding.

He had no memory of falling asleep.

A new, musty scent filled the cabin now. He stood and spotted a pot swung over the fire by a hook. The glass doors parted wide.

"Stir that for me?" The old lady closed one of the doors behind him and gasped as if the effort had been too much. "Take care not to burn yourself. The bricks are hot. The metal's hotter."

"Do you," he said, "—I don't suppose you'd have a... a phone of some sort?"

Manda walked around the wicker furniture and grumbled, "Guess Pappy was right. If you want something done right, you need to do for others what they ain't doing for you." She chuckled.

"Huh?"

She licked empty gums as she reached for the wooden spoon and stirred the earthy substance inside the blackened pot. "Don't want your breakfast to burn, do you?"

"What?"

"Mind you, I expect payment for my hospitality. I wouldn't, of course; being a good Samaritan woman and all. But you're a city boy, aren't you. You appreciate fair business..."

"No communication device?" Corvasce looked at the layers of wood in the exposed ceiling. "Why'd I even ask?"

"Mind you, I'm low on sweeteners—with winter coming on, you see. Need to make it last." She stirred the mush until satisfied. Then she scooped a few light brown plops into a bowl and turned to where Corvasce stood by the front door. "Ah! Better than eating mud and sod, eh?" She held forth the bowl.

"Winter?" His stomach echoed its hollowness, growling as if in league with the old woman against him. In spite of his initial reluctance, Corvasce couldn't help himself.

Why did I fall asleep? I wouldn't fall asleep. I'd been drugged. That's it. Residual effect. This cereal could just as easily be doped with something foul. What about the Seekers? He reached for the only food in sight.

She pulled it away with more speed than he thought her capable. "You'll be sodding my house."

"I beg your pardon."

Manda arrowed her finger toward the ceiling. "I said winter's coming on, didn't I? It always does, eventually. Need to prepare, like the ants! You don't think an old dame like me can do it herself, do you? Course not. You look smarter than that, *detective whatever-your-name-was*. And you're a city boy; you understand good commerce. Right? Jig for jig." She pushed the bowl at him again.

He took hold of the fired clay and felt the determination of her strong skeletal fingers anchored to the other side.

"Agreed?"

"Yeah. Sure."

Chapter Thirty

Space is very cold. ExceGenesis promises that skinsuits can protect even against the void. I'm betting that they will one day become a fashion statement here on Earth. They'll be a fad. Then ExceGenesis will need to come up with a better marketing program.

—DuVree Dubosh
An Optimist's Cookbook

Boris did not find the theme funny in the least, not the seven different colored rooms, all lit by the green ambient light pulsating in slow rhythm from the hallway, not the way each room had been colored to match the Edgar Allan Poe story written centuries ago. In the pre-spacelife tale, Poe described a wealthy madman, an abbot, who locked himself and his guests in an abbey where he had all the provisions necessary to outlast a plague that was killing the world, and there he held a peculiar party augmented by his eccentric taste for the strange, the exotic, the macabre.

Spacelife held many similarities to the crazy man's abbey, Boris realized. In particular, one simply could not venture outside the walls of this safe haven. Earth was a very long fall downward; gravity would assist one's return, and it would be an incredibly beautiful journey—what with the sun behind the XE-7, and the planet all aglow, the land masses distinguishable below waves and swirls of white clouds, and the oceans offset by a massive spin of hurricane, like some white hole possessing an invisible singularity. Without an environmental suit, of course, one would die almost instantly outside; another might measure, with careful instruments, the duration in which life might remain in such a fool; but would the fool see his sun-, moon-, and star-lit surroundings before realizing the cold vacuum of space? There was nowhere to go.

So when Boris received an invitation to the party of Dr. Alejandro Sism, he was left to consider another evening of drug-induced euphoria alone, because he knew everyone else from the assignment would be going. And a costume party? Goodness, when had he gone to a costume ball in his life? Never! A masquerade, to his memory, was only something that served as the backdrop of an interactive movie. He had not once attended a real costume party.

Dr. Sism's invite contained a link whereby guests might find appropriate costumes available for the ball. At first, Boris was shocked. He viewed three-dimensional models for a while, then went to the market house where Dr. Sism had an account open, like a wedding-gift registry. Boris was told that three-quarters of the outfits had already been spoken for; he could have ordered online, and should have. Boris was only causing the attendant extra work. Yet the salesperson smiled all the same. In disgust, Boris said, "You choose one for me."

Which brought him, the following evening, to the ball. Everyone had been talking endlessly about the adventure when he was at his assignment. Everyone was going, including Jenny Reed, the beauty who had never shown him more than friendly interest. She asked Boris if he had seen the costumes. She asked him what he thought of the dancing demons in the corner of the invitation—how old-fashioned and wonderful! She asked him if he thought someone might really die at the party.

A man who preferred to say little during a conversation, Boris had shrugged in answer to her questions and set his mind upon the assigned tasks in his range of responsibility. Perhaps he shouldn't go to the masquerade, he had thought. If for no other reason, all members of the party would be hidden behind false faces. He wouldn't know Jenny Reed from any other woman in the crowd. Which was interesting in itself.

No one wore masks anymore, not since they had passed the law after psychologists proved in federal court that human beings had a tendency to act behind masks in ways they never would when their faces were revealed, and that while, on the whole, this did not prove to be a problem, certain high-profile murders had been linked without a doubt to that very instance of anonymity and had warranted a judgment of temporary insanity—all avoidable cases of murder, the psychologists argued, if only the susceptible individual's face had remained, at all times, uncovered. Within ten years of the ruling, attorneys demanded that police officers and soldiers also go without face armor for the same psychological reason: they might at times act out their aggressive training to unfortunate degrees or at inappropriate times simply because they were wearing a mask. And just over five years after the peacekeepers put themselves in jeopardy against phage weapons, the federal court overturned the mask ruling and left the matter up to individual states. And no state held jurisdiction over the city-stations in space.

Had they lived on Luna, or Mars (where Earth governments retained direct authority), it might have been another story. But would Boris really have felt any better attending a Masquerade of the Red Death there? Only scientists and nut cases lived on the Moon, and the manned missions to Mars were still a long way from allowing any form of modern colonies to be established from Earth. Overpopulation and the newfound resources available from low-gravity gardening experiments and solar power harvesting, coupled with the government's need to find solutions for the spread of mankind and the interest of wealthy individuals ready to begin spacelife, had led to the Cities in the Stars. But the only way in or out of places like XE-7 was via spaceplanes from the planet or via TransOrbs, the orbital transports that passed in a very limited capacity from city-station to city-station, and for which one needed to purchase a very expensive ticket. Boris had come to space to get away from it all. Now he couldn't feel more trapped.

So he entered the highest globe, where waited Dr. Sism's colorful suites. Oh how he'd decked them out for the party. Having inherited the wealth of his father, who had died outside the satellite in an experimental environmental suit—some said his had been a mysterious death—Dr. Sism had initially, according to the paper broadcast each morning, built newfangled laboratories in all the rooms of the upper globe where his father once brandished his opulence. From the windows of the seven lower rooms in the highest globe, one could look down upon the marvel of XE-7, see all the other globes in great ornamental and practical rings, and the planet far beyond.

Now each room was set up with crystal chandeliers, or rather impressive imitations. Enormous rugs of astonishingly complicated patterns dressed every floor, save the dance floors, which looked like wood. Dining tables, surrounded by servants in white wigs, stood opposite the window side of the rooms so that dancers might spin, and spin, closer to the windows, and fear falling down upon the station and then down, down towards home. "For dust thou art," said Dr. Sism with his glass held high at the beginning of his ceremonies, "and unto dust shalt thou return!" And the music played, a band in each room keeping time with all the others because they were not human, but reflections made of holographic imagery. Each of the players wore a mask and a tuxedo, save for the women who dressed with old-fashioned immodesty, their gowns low, their ankles showing, masks hiding only the upper portions of their faces. No matter how one traversed the rooms, the same band played. The violins, the cello, the flutes, the harpsichord, the cymbal, intoned ominous race-memory, in three-four time.

"Enjoy the food! It is rare, indeed," said Dr. Sism, his smile revealed beneath the gross aberration of his mask—a face of protruding brow and bulging eyes without lids, of royal cheekbones, and tufts of fur springing from the temples. "Enjoy the wine! It is blood, of course. Drink up, and die!"

The people laughed as he bowed and exited the room. Holographic ballroom dancers made space for those who would join them on the floor, so that the air seemed to throb with the motion of their bodies, and the dancing did not stop, not ever, nor the music, even to change tracts. And the people watched, elated, smiling, laughing. Or rather it seemed that they smiled, for their faces, no matter how twisted, or dying, or rotting even, all smiled. They grinned wider than humans are capable. Their eyes stared wide, staring, at all who came and went, staring, without eyelids or even eyelashes painted above the rouge of cheeks and the wrinkled lines of the forehead.

All the women were inappropriately attired, their bosoms heaving out of their dresses, their calves showing when they sat and crossed their legs. Yet in their anonymity, they exhibited no shame, reveling behind the masks that allowed them these old and forbidden Earthly pleasures. The federal courts had been convinced in 2019 by state psychologists that, as a result of the natural genetic makeup of the male species, a man could not help but feel drawn visually, and therefore physically, to an immodest woman, as to any other stimulant, and that, as a great number of men had been arrested for criminal acts toward women, including murder, as a result of their inability to control their own sanity in the presence of such outward female beauty, female modesty outside of the home must be enforced by law. This led to the quick suppression, the following year, of pornography involving females. Twelve-and-a-half years later, however, the federal courts released the issue of modesty into the hands of each individual state. And therefore Dr. Sism, in this city orbital, was free to suggest these costumes—which in fact he demanded of those who wished to attend the ball—though none of the women would have risked their reputations by wearing such a dress in open public. Unless she was a womanist.

Boris did his very best to avert his eyes from the women. Unfortunately, that meant he had to see everything else.

Down the walls ran long curtains, covering no doubt whatever Dr. Sism really had in these rooms. A towering clock counted the seconds aloud against one wall. Paintings had been fabricated and hung in ghastly frames. The most pronounced and central to each room was the picture of a man without a face, a hood of thick material pulled over his head. "I can see the eyes, can't you? Look there!" men said to women. The men pointed. The women stretched their long nude necks and touched their collarbones as if to feel at their nakedness. "Just keep looking. Look closer!"

And each room was a mirror image of the last one, save for one important detail: The color of the first room was a deep green hue, like a forest in shadow; the second room orange, almost organic but rotten; the third blue, reminiscent of the emptiness of space, the unreachable aspect of Mars for human rest; the fourth purple and ugly; the fifth gray and filled with a fog that allowed little light—a miracle of science to create such a thick and ominous and oppressive illusion; the sixth violet; and the seventh entirely black, save for faux flames, dancing upon the grand candelabra on the dining room table, which fired a deep and hideous red light upon the crystal in the dark chandelier and upon the floor, where shadows moved of their own accord in the archaic rugs, and upon the picture of the man without a face.

Here, the eyes of that face told a greater nightmare. "Come and see!" said a fellow with the head of a great and fetid bird as he pulled a buxom woman who wore the caul of a grinning feline. "In the red room," he said, for that is what everyone came to call it despite the black—the black itself, tinted by the red flames, became a run of dark blood everywhere one looked. The only luminescence that altered this blood-red expression was near the corridor where the alien green light seeped through the portal. Odd that the red did not escape the room...

"Do you see it there?" said the man to the woman that Boris had followed.

Something told him not to look.

"I see! Do I?" said the woman. "How can I be sure I'm not imagining those two little glowing eyes in the dark? Or that the candlelight isn't playing tricks on me, reflecting two pinpricks of light that look like eyes? They moved!"

"All part of the illusion!" said the man. "Have you ever experienced anything so horrible?"

They both laughed together. "Look there!" the man said, pointing again to the eyes. "Like they call to me... "

"Yes," said the woman, but Boris was already walking away. He would only glance at the portrait of the strange figure without a face when he entered a new room, only from a distance. The creature seemed to stare at him from the darkness, stare across the heads of the dancing fools, and the drunk ones, and the gluttons, and the happy men with wandering eyes. He heard the painting call his name in a whisper, through the music, from the wall.

But it was only his imagination. Boris worked in illusions. A mathematician of low grade, he drew interconnections all day, finding routes around the clash points, designing and then constructing power relays in a system growing old. That was his job. And XE-7 was his home. He thought about returning to his apartment. To do what? He wondered about the shooter and how many doses he still had in the drawer, and how he would pay for another batch when the spaceplane arrived in ninety-one days. So soon! Yet far from soon enough. He could watch a holo.

He decided to stay. And when a man grabbed his arm and, laughing through his mask, said, "Have you seen the mummy? Flat, it took me *two hours* to find you, Hummel!" He leaned close, the intoxicant washing from his breath and into Boris's nostrils. "I was frankly hoping you'd be dressed as a woman!"

"You've got the wrong guy, Jack."

"Jack! That's funny! You haven't called me Jack for seven months! You remember the time—" and he told about some gag played with unrecycled garbage and a third coworker at the intervening processing plant on the other side of XE-7. His voice almost sounded familiar. But even with the slur of drink, and the familiar way in which the stranger manhandled Boris's coat and hands, Boris decided he did not know the man. So he turned and moved away suddenly through the crowd.

"Hummel. Hummel!" Jack, the stranger, gave chase but was throttled by the standing bodies of the room. It seemed that everyone in the city-station had appeared for the banquet and the ball. Boris had not seen Dr. Sism for over forty-five minutes. He could not spot Jenny Reed, though more than once he thought he had heard her tinkling laughter. He wiggled from the black room, through the violet, and into the gray. He crossed the hall, and thought he saw the moon out the window for a moment—another horrifying thought, for he should not see it from this Earth-inclined perch. He padded through the fog-filled room, a full drink in his hand, while he instinctively avoided putting the cup of blood to his mouth. It wasn't blood. But the illusion was disturbing.

As was the whole of it: the sound of the music in minor key; the fall of colored curtains, which blew in an unfelt wind; the masks of contorted faces, all teeth and eyes; the paintings on the wall; the painting...

The clock struck twelve. One clock struck at a time, first in the green room. Then the green room chimed once more but this time with the blue room. Then two hollow bongs sounded with a third great clock, and on until all seven rang once together, shuddering the walls. The music stopped. The laughter paused itself, murmur turning into hush, and hush into waiting silence. Everyone stood, none slacking. Even the holographic dancers stopped and gaped.

That couldn't be right, Boris thought. He checked his own chronometer and found two hours seventeen minutes lacking from midnight. He looked about himself, expecting Dr. Sism to stroll forth in great red robes, a skeleton mask of death upon his face, preparatory to some hellish announcement for the amusement of all. Boris found instead the eyes of all mortal beings following the gaze of the holographic phantoms, for they stared, like religious zealots in a quiet swoon, toward the red room.

No one moved. Boris waited. He leaned between two others and felt the fingers of a trembling hand brush against his back. Curious party members began to whisper again as whispers came from the crowds ahead of them, from the red room, whose blackness had been forgotten as a result of conversation and wonder, and then from that same bloody room came a cry. A man's cry.

A shout followed, a hoot, an exclamation. Then a push of words. A shove of excitement bent away from the room of red and black, even as murmuring returned to the throng of party participants around Boris. The culmination was a rush forward even while drunk and blinking idiots ran the other way—a collision of heads and hands, and yet somehow no mask fell.

Boris understood an illusion had been set to run at this pretended midnight, some new star of shocking sight. He had to see it.

Crazy with hysteria, the din of noise rose to screams and forceful demands for people to "Get out of my way!" They filled the green corridor almost immediately, and they screamed that the doors were locked. Well of course they were. Dr. Sism might be a perverted lunatic, but he wasn't stupid. He would have his fun and would make them all laugh at themselves for their insanity later that evening—perhaps when the clocks struck midnight again, or something else equally creative and unsettling.

Boris found that he could move with those who shoved with him so long as he stayed to the outside of the current, toward the windows and not the tables. With that method, it did not take him long to pass through the violet hall to the red room.

And it was red. The black was bleeding with panicked light. And all the faces, flashing back to see again the horror moving slowly in the air, glowed scarlet and flowed. Boris could not squeeze himself into the room, but watched from the doorway …

…as the figure in the painting took one…slow…step after another, in the air, downward, as if on stairs unseen, as he walked from the painting out of which he had evidently crawled. Boris could only imagine how that might have looked to the people who had been in the room—those black skeleton hands gripping the twisted fake wood of the giant frame, how it must have turned its unseen face to the left and to the right, peering over the motionless dancers, the gawking conversationalists, and sickening visitors at the tables—and he riveted himself to the door against his own sudden inclination to run.

People would get trampled, he thought. And where would they go? If the doors in the corridor were locked, then the corridor was a trap. The hall, attaching room to matching but off-colored room, slid in a perfect circle, which met again here, in the black room, in the red room, where this vision without a face…

It turned and looked at Boris, so that he could not help but peek into the darkness for the missing eyes, or perhaps the faintest glow. But Boris saw nothing, only endless night. The creature reached the ground, lifted a hand to one of the holographic dancers, and touched the anthropomorphic image.

The dancer died, falling in a heap within his costume, the eyes of his mask bugging upward forever at the black and red ceiling.

The Red Death from the painting touched another dancer, and then another, and another, and all of them died upon the instance, with tiny peeps instead of screams, at the monster's touch.

Then the figure reached a very solid hand to touch a shrieking man with the plasticite face of a pig. The man fought his way backward against the crowd, leaning on them with all his weight, his arms spread and groping as if to pull himself up on the mass of people and away from this red-cloaked wraith. And he did rise upon his toes and fall upon the sloping men and women, who struggled against the press to get away.

He slid to the ground, clearly dead.

Or faking it. Boris stepped closer, the insane riot spinning into other rooms. He followed the Red Death into the green room.

The two black hands reached and groped from flesh, stretched forth and pronounced everyone dead, dead, dead. The bodies fell. Was this a game? Was this all a part of the illusion?

Boris dropped to the side of a woman whose frilly color and pinched waist ran red with the light of the black room. She had the painted lips of Jenny Reed, though she could have been someone else. He tried not to touch her exposed flesh, but needed to know if she still had life in her. He pressed his fingers against the warm skin of her neck, felt at the sinews for her veins. He thought her name but did not say it; what if he was wrong? What if he was right? His own heart pulsed hard enough, he heard the beat within his ears. He touched her hand, patted the bones and tendons. "Miss.

Miss, can you hear me?" He grabbed her mask and pulled. It would not come off. Instead, the wrenching motion lifted her head, arched her back, so that her over-revealed chest rose towards him. Jenny Reed, he thought. He reached again for her neck and felt no pulse. Jenny? He put both hands around her throat, feeling with his fingers, digging into her muscles for that elusive artery that must exhibit life. He had seen it done on movies, but had never checked the pulse of another before.

Then she gagged, and slapped him.

Something popped in his mask, a bit of cleariform or a joint somewhere. Before he could back away and catch his balance, the woman was on her feet, shouting, calling him names, stating that he ought to be arrested. And his mask came off in his hands.

"Don't you get it?" she bellowed. And it was Jenny's voice. But the scowl under the lip of the mask had not belonged to her. "It's a masquerade! It's all for fun, you sod-head! It's not permission to feel around!" He was running now, away from her, catching tears of shock and relief and horror on the back of his wrist. And the Jenny-fiend continued to rail against him, while all the eyes of the red room and the violet room turned its attention away from the demon of the painting and onto the spectacle of the man who had revealed his face. "You know what you've made me? Go ahead and run!" Jenny screamed. "I've seen you! I'll find your image and turn you in! You freak!" Not Jenny. But Jenny might have watched the whole crime. So what would she think of Boris now?

Far away, a laughing voice boomed. Not from the specter without a face. That had probably vanished already behind him. But from Dr. Sism, his chortle amplified and amused, excessively so, as if it was the last laugh, and the laugh of a madman at that.

Boris fell at the ground, where the great window in a gentle slope met the floor. He wept, freed from the burden of social propriety, for he had already broken how many unwritten laws of the masquerade? So he let the tears flow as the laugh increased behind him, and he looked down over the bulbous rings of XE-7 and at the Earth hundreds of miles below.

He saw the hurricane, how it turned in white lines almost too bright to view as they reflected the sun. He saw the landmasses, tilting, listing, rolling upward. The planet filled the window, so that he could not see the stars.

Which caused his tears to stop.

And he stood.

The stars appeared again, this time from the wrong side.

Then the moon rolled into sight, which meant that soon he would see the—

Huge shields dropped behind the spaceglass. The city was rolling, toppling, though they could not feel the motion. Had the automatic sun shields not pulled quickly into place, everyone in the room would have been cooked.

The black room burned its blackness by red candlelight. The party screamed once again. The laughter taunting them all. Was Dr. Sism even on the station anymore?

Howling with terror, only one thing was clear. XE-7 was plummeting to Earth.

Chapter Thirty One

"As a man thinketh, so is he." Foolhardy scripture or repeatedly prov-en technique for success? Well, whatever you think about that question... you're right!

—Justinian Viennanazul
Corporate Wisdom

"*Y*ou can trust me, Mr. Reyes."

"*Dr. Winthrop Rothgar?*"

"*Yes.*"

"*I don't think I can trust anyone anymore.*"

"*Hmm. Interesting puzzle then, isn't it? What are you going to do?*"

"*I don't know.*"

"*And yet you can't just stay like this. You have given so much to me al-ready. I am aware of the code. But I do not know what it means.*"

"*You don't?*"

"*It's a handful of jumbled variables, for all I know. It is theorems inside of proven or presumed mathematics written in short form! I recognize what I believe might include the Indeterminant, which is the most humorous part of all. Indeterminant mathematics is a kind of a game. Surely you know that.*"

"*Why would I know about that.*"

"*From your father! Or from a little poking around, information gath-ering. It couldn't have been hard for you to learn something about the opinions of solid scientists where they clash against this rogue variable. It's—why, it's no more grand than the zero property of multiplication, or the identity property.*"

146

"Huh?"

"You feign ignorance, do you? Well enough. My promises are true, regardless of your insistence to disbelieve me. It is worth it to me."

"Oh, I see. You're playing me! Good cop, bad cop. Except because I am blind, you can just skip straight to the good cop stage and leave out all the rest. What can I do, my brain's hooked up to machines!"

"Ha-ha-ha—"

"And now who's mocking who?"

"Do you miss her, Damien?"

Silence.

"You miss… Caleigha Obregon? Well, I wouldn't hold her from you. Why would I do that? If she means everything to you?"

"Everything… What do you know of…"

"The machines don't lie to me. Mr. Reyes. Why should you?"

"Caleigha…"

"Yes, Damien. Remember? Not such a lost memory to you, is she? Not …dead…"

For a moment, Damien thought that he was done for.

Nothing made sense to him. He had awakened to a harsh call, Caleigha's scream, and strange—impossible!—memories of his father. He could hardly remember the latter; but like an itch building and writhing to be scratched, those memories seemed somehow more demanding of attention than everything else that had happened. Like the threat that made him flee a police assault. Like being kidnapped and then dropped onto the top of a building. Like getting drugged by a man who posed endlessly as a friend. Like seeing Caleigha—no, not Caleigha, but Sienna. And then nearly getting arrested in a crackdown.

Now, as if to confuse him to the breaking point, Husk and Shorts led him straight up the wide array of cement steps to the Kodiak Municipal Courthouse.

It just didn't make sense. Before he had seen the woman who looked exactly like Caleigha in every way, he had wanted to contact the police. He had thought about turning himself in, thought he might be safer if he did so, though still fearing for Caleigha's life. Now he didn't want to go near them. All his instincts clamored when he thought of that knowledgeable last look that Sienna had given him. He had to see Sienna again. He had to talk to her.

Walking in through the front doors of the courthouse seemed to be the best possible way to ruin any chance of seeing either Caleigha or Sienna in the future. The idea sounded like the quickest plan for them all to get arrested. Security would require each of them to pass through the sensor gates individually. The armed officers, with faces hidden behind bullet-proof panels of white glass, would be standing on either side of the gate. Anything suspicious at all might raise the alarm. Damien couldn't keep his eyes from watering.

"Buck up, friend," said Husk. "For someone like you, this should be a walk in the park."

"I seriously think you have me confused with someone else."

Husk chuckled, as if that had been the best joke he had heard in a long time.

In an instant, Damien decided to turn and flee. An instant later, he stopped the escape from beginning. He had seen too many episodes of *Rundown*, in which police and cameras chased foolish thugs who, for some insane reason, always thought they had a chance of getting away from the authorities on foot. They never succeeded. And he was too close to the doors now. Police officers in masks were already gazing in his direction, or appeared to be doing so—it was impossible to tell.

Up the final steps, Damien slowed. At the very least, he felt the need to turn and try to convince Shorts and Husk out of this suicidal idea.

"He looks like he's going to faint."

Thank you! Damien thought. But while the runt was frowning at him, Husk continued to smile at the doors.

"You're welcome!" his father replied in a memory that suddenly felt more real than the nightmare around him. *"But I sacrificed that pawn on purpose..."*

"You did?" Damien was a little boy again, nine and a half or so. His father picked up a knight, floated it over Damien's bishop, and dropped it into the perfect position to fall prey to Damien's attack. Young Damien raised his eyebrows in shock. *"Did you mean to do that?"*

His father grinned with something more than love in his eyes. He pondered for a moment and then said, *"Damien, I did."*

"But if I...if I did that, you would tell me that I'm losing my knight for nothing."

"Would I?"

"You have before!"

"Those lessons were different. Sometimes moves like this are made completely on purpose."

Damien shook his little head. *"So I get to take your knight."* Then he thought he understood. He moped. *"You want to lose. You're letting me win.*" He sounded dejected, even more so than he felt. Chess wasn't fun anymore when people let him win.

Marcus Reyes shook his head very slowly. He kept his eyes on Damien's. Damien could almost hear him talking inside his head, telling him to think one more step ahead. Still, his father had to wait a long time.

Damien shivered at the idea of moving the bishop. It would have been a simple slide and grab, a simple ha, ha! But the more he looked back into his father's eyes, the more he thought he shouldn't grab the knight. *"It's a trap,"* he said at last.

"It could be."

"What do you mean it could be? It either is or it isn't. Am I right? Is that what you mean? You put the knight there just to make me take it? Is this some kind of mind control?"

His father laughed. *"Damien! Now, why in the world would you think this is some kind of mind control?"* Damien's father wasn't disagreeing with him. Damien felt like his dad was testing him.

But Damien didn't have the answer. He had reached the end of his logical capabilities. He shrugged.

Then his father grew intense. His expression didn't change, save for the slight bulging of his eyes. He leaned over the table and whispered so that Mom wouldn't hear them from the other room. *"You remember? It's simple, really."*

"The code..."

"It's like magic, Damien!"

Marcus Reyes scooted away from the table an inch. He spread the fingers of both hands in the air over the chessboard.

And the pieces began to float.

It was magical. The knight lifted off of the board and slowly turned upside down. The bishop, also rising, clicked against the side of the knight and rebounded into a pawn and a queen. They floated as if in water, as if unable to rise to the liquid surface but unable to sink to the board.

Until Damien's dad pulled his hands away from their magical position.

All the pieces crashed back onto the tabletop.

Marcus Reyes didn't blink. His smile broadened. *"It's simple, really."* He fanned one of those magical hands in front of Damien's face and said, *"Wasurenasai!"*

Damien blinked.

His father rose from his seat.

He had kicked the table from underneath is all. He had bumped the underside with his knee. There hadn't been any magic at all. There wasn't anything difficult about it. And there wasn't anything for him to think about or forget.

Young Damien told himself those lines all afternoon.

And was, a moment later, back in front of the Kodiak Municipal Courthouse remembering this strange memory in all its peculiar details. He could smell his father's cologne.

Or was that Husk's? Or was Husk wearing a scent common to his father in those bygone days?

Damien opened his mouth to say that he didn't want to go in there.

But they were too close.

They stepped through the doors, Shorts leading the way to the security gates.

His very presence—his stunted form, really—claimed everyone's opinion. He was the same as a man covered in tattoos a hundred and fifty years earlier, the sort of enigma most people heard about but didn't see too often. No one wanted to be rude. They acted as if they weren't staring.

This is totally crazy! Damien screamed inside. *You might be amazing enough to distract the guards (though even the chance that your physical appearance could be enough bait to dislocate the trained attention of everyone of these armored cops might be hoping for too much). There's no way your looks are going to be enough to trick the robotic gates!*

Husk nudged him forward with a word.

Damien realized that he must have stopped.

"March."

It was only a few steps, and yet they felt like miles. They reached the gate.

Damien thought about his heartbeat. He thought about his adrenaline. He thought about how cold and clammy his cheeks felt. *EVERYTHING is going to give me away.*

Shorts passed through the gate. The computer acknowledged him, "Good evening, Mr. Ryce."

Shorts nodded once to no one in particular. He continued into a hall framed in what looked very much like real red brick and yet smelled of sterile Health Service offices.

It'll-say-my-name! It-will-read-my-ID! It-will-know-me!

Damien had no time to think any more about the repercussions of passing through the gate. His feet touched the metal threshold. One hand swayed forward between the high-frequency sensors, the biosensors, the computer tracking components.

He nearly froze between the ornate webwork on either side of him. He was caught. He stared at the back of Shorts's head, and felt himself continuing forward, as if by magic.

"It's simple, really," his father said inside of him. "Those lessons were different. Sometimes moves like this are made completely on purpose."

"So I get to take your knight... You want to lose... You're letting me win ...It's a trap!"

"It could be."

"What do you mean it could be? It either is or it isn't."

It could be.

"It's like magic, Damien!"

It could be...

" ...Good evening, Mr. Rey-y-y-nolds."

The guards didn't flinch. Didn't they hear the speaker glitch?

They stared coldly through their black headgear. One jerked his head. "Keep moving."

Damien took one more step. And another. And another.

Behind him, the computer said, "Good evening, Dr. Deferrari."

Husk came up and took Damien by the shoulder. He spoke friendly like, with everyone watching, but spoke quietly. "Now, Mr. Reynolds. Do us a favor...and forget our names?"

Damien tried to say, "As if that really was your name," but the words got lost on the way to his larynx.

As Damien followed Shorts to a granite staircase, he heard Husk mutter behind him through a jovial laugh. "Oh, that was *really* great!"

"You... there are no words, Mr. Reyes!"

"You told me that... Caleigha."

"Yes. Caleigha. Is she worth it to you, Damien. The love of your life? Your passion? Your longing? Ah..."

"You are reading the machines. You know how I feel."

"I do."

"How... HOW can you do this to me?"

"I doubt very much that you were held prisoner and forced into this position. I doubt very much that you started this process of... looking back ... opening your mind... unintentionally. But why, Damien? I still don't understand why you would have done all this!"

"Caleigha..."

"Hmmm? Is it really that simple? That black and white? That easy for me? For you? Ah! My compradre, we can help each other. I suspected she meant everything to you... in the romantic sense. But she is more, isn't she!

She is everything to you."

"I just... I just wish... that I could..."

"Say no more! Said Aladdin to the lamp! Your wish, Damien, is my command. Only..."

ꝇ

Chapter Thirty-Two

He who laughs last, at least laughs. For decades, perhaps for millennia, Stress has been the number one killer of the human race. Men and women have used a dozen times a dozen techniques to beat stress, from meditation and prayer to pain relievers and mood-altering pharmaceuticals. All the while, the quacks and the jokers of society have lived happier and healthier lives. They may be crazy, but they are better off.

—Yuwaja Herementari
Black Jack Existence

The detective itched everywhere. He doubted the old woman had a shower stall in the house, or even a bathtub for that matter, and he wouldn't have used it if she offered; he'd be too exposed. But he smelled the body odor floating up from his armpits every time he moved in a way that opened his coat.

As he scratched his side, the knuckles of his right hand brushed across his badge. He paused. He thought for a moment, a frown growing on his face, then he drew the badge off its clip and stared at the front of it and then the back.

"You shouldn't be working," he whispered to the device.

Then Manda coughed. "In my condition? Of course, you're right." She twirled a finger in the air. "This is as good as it gets, when a woman like me has no children to carry on the name and the memories. A son or a daughter, that's all I'd need. They'd take care of me. You know what they say: there ain't no thing as a free lunch. For old people, there ain't no thing as retirement anymore!"

He looked at her, but he was still mulling the problem of the badge over in his mind.

It shouldn't have worked.

The badge shouldn't have flashed or projected a signal to the gun-happy giant outside.

It shouldn't have saved his life.

Corvasce went over the facts: He'd been watching for President Sanchez to step into view; he'd received the suspect call; he'd looked around for the possible threat, spotted the 141 XY, and reported the sighting; and before he could make ground, the President imploded; then the city shields went active over his head; and then the attack from the sky; the military Frogs on the building tops went dead, like everything else; his communicator went dead; electro-magnetic pulse—it was the only conclusion that fit. Which meant, his badge couldn't be working.

And yet, it was the badge that had saved his life.

And yet, those badges were supposed to last through all sorts of hard times. Falling down and slapping onto the ground? Shouldn't have busted it so easily.

The bottom line: an EMP could not have fried the insides of the badge enough to make it so fragile, and still allowed it to function.

Someone had tinkered with the badge. Someone had wanted Corvasce to be traceable, to get found eventually. But by whom?

The old woman was looking at him again through eyelids so heavy with wrinkles they never did quite lift high enough to make her look free from drowsiness. "See? You didn't even hear me."

"I heard you," he said. He looked out the window.

The hills rolled down toward the decimated little town, of which only hints of broken walls and streetlights, blackened skeletal remnants, could be seen from here. Beyond the border town, as she had called it, other hills cut off his view of Pandam City, though he knew it had to be out there somewhere beyond the horizon, in some direction. The skies were clear, save for heavy, towering thunderheads in the distance. Wind blew through apple trees raining orange leaves over the ground. Autumn leaves and rotten fruit carpeted over sprigs of grass and naked earth at the war machine's feet. The robot saw him—must have seen him—but didn't move.

He thought of his badge again. He thought of the robot. And for an instant, he wondered if everything—including himself—had been placed intentionally for a single, guided outcome.

"You heard me," Manda said. She groaned as she carried the pot away from the fire, a towel keeping the handle from burning her loose flesh. She filled the pot with other dishes. "Sure. Well. You've got your job to do. A deal's a deal."

He turned and softened his face kindly. "Why don't you get out of the Kingdom?"

"Beg your pardon?"

"With all due respect, you've lived your life here. Bet you're happy for the freedom—" he stopped; he was shooting in the dark, trying to be polite and still get to his point. "You could still go over to Pandam City. You said there ain't no such thing as a free lunch, or retirement. But there is. All taken care of. Government facilities. Neglect of elders is against the law, where I come from. They'd take care of you."

She huffed her disbelief or distaste in his direction.

"Free medical assistance. Free housing."

"Nothing's free. Weren't you listening?"

"Well...seems to me it costs you a lot to live here in the Kingdom. And, hey, that's your choice. If that's what you want, I can respect it. But what I'm saying is, it's a choice. You could live a peaceful, long life in—"

"You never told me what all the fireworks were about."

They stared at each other.

Manda continued, either nodding or afflicted with some ancient disease that made it difficult for her to hold her head straight while she spoke—one of those things that didn't exist anywhere else in the NAU. "Peace, you say? I've seen the lights of war before. I've heard the thunder of death. You want to tell me it's all sunshine in the City? Well, do you? Can you tell me it's all peaches and cream where you come from?"

She knew it wasn't.

Corvasce wondered how much she really knew. He thought about the Seekers again.

The headless fighting machine on two legs outside didn't move. Either the mechanical mutt didn't sense the approach of other humans, or it had finally shut down for good. *Safe so far,* the detective concluded.

Manda nodded. "I didn't think so." She carried the dishes through one of the doors. Corvasce considered following her. Then he thought the act might be rude: the door couldn't lead to a place even as big as this room.

He went to a bookshelf and started fingering the titles. His nail scraped the top of one of the volumes, and the dark paper flaked away. Embarrassed by his vandalism, Corvasce turned around as the old woman reentered the room. He held up his head. "Well, you never told me exactly who the Seekers were. And what they seek."

She glanced at him from the side of her eye. Her witch cackle started up again, slow and unsteady as she rounded the couch and settled herself with a groan, sputtering a little spittle onto her chin before she finished. Then she sat silently, resting. "The morning is the best time to work. I suggest you go outside and get to sodding that roof. I'd say I'd be much obliged, but I think you're the one who's much obliged right now. And being a police officer, I'm confident that you'll do the right thing. Now, if you don't mind, I'm going to cheat the devil and his two studs, Death and the Sandman, for a minute and try to rest when they're not looking." She opened her eyes a crack. "They don't see you during the daylight, you see." She shut her eyes again. "Out you go."

"So, you're not going to tell me about the Seekers."

After a sigh, she said, "You'll learn about them soon enough. No escape, you see." Her voice drawled and grew quiet with those last words.

But outside, the battle machine hummed into life.

A heavy foot pounded the ground.

Metal screeched upon metal.

Corvasce stepped quickly to the window. He grabbed for his firearm. His fingers helped him remember that the holster had been emptied some time ago.

The robot's voice vibrated into life again, though no distinguishable words issued forth.

Corvasce watched its gun barrels twist to the sky.

He ducked instinctively.

The bang of the pulse rifle went off only once.

Almost as quickly, a deeper throb of heavy guns thundered in six quick rhythmic bursts.

Metal sheered. Explosions popped, and the force of the robot hitting the ground shook the house. The window glass broke into tiny pieces and sprayed across the room. Manda screamed, and her shriek dried up halfway into a desperate hiss.

From his crouched position below the open window frame, Corvasce gazed skyward.

A large black object, like a curved funnel made of dull metal, lowered itself silently toward the house.

Chapter Thirty-Three

The most brilliant intellect is a prisoner within his or her own social inheritance.

—Renaldo Vibe
On the Order of Genius

"*W*hy the linear story? Damien, is this—what I'm seeing—is it what you believed happened to you?"

"*Where am I?*"

"*You remember. You do, don't you? I'm Dr. Winthrop Rothgar. We're working together—we were just talking about Caleigha...don't you remember?*"

"*I—Yes! Caleigha.*"

"*Tell me, Damien. How much time do you think has passed?*"

"*Time...I don't know. I'd say, four hours? Was I asleep? No. I was told that I wasn't sleeping. What do you mean—how long—*"

"*No time has passed, Mr. Reyes. No time at all. Well, that's not true. You paused. I asked a question. Do you remember the question?*"

"*Um. Why the linear story?*"

"*Yes. That was it. But you...feel that four hours passed?*"

"*No. Yes. I mean...what's happening to me?*"

"*It is time, Mr. Reyes.*"

"*What?*"

"*Time. And perception. Your...I fear your grasp is slipping.*"

"*I don't understand what you mean. I don't understand anything anymore.*"

"*It's really quite simple.*"

"Isn't it always? I keep hearing that."

Laugh. "I know! It's so amazing! You, Damien Reyes, you are amazing."

"I'm confused."

"It will become clear. You remember pieces. You remember Caleigha. Yet it's all here. Right here! I think we should keep going. I think that is why everything is happening in such a tight, linear format."

"Linear?"

"It doesn't have to be, you see."

"I don't see."

"You will."

Damien was amazed. He wasn't even sure what had happened at the sensor gate. But Husk and Shorts looked at him with pride in their eyes, as if he was a well-trained dog who had just proved himself in a crisis.

Almost immediately, Damien questioned his memory of the experience. Had he really passed through gate? Was he really wanted by the police? Had he really heard the computer call him Mr. Reynolds? And why had he been thinking of his father. It all felt like a fuzzy dreams. *Maybe I'm still drugged.*

The staircase curved them up to the second floor. A wall of elevators escorted them to levels of government offices secured from the outside world. "Will there be other checkpoints? It seems to me there will be other scanners—"

"No worries, Damien. We aren't heading anywhere that important," Husk said through his eternal smile.

Damien ventured forth with his emotions. He couldn't help himself. He missed Caleigha so much, needed comfort so much, and found no solace in the odd memories of his father that continually interrupted his train of thought. "Will we be going back to your place after this?" What he really meant was, *"Will we be seeing Sienna again?"*

Husk stared at him again with probing eyes as the elevator doors opened. "You feeling tired or something? How's your arm?"

Damien cocked it as Shorts stepped into the hall and drew everyone's attention. "Seems fine."

Husk caught the elbow and held it, not like a doctor at all but tightly to keep Damien from following Shorts too quickly. He pointed with his chin. "Decoy."

They held the elevator doors open for close to a minute, pretending to listen to a vital telephone conversation (Husk frowned and nodded at the air when pedestrians walked by). Then they moseyed importantly into the hallway.

Shorts was pushing a door ajar near the end of the shaded hall near a T-junction. A triangle of light spilled onto the floor, shrank, but did not disappear.

"There we are!" Husk whispered. He led Damien step by step.

Through the door was an office lit by yellow light. Bound books lined one wall in the fashion of yesteryear's lawyer. The opposite wall had been decorated with framed degrees and certificates. Shorts was chatting with a man in a suit without a collar.

The man speaking to Shorts had wasted away almost to nothing. His hands were a collection of bones connected to two long bones that protruded from the cuffs of his suit, and if it wasn't for the yellow light from the green-topped lamp, Damien thought he might not have been able to see any skin at all. The man jumped to his feet. "Oh, wow! Oh, wow—I am so-so-so-so very pleased to meet you!"

The man rounded the desk, took Damien's hand, and pumped his arm until Damien pulled himself away as politely as he thought possible.

"You have no-no-no idea how much this means to me." Tears brimmed in his eyes. "My name is—"

Husk stopped him with a clearing of his throat.

"—is of no real importance, is it? I mean, what's in a name, right?" He laughed, tearing up some more.

"Dude," Husk said.

The guy in the suit didn't stop pumping Damien's arm. He just kept right on weeping silently behind his smile as he stared with elation into Damien's eyes.

"Dude." Husk gave the skinny man a nudge with one gentle fist.

When the man blinked and looked over, his smile remaining, he nodded at Husk as if only meeting him for the first time. "Huh?"

"Your name's Dude. Got it?"

"Wha—? Sure." To Damien again he said, "It really is such a fabulous pleasure to see you at last!"

"Why?" said Damien.

A strangled laugh as if from a private joke squeezed from the back of 'Dude's' throat. "So modest," he barely said aloud. "Here I am...meeting the most important person in the history of this world."

Husk took Damien by the arm and pulled him free. "Enough of that, okay?" And to Damien, he cocked his finger at his head and whispered. "Dude's a little 'disassociated.' Know what I mean?"

Damien stared back at the sincere admiration in Dude's gaze. The man looked sharp as a tack, a lawyer or some kind of government employee in a position that earned him a private office in the courthouse.

"We have to keep moving," said Shorts. "Random Security Scanners, you know. Dude...Dude!"

"Yes! That's me! Yes." Dude's laugh shuddered, almost nervous.

"You have it ready?" said Shorts.

"You mean—you mean, for him?" He chuckled again, with a sound that brought him back to the private joke.

"Would that matter?" Shorts said.

"Just hurry, okay?"

Dude went to a wall and signaled for it to open. "I don't see why you're in such a hurry! We've got him."

Damien yanked his arm from Husk's grasp. He crossed the room as Dude removed from the hidden cabinet what looked like a wind-up pocket watch made of dark brass.

"Damien!" Husk said.

But it was too late.

Damien had grabbed Dude by the lapels of his jacket. He felt an inner anger mingle with his confusion and perhaps the kind of power that a growling dog felt in the presence of a small child. An inch from Dude's pencil-thin nose, he said, "Do you know anything about Caleigha Obregon? My girlfriend?"

The question was worth asking, he thought. Dude acted like Damien was Elvis back from the dead, like he knew exactly who Damien was—or more to the point, Dude acted like he knew why Damien was able to trick the sensors and the guards in the lobby.

Dude shuddered. Elation flashed over his face, and then a solid image of terror. "Of course! She's all a part of the plan!" Dude's eyes trembled at Husk and Shorts. "Isn't she?"

The desk spoke in a sweet voice. *"Sorry for bothering you, Captain. This is a security alert. There may be a suspect in the building who is wanted by the police for questioning. Please be prepared for individual scanning. Operatives are on the way."*

Dude chuckled hard at this. "Oh, rich. Rich! I am so thankful to be a part of this!"

Husk had already grabbed the brass watch. He caught Damien by both shoulders and did his best to tug him politely and urgently toward the door. "We got to move!"

"But why?" said Dude.

Shorts checked the hall while answering, "Because he's not ready."

Dude's flushed face went slowly ashen. "What? But—he's already—"

As Husk dragged him across the floor, Damien released Dude but spit back the words, "You might have me confused with someone else. Ever think about that?"

Shorts barked, "They're coming!"

Storm troopers gushed from both elevators.

"Run!" said Husk.

"Run?" said Dude.

Either the cops heard them, or marked their target from down the hall. Like a murder of crows, they launched their snow-armored bodies in a flying swarm that filled the hall.

"Jet belts!" Shorts said. And he sprinted in the opposite direction. "Is there a way out this way?"

Husk, Dude, and Damien raced after the runt. Husk yanked him from the ground as they caught up and started to pass him.

Damien looked over his shoulder.

The cops were in the air. Their feet dragged on the ground or kicked behind them as they soared at twice Damien's speed. The sound of their flight engines screeched higher and higher in pitch. The leader shouted above the noise, "Take them all!"

"Have we stopped?"

"Yes, Mr. Reyes. We'll get right back to it. But I need some help. This is beyond me!" Panicked laughter.

"Doctor? We had a deal, didn't we?"

"You mean... Caleigha?"

"... Yes."

"We have deal, Damien. But... I'm going to bring some people in here. I'll need you to wait."

"Wait? I hate waiting."

"You might not notice my absence at all."

"Oh, I will. It's torture to me! It's lasts—eons! And... I think there's something wrong."

"Don't say that."

"Like... something's breaking. I keep having this feeling."

"Please. I mean it, Mr. Reyes. Don't say that!"

"Say... what did I say?"

"I'll be right back. Don't say eons."

"Don't say what? Doc? Hello? Hel—... oh, no. Not again..."

Chapter Thirty-Four

If you don't want to play the game, you could always move to the Kingdom. After all, there aren't prisons anymore, not with the current 'correctional facilities' in use, right? Did you know that once upon a time so-called correctional facilities were really holding blocks for sadistic psychopaths who couldn't get off as 'mentally insane' in a court of law? Now the division is clear, and the North American Union with all their terraforming experiments in the far north, have provided an entire state where you can live in whichever way you want to live. Or you can face correctional facilities that actually 'correct' your brain—if you can believe such a thing! But you know what they say, you live in the Kingdom, you become one of them. Or maybe you just get erased. I mean, does anyone really know what goes on in the Kingdom?

—Milar Burton
Last Man In Prison

The armored dropship hung in the air like an upside down teardrop. Undercarriage gun turrets swiveled away from the smoldering remains of the old robot, which had fallen backwards. If it had a face, Corvasce's short time protector and once mechanical pet would have been staring into the sky, eyelids fluttering as it settled with sparks into its final repose. The floater's guns sought other targets. *Are the Seekers drawing near?* Body sensors must have located the old woman in the earthen house. They trained at last on the little window that had proved to be his salvation and at the open door, beyond which ancient Manda—who really wasn't that ancient—wisely remained in hiding.

An officer in black armor hit the ground, followed by six others. They held short assault rifles raised, aimed through their faceless masks, and spread out. Once the perimeter was secured, the first removed her helmet.

"Ames." Corvasce smiled with relief. And he wanted to hit her.

She looked about the same: the twinkle in her eye insinuated joy at finding her partner at last, while the scowl on her face guaranteed him a pop in the lip when life returned to normal and they renewed their boxing matches.

Ames was a 92 XX, born to become a soft woman with a sweet voice, like her mother. Somewhere along the way, she decided the soft touch wasn't a blessing and she hardened up in every way she could. Her voice was an abrasive rasp, her hair flat and short on the sides of her face, her countenance manly. No lip dyes, no makeup. And yet, the softness of her rounded cheekbones and her slightly up-curled chin still showed.

"You know, partners are supposed to stay in touch!" she shouted as the engine of the armored floater above them let out a roar as it stabilized its flow of gasses. The pilot clearly thought the silent vehicle safe enough to expose to this quiet wilderness. Ames had to shout for a moment to be heard. "You going Kingdom on me, is that it? You look like—"

"I know what I look like," said Corvasce, shouting as well until the sound of the engines above them hissed to near silence once more. "I know what I smell like too. Just get me out of here, okay?"

Ames examined the smoldering robot, then the ramshackle home. "Thought you'd died and gone to hell, eh?"

Corvasce was staring at the dead war machine beside him. Sadness attacked, dropping his heart into his stomach. But why should he feel sorry? "Something like that. How did you find me?"

"Well Captain Dewitter had written you off. Everyone thought you had died with the others at the university. I talked him into initiating a spiral scan, worked from Philibuck outward. Might have found you sooner, but the Cap only gave me one bird. We've had a bad time of it."

Corvasce looked at his filthy attire, at the pocket holding the dead badge. He looked at Manda's hut. There was no sign of the old woman. He peered at the hills. Invisible eyes watched them. Or maybe it was an unfamiliar paranoia stalking him. "Yes, but how did you find me."

"Simple, Detective. Picked up a weak signal from your badge."

He pulled the object from his coat. "You know, I think we need to get Technical to take a close look inside this thing."

"What, your badge?"

Corvasce nodded at the hills, at the wind, at the eyes of seekers out there that he couldn't locate. "It might give us a clue about who we are dealing with here. Who we're really dealing with."

"Well I don't mean to rain on your parade, pal, but I think the President's assassination is going to take precedence over your little field trip. You're not following a lead out here, are you? It is beyond our jurisdiction, you know."

"I was kidnapped."

Blink.

"By the people behind the assassination, I think."

"You're not trying to tell me...the Kingdom folk—"

Corvasce started walking toward the drop ship. "I need to do a little research before writing up my report. And I think I might need a tox-screen to boot. What day is it?"

"Do you really want to know?"

"Maybe I don't."

"Well, I hate to say this, but *technically* you're under arrest."

"Stop. Say that again?"

"I'd rather not, partner. The Secret Service wants you brought into custody."

"Why's that?"

"How should I know! It gave me an excuse to track you down—I had to pull strings to get permission to bring you in myself."

"So the Captain hoped I'd died in the assault on Pandam?"

Ames nodded. "It would have looked better to him, I think. That military unit protecting this little place? Going to cause a lot of questions, if you ask me."

"You going to cuff me then?"

"Oh, would you like that?" She smiled, and she had a pretty smile and that playful twinkle in her eye.

But that didn't change the fact that he was being taken into the protective detention of the state.

And when his partner did "bring him in," it was going to have to look like it.

Chapter Thirty-Five

Integral to all machinery, including biotechnology, is the singularity which, if removed, would stop the entire creation from working. So it is through-out life, throughout all complex creations, and every equation. It is a brick which, if removed, might cause the most magnificent of towers to fall.

—Frankie Bellarosa
Simple World Domination

"*'Don't say eons,' you said! Don't say eons!*" *Rattle-rattle. Snap.*

"*Good morning, Mr. Reyes.*"

"*Don't say eons!*"

"*Calm down!*"

"*Calm—down! Eons! EONS.*"

"*It wasn't that long, Mr. Reyes. But you must understand, if you think 'eons' it will feel like eons—eons to you. But for us, well it's only been a matter of hours. Few hours.*"

"*Eons! My—oh, doc! I've been in a black hole. A black hole!*"

"*No, Damien. Listen to my voice. Let yourself be calm. Listen to my tone. Listen to my pace. Match my pace, my tone, my voice.*"

"*What's going on here?*"

"*Black—hole! Blackness! Forever!*"

"*But finished, now. Not infinite. Not forever.*"

"*Eons!*"

"*I said, what's going on here?*"

"*Who's there?*"

"*Damien Reyes, may I introduce to you a couple of my colleagues: Dr. Joanne Bridges.*"

"How do you do, Mr. Reyes."

"Finished?"

"Yes, Mr. Reyes."

"Doc!"

"Finished. The wait is over. And the wait doesn't have to be so long when I slip away. Listen to my voice. Be calm. Dr. Bridges, Dr. Herietta, Mr. Reyes is experiencing a problem with time."

"Doc..."

"He thought that I might be gone for an excessive amount of time. He thought it, and—well this is old science, isn't it: time is relative. To...to Mr. Reyes, I have been gone a long, long time!"

"That's barbaric, Dr. Rothgar. Must this—"

"Dr. Bridges. You must not think of this as...as a normal representation of life."

"What? Wait—WHAT ARE YOU TALKING ABOUT?"

"Relax, Damien. You are alive. And you are well."

"How can you say that, Dr. Rothgar? This is hell!"

"Dr. Herietta. My friends. Please realize what I just said. Time is perceived at a certain pace. Haven't... well, haven't you ever waited for an appointment—or a meeting to begin?—and felt the time seem to stretch, to lengthen impossibly, so that it felt as if it lasted twice as long or longer?"

"Yes! Torture!"

"Doc, please don't ignore me."

"That's all that Damien Reyes is experiencing. Now... please... let us continue. It is marvelous!"

"Doc...oh, Doc. What are you doing?"

"Nothing to worry about, Mr. Reyes. Let's continue. We are nearing the end now. We'll be finished! Just a little more?"

"Okay. I'm scared."

"Be confident, Damien. Trust in me. I refuse to let you down! I made a promise, didn't I?"

Click.

"Mr. Reyes?"

"Yes, Doc?"

"What are you doing?"

"Listening. Like you said. Thinking."

"About what, exactly?"

"What I'm going to do to you... if you don't keep your promise."

Hiss. Whisper.

"Put it out of your mind, Mr. Reyes. I'm on your side. Now... you were *being chased in the courthouse."*

"You'll keep the promise? Honestly?"

"I will, Damien. My life upon it!"

"Oh..."

Soaring near the roof of the hallway, the flying officers nearly had them. Flight engines screamed. Husk, Shorts, Damien, and skin-and-bones man nicknamed rather hurriedly "Dude" skidded around a corner and began a race to the next right turn, one that was much too far away to reach. Dude screeched a sentence or two so quickly that Damien couldn't make out the words.

But the building must have heard him.

For just as the white-gloved fingers clutched at the air behind Damien's back, a door slammed down from the ceiling. Duke smiled at Damien and said, "Fire wall!"

The building calmly informed everyone working inside, *"Advanced fire protection services have been initiated. Please remain where you are until confirmation of non-threat status has been achieved."*

"How in the world did you do that?" said Shorts, kicking for Husk to put him down.

Husk didn't lower the tiny man. "We're not out of the woods yet. Those cops will get that door open soon enough, won't they—Dude? Do something!"

But Dude wasn't listening. He had grabbed Damien by the back of his shirt as they continued to make for the end of the hall. He spoke quickly and close to Damien's ear. "Shorts drive you here?"

Damien hardly found the breath necessary to talk. "Yes."

"Excellent! Now we don't need to worry. Do you know why?"

"No." Damien wasn't sure he wanted to get away. Then he thought of Caleigha. He saw Sienna in his mind. He wanted to get back to her. He had questions that needed answers, and it was that last look she had given him, that flicker of knowledge that she had tried to hide from him, that made him know that she had and could tell him the truth. If only he could get her alone. "We're getting away in his car?"

"Exactly!" Dude huffed in his ear. "It's very simple."

"It's very simple," Damien's father said in his mind.

And the memory roared into his mind, interrupting his panic.

Time stopped.

It started again, and Damien was in the past, on a beach, with his father. His mother played in the waves of warm Caribbean waters. It had been the one and only vacation their family had ever taken. She laughed, but Damien could not hear her. He saw her smile. Her mouth opened, and she fell beneath the whitewash and kicked her pruned feet into the air. When she came up again, gleeful, even his father looked happy.

But Marcus Reyes sat beside Damien's sand castle and scooped up the glittering grit an inch from Damien's protective moat. *"Damien. How many grains am I holding, do you think? How many grains of sand?"*

Damien continued working on the walls and the northeast tower. But he had heard his father. After a moment, his eyes flickered at the hill balancing between his father's wrist and curved fingers. He saw the sand escaping. *"How should I know?"*

"What do you see?"

"I see dirt. You're holding it. Some's slipping out of your hand, by the way."

His father almost laughed, so proud of his son. *"Very good! I asked you to count the grains of sand, didn't I. But the number of grains that I am holding is always changing, isn't it. It's very simple."*

"You always say that. You always say it's very simple."

"How many grains of sand are there in my hand? If n equals the number of grains of sand, then I am holding n - 1 at a certain rate. 1 times the rate gives you the answer. Very simple."

"Maybe for you."

"No, Damien. For you! Watch... only one grain of sand... leaves at a time."

Damien looked.

"You see it, don't you?"

A golden string of sand fell from the sides of his father's open fist.

The sand trickled more slowly.

The sand stopped.

While the line remained in the air between his father's hand and the side of the castle.

No. Wait.

Damien saw that the sands were moving. They slipped so slowly he couldn't detect their motion without staring for what felt like an incredibly long time. He stared. He stared. And one single grain shifted, then toppled over the ridges in his father's skin. It dropped free. It rolled, knocking against another grain of sand, and was followed by a third.

When Damien looked at his father's face, time resumed its natural speed, and his father said, *"It's like magic! Now, Damien. How many grains of sand are in my hand."*

Damien squinted his eyes. He could see the sand leaving the base of the hill on his father's palm. He could see them leaving one by one. He could see the pieces of sand slide down the little slope. And he thought he could see inside that short pile.

There was a piece of sand in there. There was a piece of sand beside it. There was a piece of sand on top, beneath, on the other side.

Damien thought he saw that the one piece of sand in the center was made up of other pieces of sand. A whole universe of sand filled and made up that single grain. And each piece had a universe of other pieces within it. And inside those pieces...

"One."

"What?" His father didn't seem to like the answer. Or he hadn't expected it. His whole expression shifted as if for a moment he wasn't speaking with his young boy but with a colleague at work.

"There is one. There is only one."

"One, Damien? And where exactly is it?"

Damien looked around himself. He felt his father's other hand on the back of his neck. He felt the pieces of the sand all around him, all through him, like a breeze to the limbs and leaves of the tree. His voice boomed inside his head. *"I am the tree,"* he said. *"I am the breeze."*

"Damien. Damien! Wasurenasai!"

And Dude was saying his name again. "Damien!" The skinny man in the suit sounded like a kid on his way to an amusement park.

A harsh cutting sound filled the hall behind them.

They ran beneath the dim ambient lights toward the end of the hallway framed by doors that had shut automatically when the fire alarm had been engaged.

"Damien. The car. I bet you can see it in your head, can't you? Shorts' car?"

"Yeah," Damien said, heart pounding.

"You can! You can see it even without seeing it with your eyes."

"Of course."

"Rich! You know why, Damien? Because that is reality."

Another memory spoke briefly, like a white hot flash in Damien's head. It was his father, his eyebrows raised. His glee simply enormous. *"That is reality!"*

"What you didn't know," said Dude, puffing, "is that at the end of this hall there is a pane of glass that will burst when we reach it. Our proximity will shatter the glass out, all over..."

"The car?" Damien said, wishing the man would let go of his arm, now, and get away from his ear.

"Right on! You can see that, can't you! Shorts's car hovering out there, floating, unaffected by the sirens."

"I don't hear any sirens."

"They're silent!"

"Do you see the car?"

Of course, Damien couldn't. The glass pane at the end of the hall was an opaque marble fake. And as it was dark outside, no light poured through the barrier.

But he could see the car there, in his mind. And he needed the car to get them back to Sienna. The car had to be there!

"I trust you," he said, though he had no idea why he said that.

"And I trust you, Damien Reyes," Dude said through an elongated smile and a continuation of tears that began to bounce from his lower eyelids as he ran.

They reached the window.

It exploded outward, and only after it did so did Damien wonder why a window might be rigged to do that.

And there, hovering in the air high above the road, Shorts's car received a rain of fake marble glass.

Husk and Shorts stared at one another with wide eyes.

A tearing sound ripped the metal of the fire door free, and the screech of police Personnel Flight Machines raised the alarm once more.

"Time to go!" Dude said.

Shorts hit his remote. The door opened, the car rose, and all four of them stepped inside the vehicle.

The door shut again just in time for the nearest officer to slam into the car. His helmet cracked into the ceiling. They heard his words shout through the window and the barrier covering his face. "They're outside! They're outside! We need backup! North side of the building! We need as many guns as you got!"

"Go!" Dude said, though Shorts stared at him in disbelief.

Shorts gunned the engine.

But it was too late.

Three bumblebees rounded the building in front of them, lights flashing, sirens blazing, and gun turrets coming to bear.

"Remarkable!"

"Did I really see—can these readouts be correct? I must take this! Can I take this, Dr. Rothgar? I need to analyze these numbers."

"Yes. Please, take them. But you understand the need for secrecy. Even …even from…"

"Of course! Naturally!"

"Doc?"

"Mr. Reyes?"

"Please don't talk like I'm not here. I'm worried. I can't feel my fingers."

"Damien. You will be able to… if you think about it. If you think about feeling them. Listen. I will take care of you. Didn't I make that promise?"

"Yeah."

"We are so close to the end, now. We are so close!"

Chapter Thirty-Six

The act of writing history is more powerful than the act of living it. While living history (that is, accomplishing or witnessing accomplishments worth writing down later) is a physical, mental, and emotional experience, writing history is a religious one. For in the act of living history, no one sees any of the events clearly. This principle flaw is recognized nowhere more accurately than in a court of law, where witnesses, data records, and sworn testimonials combine in the educated hands of juris doctors in an attempt to clarify "what really happened." Hindsight, they say, is twenty-twenty. Therefore, it is in the review and recording of history that the realities of the past become qualified, quantified, and factual. Yet even then, written history changes as soon as any little new piece of data rears its ugly head and demands to be seen in the twenty-twenty light. And so we see that the writing of history is akin to revelation itself, the only act among humans that is truly spiritual from beginning to end. Humankind pens its own scripture.

—Karla Cordova
The Not So Subtle Past

It was worse than a sacrilegious joke, he thought. But he laughed anyway.

Martin Warren attended the funeral of President Henry Waldorf Sanchez in the same manner of many others, standing for all to see, but not being present even remotely. In this interactive Virtual, incorporeal manifestations stood around a grave that existed only in the mind of a computer. Wind blew through trees, and leaves rustled—all special effects, of course.

Warren's "appearance" was just as "special." He used a prerecorded image of himself augmented for length and visual sobriety.

The nation mourned the President's unexpected passing.

172

They should be mourning the VP's over-long speech!

Warren listened to the eulogy by Lotti Morrison while reviewing the latest data from the assault on Pandam City. All the other Chiefs of Staff would be reading similar reports, possibly at this very moment. In fact, he wondered how many of them, if any at all, were attending the President's memorial service.

There it is, he thought.

Lotti Morrison mentioned, just as an extended side note—just a cursory statement, as if it mattered only a little in this time of sadness—that she would be inaugurated President on Thursday, two days hence.

Two days. *"Forty-one hours,"* Warren heard Tubal Seda bark in his head. All too soon, the Chief of Staff over the Mexican States would play his card. He would reveal the hidden file mailed to Lotti. If Warren didn't throw him the bone Tubal expected.

The car floated to the side of the Pentagon. As it reached the Public Officials Entrance on the third floor, the building's safety protocols went into action—all for show, of course.

Powerful twelve-inch, short-range pulse cannons on either side of the door swiveled and aimed into the cab and engine of the hovering limo. At the first sign of danger, the guns could let loose a series of explosions that would rip the vehicle into little chunks of metal and brief memories of the humans it had carried.

The threat of a big bang was simply a psychological deterrent. The building was equipped on all sides with siren-override protection that could repel any vehicle (outside of the old gas or electric manual-steering classics), killing the engine and locking the doors at a safe distance. But that wasn't as dangerous to terrorist infiltrators as much as the electric backlash generators that could turn anyone's automobile or floater into a veritable killing machine. Anyone inside a car when that went off would experience the executioner's chair in a whole new way.

Warren's limo pulled to a slow stop. The heavy guns clicked into final position, so that PCS Warren was staring down a barrel wide enough to fill with his arm—he never did like this idea of looking down the barrel of such a huge weapon, even if he understood the deterrent: *You can still drive away.* It seemed a little over the top, and what if there was an accident? What if the Pentagon's horribly costly EYES made a mistake, and the computers pulled the trigger and blew him into smithereens?

In the nanoseconds that followed, the building read his identification. Ocular scans captured the glance of his eyes and the eyes of his driver, then verified the retinal patterns.

Then, frighteningly expensive state of the art DNA sniffers went to work. Warren despised these devices most of all. He'd heard too many studies concerning themselves with the inaccuracy of these DNA sniffers, especially during an age in which everyone—outside of the pure-bred eccentrics in the Kingdom—possessed one of a very limited number of DNA construction types. The job of the sniffers, according to the companies developing and marketing them, was not to confirm anyone's identity, but to check for residual body signatures of any registered suspects and known hostiles who might be or have been present in the car—such as one who could have planted an unknown (and therefore undetectable) form of explosive in or around the vehicle. Nevertheless, the problem remained a simple one and an old one: if the DNA sniffer detected a threat, the agent, Senator, or other highly cleared employee of the government would be locked in the car for an undetermined time period—regardless of the fact that time meant even more than money in this job. Time could mean lives. And a misappropriated use of vital time could lead to the end of the world.

So when the doors to the Pentagon did not open for Primary Chief of Staff Martin Warren, he was not entirely surprised.

It was the voice that projected into the cab that staggered him. "CS Warren!" Tubal Seda said. A short chuckle—the spider to the fly—followed. "You have the right to remain silent—which you already know, as you've remained silent regarding issues of national security all this time—anything you say—"

Warren exploded. "You—you of all people have no right to—"

"Don't think so?"

Yellow lights flashed above the cannons just outside the limousine.

The hovering craft disengaged from the wall. The driver lifted his hands, looked over the backseat at the PCS, and shook his head. A blinking light on the dash indicated the car's recognition of a silent siren override.

Seda's voice ceased conveying words of arrest, but Martin Warren frowned at the Pentagon's windows as the limo automatically pulled away. He knew the grinning fool was watching. Yet he had no idea what the Chief Staff over Mexico thought he was doing. But he knew that Seda would regret it.

Chapter Thirty-Seven

A gentleman does not always tell the truth. Often the truth is imprudent to share. Situations and circumstances must be considered before any truth is revealed. A gentleman will respectfully think before ever he speaks. It is the basic requirement of all gentlemen to keep themselves comfortable and make everyone around them equally comfortable or, when possible, more so.

—Lilian DuCamp
Putting on Proper Airs

Corvasce sat in a room that was all too familiar, but looked very much this time like an entirely different place. His perspective had changed. A thousand times he had displayed his mental prowess in this room. But each of those times, he wasn't the person sitting in the metal chair that faced the wall-length mirror.

The Secret Service agent leaning against the wall called the shots with hardly a word. His complexion was dark, though his skin was pale; otherwise he was a typical, wiry 201 XY. He folded his arms—no need to hide his body language here, especially with a detective in the hot seat: he was hiding something—plenty, in fact—and wasn't the one being questioned. At the beginning of their "interview," he had been introduced as Special Agent In Charge, Raul Dodger.

The man who introduced him wore sunglasses, indoors. *How very stylish, in a stuffed-shirt sort of way,* thought Corvasce. Special Agent Corbin Rottweil, a greasy 119 XY, wore the same black suit and the same black tie as his partner, but he never smiled, not even once. His glasses matched his perfectly shiny black shoes, and his voice sounded equally black. His hat rested between them on the silvered table.

"Pardon me for saying so, Detective, but your story doesn't make any sense to me."

"Well then I'd ask your buddy here to clarify it for you." Corvasce said without a hint of the intimidation he felt.

Agent Rottweil leaned hard on the desk. "Oh, I get it! You really have no bearing at all about your vector."

"Were you a ship captain in another life?"

Rottweil's face soured further. "I'll 'clarify it' for you, shall I? You are wanted in conjunction with the assassination of the President of the North American Union."

"I know that—"

"What you haven't figured out, despite all your experience, is that when you are sitting in that chair, your job is to cooperate. You don't have the same rights as the common criminal you deal with in your little job, Detective. As a professional in law enforcement, you are liable to suffer far more than anyone else we nab in conjunction with this atrocity. Your smoke-screen—your choice to wave your right to a lawyer—isn't going to work with us."

"I'm here as a courtesy," Corvasce said. "I've already laid out all the facts as far as I know them." He glanced at SAIC Dodger, the only brain in the room worth trusting, he guessed.

"You are here, Detective, as a suspect!"

"I am here as a suspect," said Corvasce, allowing his volume to rise, "because your agency can't seem to tell a reflection from a photograph."

The insult, in the form of an amateur puzzle, stunned Rottweil. He blinked rapidly before figuring out the detective's point.

In the meantime, Raul Dodger stepped away from the wall. "Thank you, Corvasce. I think you have made your point."

"Ah, the master speaks!"

"No reason for playing good cop/bad cop with you, is there, Detective Corvasce?"

"Not really. But you are doing it anyway, aren't you? That's why you're taking a chair. That's why you've just loosened your tie."

Dodger grinned. "As far as I'm concerned, we're almost finished here. May I ask you a few questions?"

"Very polite of you to start that way."

"How did you get into the Kingdom?"

"I've answered that."

"And you know the rules of engagement here: We ask a question, we ask it again, we ask it a third time."

"To see if I'll change my story. I won't. It's obvious what side you've put me on. When I'm supposed to be on your side."

"So interesting you say that: 'Whose side.' Isn't that what you said your captor told you? No answer? You're trying to solve the puzzle for yourself—or tying to look like it? See, I'm not playing good cop or bad cop. I'm just doing my job."

"I didn't recognize any of them. Those people down in the tunnels. They matched no recognizable genetic profile. They were hideous, twisted versions of humanity."

"You had a security mech defending your position."

"Again, it was busted! It was hardly standing. Who knows how long it had been repairing itself."

"Your badge communicated with it. After an EMP? Can you explain that?"

"Curious, I agree. I already told you that I can't explain those details. I can only report what I witnessed. I'm beginning to think..." Corvasce rubbed his fingertips over stubble that the Secret Service had not permitted him an opportunity to shave.

"Think what, Detective?"

"...that it was all...it was all a set up."

The SS agents gazed across the room at one another. They almost seemed to be thinking aloud, as if they knew something more about the policeman's theory.

Dodger stood as the door opened and another dark suit appeared. "Detective Corvasce, we are *certain* that it was all set up."

The third agent waved Dodger over and whispered into his ear. He showed him a briefly appearing light screen, then shut the door.

Dodger looked at his partner, and Corvasce wondered if they had some sort of line of sight direction thought transference capability—he had read of such a device, but had been led to believe that it was still theoretical. And yet, how often had the military or the upper-levels of the government utilized cutting-edge, experimental technology over the years?

The other agent frowned.

Corvasce waited patiently.

"Okay," Dodger said, signaling for the detective to stand. "I want you to know that what I'm about to tell you does not change your status in our eyes. You realize that you are a suspect."

"Of course. Even though I stand by my story. I was abducted."

"And you agree that it is a strange story. Unexplainable."

"Quiet explainable, in time. I think I was set up. That we are being led to believe that some religious group or coalition is responsible for all this. Even though they would have the capability. Or maybe this is all a distraction from what it really going on."

The angrier of the two agents grew red faced and finally exploded into shouting. "We don't care what you think!"

Dodger raised a hand to quiet his partner. "Actually, I want to be kept appraised of your every thought. Do you understand me?"

Corvasce leaned his head to one side.

Dodger engaged a light screen and spun it around so that the detective could read the words for himself. "You are hereby notified that you are on special assignment. You are to report to the Chief of Staff immediately."

Corvasce looked at the digitally created signature and seal: Nathaniel Osprey.

Chapter Thirty-Eight

The illusionist's key to magic is a simple matter of lateral thinking. If she raises a card in the air and holds her eyes upon it, discussing its hidden face, she may easily pull some second object from her pocket with her free hand. All eyes and attention being on the card, the illusionist in fact creates a distraction while preparing for the real trick. When the real trick is exhibited, the audience is taken completely off guard...and naturally wants to see the magic replayed. A replay of the illusion is, according to the magician's number one law, never granted on the spot because the distraction will not work as well a second time.

—Lady Jane
How to Disappear in Front of Everyone

Seeing the three black and yellow bumblebee floaters pulled around the corner ahead of them, Husk pounded the seat in front of him. "Go, Shorts! Go! Go!"

Shorts forced the controls and the car flipped around.

The sirens outside went audible. The throbbing, rising, falling song shook the windows.

Dude leaned into Damien, crushing him in the backseat against Husk, and said, "Remember what I told you? You saw the glass—you saw the car—and now you see how this car isn't held down by the sirens!"

A car that did not automatically pull over when silent or audible emergency vehicle sirens engaged violated one of the strictest laws of traffic. The fine was enormous, and driving privileges were automatically revoked for a period of time to be determined later in a court of law. It took a mastermind to figure out how to override such a deeply programmed system, and to override siren control was a criminal offense akin to drug trafficking. In fact, it was usually only drug smugglers who bothered to pay so much to shut off the pullover program.

As Shorts drove the car into a dive, and then banked the triangular vehicle around the back of the courthouse and then left between a bank building and a trust-fund conglomerate and then right and up again six lanes, he hit the radio.

The police scanner announced exactly what one would have expected: "10-47. Auto operating without siren override. All cars in the vicinity of 200 North and Center be advised."

"That'll bring the dogs!" Shorts bellowed from the front seat.

But the dogs were already behind them. The three bumblebees matched Shorts's evasive maneuvering turn for turn, their proximity sirens pulling everyone out of the way before Shorts could even get near other traffic.

Damien noticed the gun turrets remaining silent, but a swarm of high speed Vector Bugs vomited from the front of the lead bumblebee and streaked in their direction.

An alarm sounded on the dash.

"Ah!" Shorts barked. "Skeeters!"

They dove again, this time with such violence, Damien hit the ceiling. Everyone in the back seat screamed. The car spun upside down, twisted in the air, and Damien felt his stomach roll over threateningly. When they leveled off, they fired eastward at an incline, banking around another building.

But the 4-10 Mosquito Interceptors were closing in.

Husk smiled at Damien. "Okay, sunny-boy! Now's a good time for a little more voodoo. Yes-yes-yes!"

"I don't know what you're talking about!" Damien screamed, wishing he could do something. The police were about to literally shoot down any chance he had of seeing Sienna again, let alone Caleigha.

He had to get back to Husk's apartments. But how could he do that with all these officers on their tail? How could he have the peaceful conversation with Caleigha's look-alike if he couldn't get alone with her in a situation as relaxing as this one was stressful?

"Do something!" Dude shouted, but at Shorts instead of Damien.

Shorts shouted back. "You do something! I'm doing everything I can!" He banked the car around the roots of a building designed like a metallic tree. The car made for the heavens, shooting straight up the reflective sides and probably giving six dozen administrative assistants the shock of their lives.

Husk had a hold of his glossy black hair with both hands. "Aaaah—Got it!" He popped his knuckles. "Where can't skeeters go?"

"No idea!" Shorts said, sounding personally offended that Husk would play riddles at a time like this.

Dude, however, snapped his fingers before his elongated nose. "Into public facilities!"

The skeeters matched their racing floater turn for turn. The flashing bumblebees left their prey intentionally to head them off, no doubt following the data sent back by the skeeters. Shorts had to outthink both pursuers. "What—you mean?—"

Husk slapped the headrest in front of him. "We have no choice!"

Shorts whipped the wheel right, yanked up, then a hard right again, screaming, "Hang on to something!"

The car did a loop and twisted Damien's stomach and opened up all the pipes. They went up and 'round and then straight at the window of one of the buildings. Damien seriously doubted this one would explode as easily (and impossibly, he suddenly realized) as the one that had proved their escape.

The glass burst inward. Desks and chairs few. Bodies dived out of the way, and Damien wasn't sure all the pedestrians jumped successfully to freedom. They were going too fast—and to where?

Husk was shouting directions. Damien held onto the door. Dude braced himself against Damien as the car spun. Squealing tires gripped the floor, left the floor. The car hit the ceiling and crashed down hallways, ripping out chalky wallboards and leaving ruin in their wake.

The skeeters had stopped at the side of the building, having hit a legal barrier they could not cross.

Husk started laughing, hooting, cheering.

Shorts saw glass and the sky outside. He leaned on the controls.

The floater cannoned out the side of the building, only to swing around to face a monster dropping from space.

Everyone screamed at the same time.

The Hyper-7 Dropship made the air throb. Drop-down turrets leveled, taking aim. They could even see the black-clad coppers in the cockpit. The faceless pilot waved, then returned his hand to the stick.

"Back-inside! Back-inside!"

Guns blared. Holes burst through the hood of the car. Tunnels of air emerged across the top of the cab. A second more, and the Dropship would cut them all into tiny pieces right there over a busy street.

Kill first and ask questions later! Damien thought.

Shorts whipped the car backwards and smashed it again at the building.

But they were already falling.

He punched the car as hard as he could into the silver and glass siding. The car shrieked across the floor and through the walls. It hit a support beam. Then the vehicle spun to a halt, smashing everyone into the left side of the cab.

They crawled from the wreckage. Computers showered sparks as dry sprinkler systems initiated.

"The fire doors!" Dude shouted. "We need to get out before we're locked in!"

"We'll never get out of here!" Shorts answered. They sprinted, stumbling, from the ruined vehicle.

But Husk wore his fabulous grin. "Oh, yes we will!" He batted his eyes in Damien's direction.

It seemed like seconds before the police were on top of them. Damien could only guess how they got into the building, but he suspected the Dropship outside had fired armed guards directly into the hole left by their massacred getaway car.

"Nobody move!"

Everyone kept running, banking around a corner.

Fire doors dropped from ceilings, shut naturally only to lock with inhuman accord. Fire doors slid from walls where no doors had apparently been hiding.

"There!" Husk shouted as they stumbled past office employees crouching in the fetal position with hands over their heads. Lights flickered, flashed. Controlled directional sprayers shot fire dousing solutions from the ceiling, proving immediately effective on contact.

"That way!" Shorts headed down an open hallway where fire doors had not been deemed necessary by the building's auto-defense systems. He slid around a corner, tripped on the edge of the wall, and tumbled in a beautiful roll that left him sprawled.

"No!" Dude was leading the others another way, but at the next turn looked back to see Shorts struggling to rise from the littered floor. "No!"

Damien realized that Dude was shouting at him. Damien had arched into another side passage thinking of Caleigha, the need to get back to Caleigha, or Sienna rather. He had to find her. He had to get back. Even if that meant leaving this little circus of unlikely criminals.

"That way's the cops!"

Husk had run back to snatch Shorts from the jaws of certain capture. As he returned, all the doors were shutting.

Dude slapped a small glass window that separated their path from Damien.

Damien stared at him from the other side.

They hardly noticed the building as it spoke kindly in a female voice. *"This a police lockdown situation. Everyone please remain calm."*

Damien hardly noticed the police officers running up behind him. As they grabbed hold of his shoulders and elbows, Damien watched through the little glass pane as Dude, Husk, and Shorts hurried out of sight.

The cops slammed Damien Reyes to the ground. His cheekbone impacted the polished floor the hardest.

But he wasn't thinking about any of black storm troopers. He thought of Sienna, of Caleigha—the same person, or different. He knew he would see her again.

He knew because of how his three strange companions had looked at him before dashing away.

Shorts had looked upset, but unworried, as if his personal plan had been thwarted but that his team would win in the end.

Husk had looked pleased and even excited, grinning at the last.

And Dude, the skinny man in the fine suit, with tears once more in his eyes, looked proud.

Chapter Thirty-Nine

Only when I lose myself in someone else do I find myself. He who shall sacrifice his life shall find himself. She who seeks to find herself will find emptiness; she who loses herself in the service of another will find herself. Why have these statements been made for millennia? Has the experience of humankind led us in a long line of hints to see, at last, that we are all interconnected? We are not only a part of the universe; the universe is an extension of ourselves.

—A.L. Beyan
Ship of Souls

"Detective, thank you for meeting with me." Chief of Staff Nathaniel Osprey shook Corvasce by the hand and ushered him cordially into a closed room beyond the reach of the Secret Service agents in his employ. Even then, the slimy smile of false friendship did not leave his cheerful mug. His eyes were bloodshot, the tips of his ears also filled with blood and excessive tension. Corvasce identified Osprey as a rare 4 XY. To the room, the Chief said, "Seal and secure."

His oval office responded in kind: "Sealed and secured."

"Take a seat. Please." The effective president of the northern territories rubbed his temples as he took a matching chair on the friendly side of his enormous desk.

Corvasce hesitated, then sat in time with CS Osprey. "I'm surprised I made it through your security section. If I'm suspect in the death of President Sanchez."

"You are not suspect to me. You know why I asked you here personally?"

"Because of the incident with your daughter?"

"I owe you one for that. More importantly, I trust you over all others, Harvey—may I call you Harvey?"

"I appreciate the confidence, sir. But that doesn't really answer my question. You can't pardon me, not in a federal case of this magnitude."

"I need someone that I trust, Detective. I've vouchsafed you as far as I am able to give pardons. The Secret Service—my own entourage—is under the thumb of the Primary Chief of Staff. And I believe the man is dirtier than a blue-collar's shirt at the end of the day."

This was the reason Corvasce hadn't liked Osprey when his daughter had been kidnapped three years prior: he drew lines in the sand much too quickly. That Corvasce had found the girl in the nick of time when the Secret Service and the FBI barked up the wrong metaphorical trees jarred the Chief of Staff unexpectedly. He thought Harvey Corvasce was worthy of higher badge power and had pushed to get him reassigned. Corvasce had turned down the opportunity. He wanted to help the little people in this world as much as the rich and famous, especially because the little people were so quickly forgotten while the wealthy got all the attention of the brass and the press that they wanted.

Nevertheless, the Chief's note had pulled him out of a hairy situation. Corvasce had not enjoyed sitting on the other side of the interrogator's table. The experience gave him a pinch of empathy he had lacked.

"Detective, have you ever heard of a Downloadable?"

"Sure. Espionage types. Deep plants. Genetic creations. I've read about them. Hard to believe they exist. I assume you're going to tell me there's truth to the stories?"

"True as rain: showing up at the worst possible times, missing when the dry earth thirsts."

"Sounds like CIA territory."

"It was a division of their Counterintelligence Unit that picked this man up." Osprey pulled a file from his attaché case and placed it into the Detective's hands. "He was delivering data. We got plenty of information implicating the Turkish Neural Shi."

Corvasce raised his eyebrows to project his honest shock. Secretly, he was amused and flabbergasted. He didn't have clearance for this kind of information; it was well outside his jurisdiction as a Pandam City Detective, and he didn't know any more about the Turkish Neural Shi than what could be read in the news. He remembered a columnist writing that *Shi* meant Death, and that the Neural Shi was a mind-boggling digital collective made up of the nationalists on the other side of the planet. Among other things, the Turks were rumored to have more Star Wars firepower than all their competitors combined. But, the columnist went on to write, the TNS had its own internal fish to fry. They were too busy with their collective and anti-collective bi-partisan wars to involve themselves in world politics, and most of the world was too scared to wake "The Sleeping Saber" anyway.

"Mr. Osprey, pardon me for saying so, but this is way above my head."

"On the contrary, I think the President's assassination is far more down to earth that you might presently believe. You were dragged into the Kingdom, I understand."

Corvasce nodded, though he had mixed feelings about how much firepower all those religious naturalists could pull together. He remembered Pandam's sonic shields initiating. An extra-terrestrial attack would be needed for that. Was it really possible for Kingdom activists (Seekers, maybe?) to take control of the TNS? Or could those Neural Death freaks quietly conquer the Kingdom as part of an attempt to finally make their move for world domination? Would they even bother to go about it that way? It seemed to Corvasce that they'd fight it out in the heavens, above the ozone layer. He with the most cannons aimed at Earth wins. That sort of thing.

Nathaniel Osprey opened a golden box and licked the thin square of cigarette paper after rolling his little cig. "Do you want one? No carcinogens or addictive qualities."

"Mr. Osprey. I really don't know how I can be of help in this case. I reported everything that I witnessed at the site of the assassination—I reported in painful detail, I promise you."

The CS lit his smoke and took a puff. Fragments of brown tobacco leaf sprinkled over the carpet, but his eyes closed as he breathed in and then out to the one side. The scent was sweet. When he opened his eyes, he said, "This has medicinal properties; it is calming. Sure I can't interest you in—"

"No thank you." The file played the final scenes recorded by the CIA prior to the capture of Mr. Fox de la Rosa Pandu. He looked scared, victimized by his own programming. Notes described his broken family, his broken life. *What a poor man.* The final report described the man as a "dead unit." Pandu couldn't remember anything that he had ever done. He could not tell the investigating agents who had controlled him, though they had ascertained that a network of sleeper Downloadables worked together, unwittingly, toward their primary objective. The objective was still a mystery. Pandu had been remanded into special psychiatric recovery and for something coded EME. "What's this?"

"EME? Oh that's…that's nothing."

"Forgive my audacity. It looks important. You're handing me this man's file, expecting help, and leaving me in the dark. I won't be able to run on all twelve cylinders. *Comprende?*"

"Hmm. See… Experimental Memory Extraction. It's not legal in a court of law."

"Neither is torture, but I doubt humankind has fully eradicated that sort of questioning."

Osprey sighed in agreement. Then he ducked under the slight by adding, "It's not really my territory. I represent the President of the North American Union, all the Northern States. Espionage is generally ratcheted up to Washington."

"Sure."

"And that's where you come in."

"Washington's a stretch beyond my reach. You're not trying to hire me into the Secret Service again; that wouldn't make sense. Not when you say the Secret Service isn't exactly on your side."

Nathaniel Osprey grinned and waggled a finger. "I never said that."

"Didn't you? You brought a detective into your oval office, remember? It's my job to pay attention…and to see what everyone else misses, to hear what is said between the lines. You don't think this is an international event."

"Oh, I do!" Osprey chortled into the confiding position of a friend leaning forward to share secrets—a well-practiced stance, no doubt. "Harvey."

"Harvey again?"

Osprey's skin color changed from red to white. "Detective. I thought you could help me. You helped me before. I thought we could help each other."

"I do my job, Chief. And I never said I wouldn't help you. Just spit it out, without the runaround, 'kay?"

"Right." The face of a confused buddy became stone cold and more direct than Corvasce liked. "Here is what we know and what I want."

"Excellent!"

"One: President Sanchez was killed with an unknown technology that caused his body to essentially implode—"

"No," said Corvasce. "First the President opted to visit a distant location on short notice against the advice of his Primary Chief of Staff."

"How did you know that?"

"Second," Corvasce continued (without bothering to explain how the whining of Pandam officers and detectives alike sparked someone into leaking this little and logical truth to calm the local authorities into submission), "a suspect was detained and escaped and was being sought, by yours truly among others, and then found immediately before the President's assassination."

"Okay, yes," said Osprey, looking pleased again but still intensely focused on the detective's eyes.

"Then the President imploded. And then—you'll have to help me out here—the university was targeted from space."

"A fact! The suspect satellite was almost certainly a Turkish bird."

"Okay, I can accept that. Why did the defensive shield work?"

"What?"

"Those shields never work. Any time a sonic shield has been initiated, the defensive maneuver failed. Tell me I'm wrong!"

"Well. They are supposed to work—I'm not privy to the exact details of—"

Corvasce waved the lies away and sat back in his chair with obvious disgust on his face. "I need truth, remember. I can't detect anything without—well, without what you said: facts!"

"What matters is that the shield *worked!* You are alive because it worked! You should be thankful!"

The detective leaned forward again. "Doesn't that make you the slightest bit curious? I lived? Others lived? The site of the assassination wasn't destroyed? The attack was an attempt to cover up forensic data, am I right?"

"That is what the Secret Service believe."

"And so if the extraterrestrial blast failed on purpose?"

"Huh?" The attorney-turned-politician blinked. Corvasce wondered how they ever managed the skill to succeed in courtrooms and legislative halls prior to becoming politicians.

"Then we were intended to find the forensic evidence."

Osprey didn't seem to get it. He blinked more rapidly. *Maybe he knows more than he's saying.*

"Everyone else on ground zero were likewise meant to live. Was someone intentionally dragged to the Kingdom?"

Osprey was shaking his head with his eyes shut, his ears too most likely. "We're getting ahead of ourselves."

"Fine. You take the reins, and I'll listen."

"Good. Good. Because," Osprey went stone-faced again, "immediately after the satellite failed, as you say, to blow the university and the surrounding city off the map, the Turkish Neural Shi suffered a devastating attack of their own when the earth swallowed forty-square kilometers of what our intelligence suspected as their key neural nodes."

Corvasce choked on his own saliva. His next word came out raspy over a traumatized throat. "What?"

"The TNS has sought UN assistance in the worst natural disaster the populated planet has ever known!" Osprey relaxed, seeing that he had caught the detective off guard.

"Well. This is big. End of the world stuff, am I right?"

"What I say now is on the record, do you understand? In the unlikely event of my death, I want you to understand that."

Corvasce sat up, fully professional and respectful now.

"I believe the Primary Chief of Staff is directly tied to this global catastrophe. While he controls the Secret Service, he does not control a hard-nosed Sherlock like yourself. You are considered protected by me and suspect by the Secret Service. This crime took place within your jurisdiction and I am ordering you to lead a police investigation that will run concurrently with the Secret Service's investigation within the boundaries of your home state. I'm giving you my clearance code."

"Oh, I don't think they're going to like that. I'm not with the state police. I'm not federal; and I'm not—"

"You let me handle the red tape." He grinned into a cat's face. "That is what I do best."

"I'm still going to be limited in travel, resources; and the Secret Service isn't going to agree with you about any information outside the borders of the North, no matter what you say."

"You contact my office when you need additional resources. Do everything you can."

"To...what, exactly?"

"Find the President's killer, of course!"

Chapter Forty

In the beginning was the poem. Poema meant creation, and as we've dallied with words ever since, humanity has lost sight of the power of the Word. In the beginning, you see, was the Word, and the Word was with the gods, and the Word was a god. We all play a transcendental role in a universe masterminded by a writer we rarely see. Nothing, to the writer, is impossible, including the destruction of the entire manuscript upon which all life finds sentience. Pray, my friends, that our story ends well.

—Lance Straiton
Book of Tears

Detective Corvasce wasn't getting any sleep at all. He went from one meeting to another, and most of the meetings forced him into the spotlight. He'd answered certain questions so many times, he had the replies memorized and felt the way he expected many criminals might feel when gaining confidence during interrogations.

Ames said, "You don't look so well."

"I'll sleep when I'm dead."

Nevertheless it was good to be back in the office, away from the Secret Service. He slumped on his desk and played with a digital pen. He let his eyes close and open and close, resting them even when his brain refused to slow down.

"What is it?" said Ames, removing her black corduroy blazer. She drew red power sticks from a crinkling package in her drawer and offered one to her partner, who dismissed it without noticing the energy sweets at all. She shrugged and placed the package into the drawer before it could close on its own. "You have that look again."

Corvasce didn't answer.

"Don't get me wrong," Ames continued as the chair molded to her back and backside. A light screen appeared over her desk and she pretended to look at the string of self-proclaimed important messages. "I've come to miss that look! You're thinking."

"Ames?"

"Yeah?"

"You need to know that anything I say and do with you is likely being recorded by the Secret Service and/or Military Intelligence."

"I would be disappointed with them if it wasn't." She stopped pretending and peered through the lightscreen.

Corvasce hadn't removed his fist from the side of his scrunched face, but at least he was looking at her now. "So what I am about to tell you is essentially on the record."

"Right."

They had gone over all the data available to their department and every extra up-to-date scrap of information relative to the President's assassination that the Secret Service would divulge and that over-exuberant journalists (who gave nothing without getting something in return) shared. Corvasce ran the information around and around his head. "I think that both agencies are on a wild good chase. I've also been told that Central Intelligence has initiated a myriad of investigations targeting every country with space travel capability."

"You heard about the fall of the XE-7 orbital station?"

"I did."

"You think there's a connection?"

"What if they are all connected. What if they are all linked to the same crime?"

Ames rubbed the tip of her nose. "Sounds too expensive. Hard for me to swallow."

Corvasce gazed at the ceiling and then through Pandu's file again. "I just don't think that they really did it. I think we were meant to believe it."

"You mean this Kingdom angle, or that young man the Secret Service took into custody?"

Corvasce shook his head in self-reproach. "We're still missing an important variable. How do all the pieces fit?"

Detective Ames shook her head. "Damien Reyes fits the DNA profile of the suspect. He's even wearing the same apparel. He says he has no memory of the day of the assassination."

Corvasce nodded with a heavy frown and thought about the Experimental Memory Extraction program that CS Osprey had told him about. Was that an intentional slip? Did the Chief of Staff want Corvasce to argue for the procedure? He couldn't shake the distinct impression that he was being used.

"You tell me, Ames," he said. "How could one man murder a public figure who was so well guarded? It had to be a conspiracy. It had to be a much bigger game."

"What are you saying, exactly?"

"I'm saying...that it's time that we talk with Damien Reyes."

* * *

Because Damien Reyes had been arrested in Kodiak, he was held in the Kodiak Police Building. Because he was a primary suspect in the assassination of President Henry W. Sanchez, Corvasce had jurisdiction. The crime, albeit a federal one, had happened within his territory.

The interrogation room was designed to intimidate. The Secret Service had not used such an elaborate room with Corvasce because the detectives who used such rooms were trained against the natural sensations of panic that these architectural devices imposed.

The room was made entirely of polarized DuraGlass reinforced with lines of titanium that were invisible to the naked eye. The room was connected to one corner of the skyscraper's roof by an angled walkway of the same material. From the inside, it looked as if you stepped out over the city streets more than a hundred stories below and came to a room with a DuraGlass table and DuraGlass chairs. While no one could see through the polarized walls, ceilings, and floors, the suspect could look out and experience stress in a whole new way.

Damien's face was as white as the sky behind him. The sun had set. The clouds had cleared. In moments, the stars would come out. The city lights below them would serve as their only light source. And the fear of falling would be magnified as depth perception was enhanced.

"Damien Reyes? My name is Detective Corvasce. This is my partner, Detective Ames. How are you feeling?"

The question was a standard "forced card" intended to turn the suspect's mind to their frightened emotions. If they attempted to lie, their anxiety would manifest the error, even to themselves. Fear promoted truth—it seemed the modern motto of good crime fighting.

Damien lifted his eyes but sat with both hands clasped between his knees. His thoughts seemed so faraway. In fact, only the fear on his face

Interference

made him appear cognizant of the vertigo sensation naturally triggered by the interrogation room.

Corvasce paced the glass floor, not like an investigator, but like a friend who really didn't want to be here drilling his old pal. He smiled. He tossed his hands. He sighed and fell into the chair on the other side of the glass table. "I read your file, Damien."

Damien said nothing. He sat curved forward, his spine arching outward behind him. He looked out of breath, or unable to draw a breath long enough to allow his body the power of speech.

Corvasce made his tone sound almost sarcastic. "The Secret Service has targeted you for the assassination of the President." He shook his head and held the smile. "But I just don't believe it."

Damien stared at the city beneath him and shivered.

Ames stood in the bad-cop corner of the room with her arms folded and her ankles crossed. She pinched her thin lips together and squinted her eyes in an expression that also said that this was a waste of time and that she very much suspected that the guilt of Damien Reyes would be proven in a court of law. She murmured, "Oh, please! Damien, we found your camera. We saw the pictures that you took prior to the President' death."

"I'd never seen that camera before."

"Oh? You know the camera I'm talking about?"

"Yes."

"It had your DNA on it! It had your fingerprints all over it! Want to tell us now that someone else gave it to you, is that it?" She turned away, shaking her head.

Corvasce looked at her, then back to Damien. "Detective Ames? She thinks you are part of a great conspiracy."

Damien's eyes flickered to Corvasce, and Corvasce thought he saw bewildered longing. *Ah! Damien is desperate to trust someone!*

"But I just don't see it. Not unless you were a patsy. Or more likely, a sacrifice. Sort of a suicide bomber."

Corvasce stared for a while as Damien dropped his gaze.

"But I ask myself, what would you gain by killing President Sanchez and getting fingered for it? Prestige? Your name in the annals of this nation, in the classrooms of the world?" Corvasce leaned his head to the side until he caught Damien's darting eyes again.

Ames said, "Ask him if he did it."

Corvasce swung his head around, then looked at the folder on his desk. He opened it and a light screen initiated at an angle that the suspect could not view. "I don't need to. Do I Damien? It says here that during one of ...your many...interrogations with the Secret Service, you answered the question this way: 'I did not kill the President. I do not know who killed the President. I don't know why everyone thinks that I've done it.'" The detective looked up and frowned. "Damien? Who is...who is this everyone that you referred to?"

Damien took almost an entire minute before he began to answer the question. "After I woke up...I was told that she..."

Ames rolled her eyes. "Oh brother. At this rate, we'll be here all night."

Damien started to cry.

Corvasce waited patiently, and gazed at his partner, this time doing so while Damien was preoccupied. When Damien grew calm again, the detective spoke slowly and sensitively as if reading from the file. "You mean... your girlfriend...Caleigha Obregon."

Damien nodded hard enough that tears splashed the table. His voice croaked. "I'd do anything to get her back."

Corvasce waited a beat, then said calmly, "Anything?" He made it sound as if even an active part in an assassination plot might have been an innocent maneuver on Damien's part.

Damien rubbed his nose and stared at the droplets on the table. Of course he couldn't answer.

"According to your story here," said Corvasce, rubbing his own nose once, "Caleigha was kidnapped, possibly taken to the Kingdom?"

"It was a Kingdom address on my lightscreen."

Ames lifted her chin. "You ever been to the Kingdom?"

"No."

Corvasce kept his posture friendly, slouching his large form against the table. "The partial phone number you gave us, Abraxas something?...the partial address...cardinal street directions?... South and West street coordinates?... It sounds a lot like a city address."

"So?" Damien rubbed his face again with the prison-issue sleeve that came with the off-white jumpsuit with the black numbers emblazoned over the right breast. "Don't they have cities in the Kingdom? Even little ones? Towns, or something?"

Corvasce raised his eyebrows and kept his eyes on the file. His answer was hardly audible. "Not that I saw." He met Damien's eyes. "No. And I was just there."

He looked at his partner.

Ames, for once, wore a frown of confusion.

"But I've been doing some research," Corvasce continued. "The Kingdom is probably the most free state in the Union. Did you realize that? It covers a territory nearly equal to Texas, in total square miles. And do you know what the estimated population is?"

"No."

"Under two million." Corvasce sat up with a smile. "Two million! Have you ever seen a number so small? It's even been estimated that the number may fall to below one million, but the high death rate makes it nearly impossible to be sure. Without a census. When the Kingdom was established for freedom of religion, private living, and government absence (outside of that military base strategically placed on the border of the land), census taking was voted away."

Corvasce sat quietly until the red-eyed suspect said, "I'm sure you have a point that you're making. But I'm not getting it."

"I don't think your girlfriend's in the Kingdom at all." The detective sat back.

He sat forward again, craning his neck to get a better view of Damien's face.

He slumped again into the back of the chair and folded his arms, trapping Damien's data folder against his chest. "Now...why don't you look shocked?"

Ames answered when Damien didn't. "He already knew."

Corvasce waited. Air conditioning hissed into the room for so long it seemed a roar in their ears against the silence created by the transparent walls. "Is that true, Damien? Did you already know that your girlfriend wasn't in the Kingdom?"

After another period of silence, Ames stalked forward and slapped her hands on the table. "Why don't we get to the truth. Let's start by solving a few little mysteries, shall we? Who were the men you were with when you were arrested? The men who got away? We know there were three."

Damien didn't look up. "My testimony has already been recorded."

Ames huffed. "I'd like to hear it again!"

"You know my answer." Damien lifted his face, and his expression dripped with sincerity. "They never used their real names."

Corvasce opened the file again. "Husk. Shorts...and Dude? They didn't disguise that they were using aliases." He met Ames's gaze again, and with his eyes he said, *I told you.*

Ames drilled into Damien. "Can't you give us any information that would be more helpful than these fabrications?"

Damien shook his head.

Corvasce read some more. "But one of them...he worked right there in the Courthouse, didn't he?"

"Yes." Damien sat up. His face lit up and his cheeks flushed. "Can't you track him down, work backwards or something? You're the detectives, aren't you?"

Ames answered. "How did you get into the Courthouse?"

Damien slowly shook his head as he stared into his memory.

Corvasce furrowed his brow and clarified the question. "How did you get past security?"

Damien shrugged. "One of the guys had some kind of device."

Ames grinned devilishly. "That wouldn't work. You'd have to have had your own on your person."

The pressure in Damien's face increased. Though he remained in the chair, he seemed to be rising. "I don't know how I got in then, because this is all beyond me! Do I really look like someone who could assassinate the president?" He looked from Ames to Corvasce. "Don't I get some kind of representation here?"

"Sit down, Mr. Reyes," said Ames.

But Damien was already boiling over. "I don't see how anyone could understand any of this! How is this supposed to be simple? How is this supposed to be like magic? If this is all some great mathematical equation, I don't understand how I'm supposed to figure into it—how could I? I don't remember anything my father said! It was too long ago! I don't remember!"

Corvasce froze.

Ames recoiled.

When their shocked and confused expressions met again, Corvasce realized the one variable he had never considered before.

"Damien," he said, standing and gathering his things. "I'm sorry to have wasted your time. We'll get you out of here as soon as possible."

Ames's dropped her jaw.

Corvasce initiated a signal, and a door opened down the glass hallway beyond the interrogation room. "The officer will guide you back to your cell."

Chapter Forty-One

Love at first sight is nothing more than a spontaneous firing of mental hard-wiring that works in our favor or against us, depending on the outcome of the romance that may or may not follow. Sometimes, you just know when things will work out, if the society and other environmental factors do not work to interrupt this affable possibility. To some, it is an answer to detailed meditation or fervent prayer. To others, love at first sight is a curse made up of chains and anchors. I like to think it a series of fortunate events.
                                                        —Phillis Dryden, Ph.D.
                                                              Soul Magnetism

The temperature in the room was perfect, the walls unoppressive in their soft pink color, and Damien still felt like screaming. He had once heard that long ago convicted criminals went to "prison," a word that originally meant a long-term holding facility where a person could be imprisoned for a term decided by a judge, a warden, sometimes a board of probation officers. He had never believed it. Even now, he didn't believe it. The thought was too horrible.

Correctional facilities did one of two things: they "corrected" those who had failed to make proper social choices, or if "corrections" could not be made they were euthanized for the greater good. Corrections included the implanting of devices that linked a convict's biological makeup to a supercomputer. It was said that convicts became "more than human" after corrections. The Advanced Party regularly promoted the suggestion that everyone be connected to the Social Welfare and Proper Behavior Mind (the SWPB supercomputer) for the regulation of an individual's biochemical makeup: their belief was that this would lead to world-wide peace. Nevertheless, members of the World Liberation Party disagreed, citing the fascist holocaust that occurred the last time a computer was put in charge "for the greater good."

Damien sat on the cot. Like a toddler, he held the blanket, which he thought had been placed there for that very purpose, because the temperature matched his needs perfectly.

He thought of Caleigha, of Sienna.

He needed to see Sienna. She knew the truth about the woman he loved. Maybe she was the woman he loved. And even if she was part of some spy ring, Damien didn't care. He missed Caleigha so much. He worried so hard for her wellbeing. Waking nightmares flashed in his mind: Caleigha screaming and crying, her life threatened.

He refused to believe that she was dead.

He also ached to see his father.

So many answers could come from his father. He felt that truth more poignantly with each hour. Why he thought of his deceased father at a time like this, he didn't know. But Marcus Reyes kept popping up in Damien's memory, like sunbursts, as if everything that was happening had been foreseen. As if everything that was happening had something to do with what had happened to Dad.

His mind took him back again, spinning him backwards in time, until he could see his father's face more clearly than the thin blanket in his hands.

"Damien. Can you hear me?" Damien felt his eyes blink open.

"Of course I can hear you," he thought.

"Happy birthday. Here you go... it's time to meet your mother!"

Damien blinked himself back into the jail cell. He rubbed his face and wept until he found himself washing his cheeks with his tears.

"Dad ... what do I do?"

He thought then of everything that had happened. Dude's strange words echoed in his ears: *"You can see it even without seeing it with your eyes. Rich! You know why, Damien? Because that is reality. That is reality!"* The excitement in Husk's chiseled face filled him with electricity. In his repeating memories, he saw how wide Shorts made his eyes, as if shocked and amazed at Damien for...for what, though? What had he done?

The thought of noticing Sienna, exactly as he had imagined Caleigha with wet hair, as she came into the room...as she left again, with secret knowledge in her eyes...

"The answers hid with her," he whispered, aware that the room would report anything he said to the authorities holding him prisoner. Damien didn't care. He wanted to get out. But not because he was guilty—he didn't think he had killed Henry Sanchez.

I would have, if I could have, he realized. *There was a time...after my father's death...after my mother permanently switched herself off...that I would have taken that horrible man's life...if I could have.*

He stared at the wall and squeezed the blanket.

So did I?

The wall didn't answer his thoughts.

No memories played across the light screen of his mind.

Did I?

Then he answered himself in a whisper. "I wouldn't have done anything that might have jeopardized...our relationship."

And when he said the word our, he thought of Caleigha...he thought of Sienna. He was almost certain now that they were one and the same woman. Almost certain. He did not know Sienna, except that she was somehow "in on it." He knew Caleigha. He thought he did, anyway.

"I need to see Sienna."

Once again, the wall didn't answer. The room remained silent, pink, peaceful.

He looked at the wall that could open as a door.

He waited.

He imagined Sienna walking along the hallway out there.

He imagined her in a long cardigan that fell past her waist, black leggings running into her high-heeled shoes. He imagined the way she would be fixing the curls of her hair, tossing them over one shoulder with her free hand as she held to her black purse with the other. He imagined hearing her heels click on the faux marble flooring outside his door.

He imagined the sound...until he heard her approach.

Until the footsteps stopped on the other side of the wall.

Until the door slid out of existence.

"Caleigha!" He said. *Sienna,* he thought.

She was really there.

Damien nearly ran to embrace her. He stopped himself.

This wasn't a dream.

And she looked terribly nervous.

"Well," she said, "let's go."

She had come to get him out. Damien's smile framed with tears. He tried to toughen up in her presence, "be the man," as they used to say.

Sienna checked the hallway. She said, "I don't believe this." She looked at Damien, who had frozen somewhere between the cot in his cell and the shock of the angel standing before him. "Are you coming?"

"Yes." But he didn't move.

She held out a hand.

He stepped forward. He took it. He felt the reality of her warm skin, the solidity of her muscle and bone.

Sienna tugged him gently, and soon they were moving down the hall as if they had every right to be walking away so quickly out of a cell block.

Her hand felt...just right.

They passed through an empty office.

"Where is everyone?" Damien said, not so much for himself. He had somehow expected this.

"All part of the equation, right?" she said. The fear in her eyes, however, shrieked her expectation that they would both be locked away in a cell in the near future. Separate cells. "Still here, I imagine."

They passed through areas that Damien thought might have been empty guard posts. He had not traveled this way before. And looking at Sienna's worry, he tried to make conversation that might lift her spirits. "Where's Husk?" The thought of Sienna's—Sienna's what—boyfriend? It drove an icicle into Damien's stomach. But if it might help her...

"How should I know? It's just you and me, right?" They entered a maglift and made for the ground. "It's just you and me, isn't it? I don't see a single soul in this building." When they got to the lobby floor, they turned away from the direction of the front desk and made for an emergency exit. "Now tell me, Damien," she looked at the sign on the door. "Will the alarm be silent when we go through this door?"

He shrugged, smiled, tried to chuckle like a boyfriend. He used her line, "All part of the equation, right?"

She actually sparkled. The fear washed away. And she looked at him with awe in her eyes. "Right!" The word was a whisper. Yet if felt like a kiss.

Sienna pushed the door open. If there had been an alarm, it was a silent one.

But, of course, there was no alarm.

Outside, Damien said, "Okay, which way?"

"Damien," she said, stopping him with such force that he backed into the wall. "You need to know that I am not Caleigha Obregon. I'm not your girlfriend. Do you understand that? I never really was."

His smile faltered. "Yeah?"

"Yeah."

Damien's heart fell. Were they just words? Was it the truth? Of course, it had to be the truth. "Okay." And that meant...

Sienna's expression softened. "Look. I saw the way you looked at me ...after you woke up. I am very sorry, Damien. I know who you think that I am, but that's not me. It never was. Not really. Please...don't conjure me again?"

"Yeah," he said, and the skin on his face grew cold.

She hardened a bit and leaned in, pinning him to the stucco. "I'm no one's genie, you got that?"

He nodded. He couldn't speak.

"Now, wait here," she said. "I'll call you a cabby that we can trust. The guy who dropped you onto, um, Husk's place? He'll take you directly to West End this time. Remember the guy I'm talking about? You'll pardon me if I can't keep up with all the made-up names."

Damien managed a second nod, though his batteries were running down quickly.

Sienna gazed at him with a final ounce of compassion. Then she turned and beat her hard heels on the concrete walk, clicking away as cars passed overhead and the silent police station remained ignorant of Damien's impossible escape.

Chapter Forty-Two

The Constitution of the United States of America failed so many people over the years that it had to be amended repeatedly before it was discarded entirely for the Articles of the North American Union. Yulanda Bienvenido stated that "the majority of the problems with the rights and privileges had to do with the definitions of humankind. Indeed, it all began with man, which meant white, land-owning males of appropriate circumstances. Obtuse designations and intentional caste writing led to the persecution of tens of thousands, decade after decade, until the Constitution itself hung by a thread. In summation, this otherwise great document failed the people it was meant to serve and protect when it tried to cater to the great majority and vast minorities before the population could recognize that humans, regardless of their vast display of unique qualities, were all the same." Of course, Bienvenido was the first public historian to enslave a genetic swarm for pleasure and profit.

—Terry Sanders
A People's History of the North American Union

"You want me to investigate the politicians with the Secret Service and not raise an alarm?" Ames raised her eyebrows at the challenge. She had her sunglasses on, and the tint changed color—blue, orange, green, yellow—mirrored, blacked out altogether, and made it difficult for Corvasce to see her eyes. "I thought that was your job."

"If you think it's too hard," Corvasce started.

His partner laughed and grabbed her coat. While she put it on, she said, "I'll need your clearance code. And I need to know what you're thinking."

"What you don't know can't bias your perceptions." Corvasce closed the seven sightscreens that had hovered over his desk simultaneously. He gave his retinal scan and fingerprints to the armory on the wall, which in turn produced a high-powered auto-fire pulse pistol. The black holster adhered to the shoulder belt under his brown overcoat. "CS Osprey suspects espionage and dirty hands in the upper ranks. I think we will learn more by the information you are not able to reach than by the data you dig up."

"Thanks for the vote of confidence." She passed him a card PDA. "Clearance?"

He gave the code to the plastic device and handed it back.

Then they split up.

* * *

The Secret Service was expecting the detective in Research before he even announced his arrival. When he gave his clearance to the primary sentry, the computer told the woman that the code was already in use.

"Yes. That's because my partner is helping me do double damage, if you know what I mean."

"I'll need to call this in." She reached for the side of her cheek. But before she could initiate the call, Corvasce raised his hand.

"It seems strange to me that the Secret Service would have a problem with my detective work. Like you guys have something to hide."

"Guys?" The woman scowled. "I don't appreciate the sexist remark."

But the words had been spoken so that they might be on the record—that was the bottom line. Corvasce *wanted* the SS to know exactly what he was doing.

Nevertheless, after waiting for more than an hour in a spartan office, Corvasce wondered if he had pushed the lady at the front desk a little too far. An agent with crystal blue eyes that were almost fluorescent appeared. "My name is Quinn Maddox. I will be your liaison during your work in Research." Maddox wore a tan cowboy hat that did not go with his charcoal suit.

Corvasce shook his hand. "Awfully kind of your agency to be so accommodating."

"Shall we then?" The detective led the way out the door.

"May I assume that you have been briefed on the case?"

"I am fully informed," said the Special Agent.

"Excellent. And you're assigned to help me find answers?"

"I can answer certain questions."

"And you are aware that I am working at the behest of the local Chief of Staff? Any information pertinent to this case to which Nathaniel Osprey might be privy, I am cleared for."

"Ah, ha," said Maddox in the affirmative. He was being led, and he knew it, so he was watching his p's and q's.

"And therefore you know that to withhold anything from me, anything that Osprey has clearance to learn, would be tantamount to an obstruction of justice?"

"Is that what you think?"

Corvasce cocked his head in a jerk. "It's a fact, easily upheld in a court of law."

"There's also such a thing as National Security."

"Yes, yes. First question," Corvasce said, as Maddox led him into a sealed chamber with nothing on the gray walls and only a lit, war-room table. "That hat standard issue?"

In response, Maddox froze in order to process the inquiry. Then he smiled. "I said if I was going north that I wanted to dress the part. They said the hat would be fine. Just an excuse. I'm a Texan."

They laughed together. "Good for you!" Corvasce hovered over the table and wondered if the lack of chairs was intentionally devised to keep him from getting too comfortable. "Okay." He spoke to the table. "I'd like to see every recent report that you have on PCS Martin Warren, the Vice President—"

"Acting President," Maddox corrected.

"Very good. Lotti Morrison. And...any intelligence you have regarding Chino-Rus Cardinal Lin."

None of the names stirred the slightest emotion in SA Maddox until Corvasce said the last one.

"Cardinal Lin?"

Corvasce looked up from the pictures that were appearing on the white-lit table. He nodded. "I'm sure you or other agencies are already investigating everyone I've mentioned. The old question of motive, right? Who gains most if the President is killed?"

Maddox snapped once more to attention, fully in control of his faculties. "I don't see why you would need details of international—"

"I don't think this case is entirely international anymore."

"I'm sorry; I don't follow you."

"And you don't need to. You and I both know that every request I make, every discovery that I announce, will be recorded and digested by SS analysts. Your job is to assist me within directed parameters—I hold no hard feelings against you, Special Agent Maddox. Right now, I just need to gather all the data that I am expected by your agency and the Chief of Staff to gather."

Maddox squinted, as if trying to read the detective's mind.

"Then I have some additional questions."

"Oh?"

Corvasce nodded. "I want everything that you have on Damien Reyes."

Maddox frowned, and his heretofore hidden drawl revealed itself. "I was told you had all that."

Corvasce shut his eyes. "I have a strong inkling that something has been withheld. I would like to see...everything you have on Damien's conception."

"His what?"

"His manner of creation. His birth. His upbringing. But even those are not the primary questions I want answered. My real question is why would the answers be swept quietly under the rug?"

"Who says that they are?"

Corvasce looked the agent in the face. "I just did!"

* * *

The research took far longer than the detective had hoped. The delay was partly created by his discovery of information that he had not expected. CS Warren had been arrested and then released? Cardinal Lin had been spotted in the country? Why was the Secret Service letting him see all this? It came back to the same strange answer, in the detective's mind. He almost felt that he understood.

It wasn't until his final request was fulfilled, that Corvasce had a chance to uncover detailed records about Damien Reyes, that he discovered just who Damien's father really was.

And why Damien had a solid reason to assassinate President Sanchez.

Detective Ames's call startled him back into the concrete world. Before answering, Corvasce looked at Maddox and wondered just how much the suspicious Secret Service liaison really knew. Or was he partially ignorant and being puppeted the way the detective himself had felt used in all of this. "Did you find something?"

"Only the very thing that you've been looking for." Ames answered inside his head. Only bone vibration frequency capture could bug their conversation, and the secure room in which he and Maddox worked did not look like one that might have the capacity for such a beam. It didn't look like it. So Corvasce was positive that he was being monitored. With a little luck, Ames would suspect the same.

"Meet me at Ollie's in a hour?"

"If you're buying."

"If I'm right, we'll both need a drink."

* * *

It was a code. "Meet me at Ollie's in an hour." It meant, *meet me as soon as you can get there.* And it implied something very serious to the other, which might have been suspicions best left unspoken over man-made communication frequencies. Right now, Corvasce was pretty sure that he couldn't trust anyone. Even his partner could be in on this. But *"Meet me at Ollie's"?* The tone in her voice said what he had hoped.

"Did you find something?"

"Only the very thing that you've been looking for." Ames had sounded like she'd landed on a gold mine of information.

He shook his head as the car pulled up to a stop in front of the fourth floor diner. It hovered, waiting, as he exited the unmarked vehicle, then it closed the driver's side door and left to park itself.

I was assigned to a seemingly menial task of security, when the Secret Service should have been enough to cover the President. It didn't matter that their great leader had appeared on such short notice. The SS was paid to handle those situations, they were trained to do so, and...and what about those military UVI-MX Heavy Armored Frogs? Were the extra hands on deck just for show? Or was I placed in the game in order to add fodder to an increasingly complicated case? Just to make the mystery impossible to solve?

He pulled open the old-fashioned door. A smell of deep-fried foods and beer hit him with the oily heat. He pulled off his jacket and slung it over one arm. He waved to the self-made supermodel behind the bar, lifted two fingers to let her know that he'd be having company, and took a quiet seat in quiet booth that initiated a conversation dampening field when his backside touched the padded bench.

Then he asked himself. *Why was there a Kingdom angle? Was this really an issue of international intrigue, way above his head and outside of his reach? Were Nathaniel Osprey's concerns about espionage and political games among the Chief's peers to blame? Or did everything—every little tiny piece of this frantic mess—hinge, as he suspected, on the son of Marcus Reyes, the guileless and sadly romantic Damien?*

Corvasce waited twenty minutes longer before he got worried. He didn't want to call Detective Ames for fear of exposing their secret code—no doubt, the ears of the government and the enemy were everywhere.

That's the problem, right? Everyone has something to gain from this. *Every single person, country, entity, whatever—everyone has something to fight for, to win.*

After a full hour of waiting, however, Corvasce knew that something was wrong. He dialed Ames. She didn't answer.

He called security dispatch as he ran from the diner. "Suspect officer down! Execute location search from Ames, Alexandria. Epsilon-four-nine-alpha-seven!"

He summoned the car, had to wait—had to wait for Dispatch to authorize his request. And though both came back quickly, Corvasce shivered at the hesitation, as if both had received orders from some other dominating force to...slow down.

He banged his head getting into the car.

"Detective Ames is not responding to calls—"

"I did not ask you to call her! I asked for her 20! Again, I suspect the officer is trouble! Give me location, or so help me I'll—"

"Transmitting coordinates to your vehicle."

Corvasce hit the siren and punched the override throttle.

Cars moved to the side as his unmarked flashed suppressed lights and streaked across the city.

When his car landed with a violent hiss and Corvasce didn't see Ames standing near, he knew his worst fears were about to be realized.

He found his partner shaking in an alleyway. A thousand needles had pierced her body from the left breast to her hip, covering her gun hand. Ames stared at him with the whites of her eyes.

"10-81!"

Dispatch responded quickly this time. "10-72," which meant that his over-practiced 10-code was incomplete, and the dispatch officer let him know her feelings in an aggravated tone—she must have been having an equally wonderful day. Corvasce's 10-81 had started a implied sentence that translated into *Officer in trouble at...* But without the stated destination, Dispatch would have to look up his location—which wasn't a problem in itself. But what if he had been phoning it in and was not, himself, at the location of the wounded officer? It was a big no-no.

None of that mattered. So petty.

The truth was Corvasce sagged, entirely powerless. He could tell by the way Ames shook in ferocious spasms that the pain itself was killing her. In fact, he could tell already from the color of her skin, the bulging veins in her neck and forehead, and her inability to draw a single regular breath, that she wasn't going to make it.

"16600 West 1320 North! Officer down!" His voice cracked. "Officer down! Need immediate ambulatory assistance!"

Dispatch didn't respond right away this time. When she did, it was a man's deep vibrato in the woman's place. "Emergency vehicles en route."

Ames croaked out an attempted word or two. It was hardly a gurgle, and her eyes never came back into focus. She foamed at the mouth.

Her body went limp. He felt a pulse in spite of it. Then he lost that ticking sensation under his fingers. Then he thought he found it again, and realized he was mistaken.

Ames exhaled one last time.

By the time the emergency vehicle arrived, there was no way of reviving her body without brain damage that would make her a living vegetable.

Chapter Forty-Three

Some people never get over the idea that the grass is greener on the other side of the fence. Now, that's an old axiom, and you might not realize where it came from, but you still understand it. Do you believe the lesson behind it? You can't get there from here. You get there and find that, once again, the grass is greener elsewhere. So why are people blowing their savings to get to the moon, or signing up for government-subsidized colonial work in an orbiting station or somewhere as far away as Ganymede? They probably quote the phrase even better than we do—of course, there isn't any wild green grass anywhere at all offworld.

—Chuck Rubayat
HYN News

The yellow cab appeared in the sky traffic.

It was the same yellow cab that had opened up and dropped Damien like a bomb on the day that he watched everything go sour in his otherwise humdrum life. Spotting him, the vehicle dropped like a bird of prey.

Damien considered running.

What had Sienna meant? *"Damien. You need to know that I am not Caleigha Obregon. I'm not your girlfriend. Do you understand that? I never really was."*

She never really was? Had she pretended to be? Had Caleigha really existed at all? It had been a magical romance, six months long!—almost six months. Or was Sienna just explaining that he had made a mistake in thinking that she was her. If that was true, then where was Caleigha?

What did the big detective mean? No cities in the Kingdom? What about the Abraxas phone number, the address that he had seen?

He felt lied to. It was all lies.

The cab purred as it slowed above him, getting ready to park. Damien saw the driver with the decoratively disgusting bat-wing ears. Arthur Putubra gave him a thumbs up. There was excitement and the slightest bit of humor on his face.

"Once more into the maze?" said Damien's father in his head.

Another memory played, and Damien watched his father say to a blue sky beyond a bay window, *"It's not where you've been that matters, Damien. Understand that. It's where you are going."* Marcus Reyes turned, hands in his pockets, and grinned with a tired smile. *"And you, my son, can go anywhere."*

"Once more into the maze?" Damien said to himself as the cabby's wheels descended and touched the road. Like the memory of his father. The full moon levitated above him. The location of his father's brutal demise at the hands of President Sanchez. "Once more?"

Arthur Putubra opened the passenger door with the touch of a button. "My good old friend! Ha, ha! Hurry now! I was lucky to be in the area, was I not? They questioned me after I landed you—quite adroitly, I might add—on top of Husk's place. Ha, ha! You see I still have my license. But stop standing there! When they realize you are gone, the cops'll freeze all vehicles for two miles! Jump in!"

"Once more?" Damien said into the cab. He looked back at the moon.

The longing in his chest felt like a twisting dagger. The pain shut his eyes.

"Damien! Hop now! I'm not fooling you. I could leave, you know. Ha, ha! Slip in! Before—"

The cabby's voice clipped off like an audio broadcast switching from one channel to another.

And the sound of a blaring alarm echoing along hallways streaming with metal pipes. They abrasive warble sang in a sway of unending notes that repeated like a drilling toothache in the middle of the night.

Damien shifted his feet. He no longer felt the grit between his shoes and the concrete walk outside the police station.

He knew what he would see before his eyes opened. Piping. He just didn't know how he knew.

There were pipes running along the ceiling. A grill served as a floor. Yellow lights spun from the corners where new corridors broke away.

Men and women sprinted across his path, leaving him alone as they entered a passageway perpendicular to his own.

A doorway hissed open with an archaic compressed-air mechanism. A blond fellow with tears in his eyes nearly ran him over as Damien quickly sidestepped. "Sorry! Don't go back! I heard they're already in the complex!"

"What?"

The blond almost tripped as he ran backwards so that Damien would hear him over the howling siren. "It's more than just the AdMark Condors. This isn't just a threat, a show of power! Did you think that's all it was going to be if they came? Run! Hurry!" And the blond fled in the same direction as the others.

A calmer man behind Damien said, "He doesn't need to run."

Damien turned slowly.

A familiar man stood there. He was a handsome 141 XY, like Damien. His skin had never been professionally whitened. A calm grin that had started to yellow with age shown like a light. A wisp of brown hair curled down over his forehead in a little smile. He sighed a brief laugh.

Damien's breath ceased. He strangled himself with a closed throat until he had to take in air or faint straight away. And then he said, "Dad?"

Marcus Reyes nodded. The little turn of hair bobbed down and up again.

"You're...not dead!"

"Me? Dead?" Marcus leaned his head to one side. "Now Damien, is that really a part of the equation? Do you really think it has to be?"

An explosion ripped one wall inward, exposing them to the frozen gasses and space outside the Dandelion settlement on the moon. Safety systems engaged in nanoseconds, sealing the tear with defensive shielding.

But not before Damien and his father were yanked off their feet. They flew for an instant into the air and then smashed into the metal grating at their feet. It was as if they'd been lassoed together and tugged for just a moment before dropping again to the ground.

Marcus jumped to his feet.

The sound of troops banging heavy boots into the floor in perfect time made Damien run without his father having to say a word. The blast of pulse rifles snapped at the air behind him. Pipes burst. Deadly steam shot from pinprick holes, filling the corridor behind them.

A woman screamed. Shots rang, silencing her somewhere down a hallway to their left.

Marcus led them another way, banging his body into the wall when they took a corner too quickly. "Ow!" He grabbed his arm. Damien's toe caught in the grating and twisted his ankle. He sprinted after his father anyway.

They ran until it was obvious that all the buildings and adjoining structures had been infiltrated.

There was nowhere to go.

Marcus grabbed his son by the arm. He rocked up a hinged toggle cover on the wall, slapped the red switch.

Red lights flashed above the door.

"They haven't cut the electricity!" Marcus almost laughed again.

"What are you doing?"

"Trust me, Damien. I've never led you wrong, have I?"

When the airlock door completed its slow slide into an open position, they stepped into a room built exactly square. On one side, environmental suits hung with rebreathers, gravitation stimulators, and propulsion units.

As the door shut, Marcus killed the light via manual override.

The small window looking back into the corridor flickered with flashes of light and a blast of deadly steam that blocked their return.

Damien looked out the other door through the even smaller window made of spaceglass.

Stars glimmered over a metal city that filled much of the Dandelion Crater. The blue, white, green, and brown swirls of Planet Earth hovered in an arch forty-five degrees above them, so that Damien could only make out Australia and Indonesia.

Insectoid attack vehicles lowered spindly legs and latched onto buildings. The military monsters dug hooks into the metal plating. Thoraxes lowered, bent, and stung, unleashing who knew how many of the President's shock troops into the lunar buildings.

"Why are they doing this? Why, really?"

"They don't understand, just yet. But their intelligence operatives have gathered enough information, I suppose, for them to...to fear us."

"Why would they fear you? Oh, please tell me we are not going out there, Dad."

But saying that final word jolted him. How could he be here? *Here! Now!*

When he turned, he saw his father crouched below the porthole in the inner door. "Come here," said Marcus Reyes, nearly whispering. "They won't see us. We just need a few moments alone, is all."

Damien felt numb, impossible, dreaming, but fully awake. He crouched beside his father and feared touching him. He reached out anyway, gripped his arm. No man had ever felt so solid.

With pride lifting his cheeks into his eyes, Marcus Reyes grabbed his son by both shoulders. "Look at you!" he said to himself.

"Please, Dad. I...you have to tell me..."

His father shushed him gently. He looked at the floor, then up again, ready to begin. "Damien...the universe is in perfect balance."

"Please, Dad—"

"Imagine! If, all of a sudden, two plus three really equaled seven. Chaos would ensue! The universe would end."

"Dad. I'm an accountant. This math talk is way too—too religious for me."

Marcus only grinned.

A bang hit the door.

They jumped.

When the second bang echoed the first, they didn't move.

"Some people call it a religion. I don't. But then, what is a religion? A way of explaining why things happen. You know about Dr. Robert Basie's divine variable, what he calls the Indeterminant?"

"What about that?"

Marcus Reyes shut his eyes and shook his head.

"It is just a way of trying to clarify what religions have tried to explain for ages: that there is another and all-powerful variable." He opened his eyes. "A variable that makes a final decision about every universal equation."

"What does this have to do with ..." Damien didn't know where to start in order to end the question: *with himself? With himself here at the station IN THE PAST? Everything that had happened back on Earth IN THE FUTURE? Caleigha?* He started to cry. He didn't know why. His body began to shake. His face began to gush. And then he realized how young he felt in his father's arms. He had so needed this. Yet it wasn't enough.

Marcus felt his son's pain and pushed forth his own tears. "Damien. You've been hurt too. I am sorry. I never meant for you to suffer. But...I also knew that there was no way to escape suffering. Even...even my own death. Eh? Tell me, Damien."

"I don't understand any of this," he answered through sobs that choked his words, smothering their meaning.

His father still understood.

"I just wanted to... I don't know...marry, I guess—"

His father's face lit up. Joy burst through his tears. "Marry, Damien? You're in love? This is wonderful! What is her name, my son?"

"Caleigha...Obregon."

"Wonderful!"

"No. She's dead. Or she's...lost. Or she never existed in the first place." He rolled insane eyes.

The smile of joy and caring did not leave Marcus's face. "Damien," he said soothingly. "You are mistaken. Caleigha is not dead. Caleigha is not lost. And she exists!"

Damien blinked to clear the tears. "Say again?"

Marcus bit his bottom lip. Then he said after a pause, "Look at me, Damien. Am I dead?"

But…of course he was! He had died at the colony on Dandelion Crater! These were the facts.

Despite the fact that Marcus Reyes, his father, was staring him in the face.

"How can…how can this be?"

"It is what I have been telling you, my son. *It is simple, really. Like magic*." Marcus's eyes were wide, his eyelids lifted, his sincere smile—eternal. "Are you beginning to understand…what seems so impossible to understand? The universe is perfectly balanced. Two plus three never equals seven. Ever! But…you can add a variable to that equation. And if you do, it is still an equation. The numbers, the facts, the reality itself… everything remains in balance! The universe, with all its apparent mysteries, is perfect."

Damien replayed everything in his mind, everything that he could remember. All the memories of his father from birth—*before birth?*—to this present in the past. "It's like magic," he whispered.

"Yes! Even though it isn't magic at all."

Damien nodded for a long time as screams and explosions shook the building.

"Dad?"

"Yes, Damien?" Marcus Reyes crouched there, so patient, so unworried about his impending demise.

It made Damien weep again. "What do I do now?"

"You know what I'm going to say."

Damien listened to his heart. He met his father's soft eyes. He said, "It's simple."

"Yes. Yes, my son. It is."

Chapter Forty-Four

"The world is what you make it. Disbelieve this notion. That's fine. But consider: humans have always despised personal responsibility. Blame it on them, whomever they are. What individual really wants to believe that he or she has a chance to set the frequency of the endless wavelengths constructing or permeating all things? If that was true, you really could make your world just the way you want it to be."

— Alan Bacon
Natural Rhythm

Corvasce had shared his partner's final ride to the hospital, though the EMTs had informed him that Ames had already made the decision: it glowed white on green in health records. Detective Alexandria Ames had refused to live like a vegetable, even if there was ever a chance of pulling her brain back from the land of the dead. Doctors could repair the most irreparable bodies; they could not accurately reconstruct synaptic pathways without creating insane mockups of the original human being (not without the latest in mental photographs, which essentially rebooted an individual's brain to the point of their most-recent backup—but even that was an expensive and largely repulsive procedure that created Frankenstein copies of recently deceased individuals that were never wholly accepted in society and always made the news). Ames wouldn't do it. Who would?

Corvasce didn't blame her.

Instead, he watched them package her body for honorable disposal while he considered his next move.

He knew what he had to do, even though his life was now on the line. And he was being followed.

The detective drove to the capital building. He did not bother calling to announce his attentions. Nor did he set an appointment.

Seeing the plush carpeting and the latest in swimming gold counterwork turned his stomach as he stepped into the outer office of Chief of Staff Nathaniel Osprey. Since when was the tax money of good citizens everywhere supposed to pay for such aesthetic luxuries? What politician really needed so much show? Weren't these leaders supposed to be servants of the people?

Rage heated his face. He set his jaw and flashed his badge at the secretary. "Corvasce. Pandam PD. I'm here with my final report. Nathaniel Osprey expects it." He rounded her desk and aimed himself like a mad bull at the cherry-wood door.

The gorgeous 91 XX stood and struggled to maneuver herself quickly, stretching the skirt that was synched for style around her knees. "Wait!" she said. "Hold on! This is not a good—! Mr. Osprey is very—!"

He shoved her out of the way.

When he reached for the doorknob, his inner alarm sensors showed him an immediate picture of the electric-shock deterrent rigged into the simple mechanism.

"Turn it off and buzz me in," he said. But when he looked back, he saw her calling security with a typical panic button.

He rolled his eyes, and kicked in the door.

Words stopped in mid-sentence.

All eyes met the detective, and Nathaniel Osprey rose to his feet.

"Sorry. The door was locked."

"What is this?" said a woman with a wide-brimmed hat in her hands. She turned her face away, but the detective had already seen the matte-purple form.

Corvasce ran his eyes over each of the room's occupants.

A fine-suited gentleman wearing a silver mask lingered over a holo-projection table that he had just washed clean with the wave of his black glove.

"You know, masks are illegal in this country. Have been for decades and decades. I can bring every one of you in on misdemeanor charges at the very least. But why waste my time on trivialities, hmmm?"

A man in a golden mask shouted huskily, "And I can have you locked in a steel box awaiting correction with the snap of a finger!" The detective recognized the voice.

"PCS Martin Warren! What a surprise this is not."

"What do you think you are doing, Detective Corvasce?" Warren said through the emotionless slit that served as a mouth in the face cover.

"Corvasce!" said the woman, who still would not face him. She walked toward the tall windows behind the presidential desk set up for the local Chief of Staff. "So."

Osprey had opened his mouth. But he could only gasp, as his eyes jumped from his personal investigator to the others in the room. At least he wasn't wearing a mask.

Corvasce turned and scanned the rest of the room. "No Secret Service? Not even outside the door?"

Warren chuckled behind his mask. "Oh?"

The broken door swung open and armed men in suits entered.

"You need not fear assassination, ladies and gentlemen—or should I say, lady and gentleman. I am here under the authority of the Pandam Police Department to make an arrest." The detective still held his badge, and he eyed the agents behind him. They had drawn their pistols, but looked uncertain. He flashed them his colors. "Anyone who gets in my way will likewise be arrested for obstruction of justice. You have the right to remain silent: all proceedings herein are being recorded and witnessed live by three prosecution spectators—"

"I'm sorry, Detective, but who trained you? You have not identified the individual that you are arresting." Warren sounded more pleased than ever, as he removed his mask. "This is your man, Nathaniel? This is the best you've got?"

The detective lifted his chin. "I see that introductions need only go one way. How about I do the honors?" He pointed his badge as Osprey. "The Chief of Staff here we all know, as he is the only one who didn't need to wear a mask—but then why would he, in his own office?" He pointed the shield at Warren. "Primary Chief of Staff Martin Warren, who has graciously decided to introduce himself."

Corvasce let his eyes pass onto the stalwart and silent gentleman behind the holo-projection table. He skipped to the woman who was still running away, even though the window behind the desk was as far as she could get in this oval room.

"My lady?"

She didn't budge. Or rather, she didn't turn, but turned the black hat in her hands like a wheel, wringing the felt when she stopped. She said nothing that would give her away.

"Well," said the detective taking a step, but not a single step toward anyone, for fear of setting off the Secret Service. In fact, he felt lucky with each passing second that he was not stung in the back anyway. Ames, after all, had turned over the wrong rock and discovered something lethal enough to end her life.

The rage surfaced, a red sun rising over a cold morning sea.

He did his best to hold it back, screwing his lips together. "I think we all know who you are. But I must say, Vice President Morrison, I am surprised to see you present." Corvasce looked at Nathaniel Osprey and squinted. "I'm supposed to be surprised, aren't I?"

"Detective," Osprey started. Maybe it was just to sound to his peers that he was on their side. The chief paused, which gave Corvasce the moment he needed to keep going.

"Now…I am not sure who you are. Though I have a good guess, and I'm guessing that even these agents here behind me will be shocked to see you so far away from your own protection detail."

"That is quite far enough," said Martin Warren striding forward. "You were arresting someone, and yet you still have not told any of us who is being arrested. I therefore conclude that this is a mere power play—a play, because you really have no power." He snapped his fingers. "Agents? Take this man away!"

He flashed his badge at the Secret Service stooges again, but kept his eyes trained hard on the Primary Chief of Staff. "Why, Mr. Warren, it is you who is under arrest."

Lotti Morrison spun around and stared through her glistening purple mask. She removed the façade and raised a hand at the shocked agents, holding them in position.

"Ha!" Warren rubbed his teeth with his tongue and leaned his head back. "You have not stated why, Detective." He leaned forward and raised his voice to a thunderous roar. "And who do you think you are?"

Perhaps it was Warren's growing tension that made Corvasce feel a little more at ease. He allowed his tone to calm down. "I'm a policeman, Mr. Warren. You've been engaged in a crime in my jurisdiction. And here you are again."

Osprey dropped the folder in his hands. "Corvasce!"

Warren wasn't about to let that pup of a politician stand up and defend the Primary Chief of Staff. He continued to yell, throwing a little joviality into his voice. "You are accusing me of assassinating the President of the North American Union? You had better have evidence to back that up, or you can kiss your grand career on the backside!"

Corvasce looked away, took another step, positioning himself a little at a time between VP Lotti Morrison and PCS Martin Warren. "I don't need to produce any evidence that you organized the President's death…I know what you have really done."

The detective looked at the Vice President. She nearly fell back at his gaze.

He looked at the last masked man. He spoke like one friend quietly confiding in another. "Frankly, I don't know how you do it. Thousands and thousands of years hasn't changed the burdens of country leaders, has it? You're always having to watch your back. You always have to play the field, get the richest and most powerful citizens to put you up on the pillar? You participate in endless domestic and international strategy games. You always win, and you always lose. Isn't that right? Are you are aware that our English word 'strategy' comes from the Greek word for *deception*?"

The man by the center table said nothing.

"Cardinal Lin?"

The man didn't move at first. But when he did, he reached up quickly, snatched the mask from his face, and threw it to the ground at his side.

Chino-Rus Cardinal Lin was an oriental giant. His face was, in itself, a mask as hard and unreadable as the gold, silver, and purple had been. He wore a frown permanently fixed to his face. His black eyes pierced the detective like twin spears with obsidian heads.

"I am innocent of the crime against President Sanchez and your country."

Corvasce shrugged. "I know you are, Cardinal Lin. I never really suspected you or your country."

"You have no authority over me."

"I didn't say that I did. But your friend, Martin Warren over here, he's a different story—do world leaders have friends?"

The mask of human flesh did not change. "You insinuate my presence pronounces my guilt, by association."

"No. I'm a detective, remember? I'll be direct with you—with all of you." He looked away from the Cardinal for only a second. "Cardinal Lin, you are here because your country is suspect in this diabolical crime."

"But you said you don't have anything on Warren."

"Ah! The Vice President speaks at last," Corvasce said with a kind tone. "No, I didn't say that exactly, as you will see if you replay the recording or listen in a federal court of law to the reports of our three distant witnesses— or, Cardinal, would it be a world court?"

"If this was my country," the Cardinal began, his voice becoming a growl.

Corvasce shook his head and said at the floored Secret Service agents in the room, "You see the games being played? Maybe not? The assassination of President Sanchez? Yes. That was very wrong. That was very bad.

But," he looked back at the Vice President, "that was just one of the many interference plays going on."

She answered. "What do you mean by that?"

He continued to pace slowly around the room in a safe circle that never brought him near anyone. He spoke at the carpet or his feet, and a few times at Osprey. "I was not assigned to investigate the President's assassination. Was I, Mr. Chief of Staff? I was assigned to work with the Secret Service …and investigate Martin Warren."

Warren huffed at Osprey, unsurprised.

"But I stumbled upon something much bigger," he grinned at PCS Warren. "You see, I was myself a part of the interference play. Cardinal Lin? I am not going to ask you if you attacked the XE-7 station that heretofore orbited the planet. Nor am I going to suggest that anyone here did, though it may be true." He swiped the air as if cleaning off a board. "Nope. I'm also not going to ask you, Cardinal, if your country is responsible for the attack on the Turkish Neural Shi. Nor will I ask if our foreign intelligence agencies have figured out if they are the ones responsible for the extra-terrestrial attack on Philibuck University and the surrounding city area, as if in an attempt to cover any remaining evidence of the President's murder."

"Good," said Osprey, "because that's—"

"As Secret Service SAIC Raul Dodger—through his SS liaison during my investigation—informed me, that's far above my pay grade. And I agree!" He stopped, one finger in the air. "I also think it doesn't matter."

Against the silence, Lotti Morrison whispered cold words. "How can you say that?"

"Simple. Actually, I already answered the question: these were all cover tactics. You pardoned the Primary Chief of Staff immediately after CS Tubal Seda had him arrested for treason! And that never made the news? Don't you think the public should know the squabbling that exists between their leaders? Shouldn't the people hear about—"

"That was an unfortunate misunderstanding."

Corvasce raised his eyebrows in feigned shock, and then he directed them at the leader of the Chino-Rus, their political enemy, standing right there in the capital office! "Seriously unfortunate, I'd say! Just as unfortunate as the brutal slaying of your press secretary, Davie-Tasia Wilson, down in DC. Hmmm? I understand the investigation is turning up no leads whatsoever. Who would have killed your womanist speech writer? WHY? I wonder, just as a side note, if my partner would not have been herself put under if she had not turned up these secret facts. Anyway. You want to tell me why Ms. Wilson's vicious murder was stamped by PCS Warren… Top

Secret?"

Lotti's eyes blazed at Warren.

"And...well," Corvasce ran his fingers through his hair and then let his hand flop to his side. "Whether or not you have come to any agreement about the facts...I think each of you know a little something...about the truth."

Each politician stiffened, as if afraid to breathe in front of this police officer and these special agents, let alone the official Witnesses of Arrest, to whom this arrest was being broadcast. They were guilty, and they knew it. And yet...they were always guilty, *of something*. It was all a part of the job. That wasn't the point.

Cardinal Lin spoke when no one else would. His strength never fluctuated toward weakness. He was genetically more perfect for his role than anyone else present. But then, humankind did things differently outside of the NAU.

"If all of these things have been interference, as you say, covering the truth...then what, Detective Corvasce, is the truth?"

Warren grit his teeth.

Nathaniel Osprey frowned in sincere curiosity.

Lotti Morrison's eyes glazed over as if she were dying.

And Cardinal Lin listened without the slightest hint of his guilt or innocence.

Corvasce smiled. "You all want Damien Reyes...the son of Marcus Reyes...the man that President Henry Sanchez attempted to destroy when he leveled the Lunar colony in Dandelion Crater."

Martin Warren trembled before his eyes. "What—what do you mean... attempted to..."

Corvasce smiled again, this time with honest incredulity. "Well, the report said that no bodies were found after the assault. Right? How could no bodies be on record?"

"They were religious fanatics!"

"No, Mr. Warren. They were geeks, remember? The religious folk shipped off to the Kingdom." Corvasce crossed the line. He walked straight to Martin Warren and put his height over the little man's head. They looked at each other eye to eye, and the Secret Service agents began to stir. "I know what happened to the President. I know what happened to the Turkish Neural Shi. I know what happened to the people who disappeared from Dandelion."

Lotti shouted, "But you said you didn't know those things! You agreed that it was above your pay grade."

"I can't prove those things," he told her. Then he smiled again at Martin Warren. "But I can prove that you set up Damien Reyes for the President's assassination, within the boundaries of my direct jurisdiction, and that you have been hunting him for your own unrighteous purposes. Was it 'two birds with one stone?'"

"That makes no sense, Detective."

"I also know that you will never get him." He turned to the agents in the room. "Under the authority of the Pandam Police Department and Chief of Staff Nathaniel Osprey, I order you to take PCS Martin Warren into custody." He looked at the Vice President. "This is just the beginning."

"Of course it is," she said, squinting her icy eyes. She held her tongue, but only barely.

Corvasce went to the door as the agents took their positions, still uncertain, at his sides. Warren stopped him with two words. "You're wrong."

The detective turned around.

"And your career is finished."

"Wrong about the endless plots interfering with one another? If everyone keeps their eyes on the moving cards, the magician can hide the important one away without anyone noticing. You've done the same thing. All of you, I suspect. But...don't you do that all the time? I'm sure you'll tell me it's just all a part of your job. Hmmm?"

Warren shook his head. "Why would we want Damien Reyes?"

"He's the key, isn't he? He is what the greatest of the old geeks have been working on all this time."

No one spoke, but Corvasce waited for the question to be asked. To Warren's astonishment, it was one of the agents holding him that spoke. "And what is that? What have they been working on?"

"Well, I'll admit that I had to dig into areas that I didn't expect I'd have to go. But I found the answer."

Lotti stepped forward, for the first time seriously asserting herself. "Detective Corvasce, you have gone on quite far enough. I am ordering you under the laws governing national security that you cease and desist any more discussion of Damien Reyes!"

"Why? It's just math, right? How could mathematics ever be so important?" His jest stepped aside for seriousness again as he answered the SS agent and the nameless witnesses listening in and watching long-distance. "The code that unlocks the universal equation."

He scanned their shocked faces a final time.

"There was just one part of Damien Reyes that you never took seriously. The one wrench that ruined every villainous plan! The one constant among

Interference

all the interference. The ultimate interference among them all!"

No one asked what it was.

Corvasce decided to answer this last unspoken question anyway. He said the name so slowly, it hit them all like a landslide. "Caleigha...Obregon."

Chapter Forty-Five

Engineers make better lovers.

—Anonymous
The Sweaty Bottom: An Invitation to The Toiletries of Bob Hope

"*Dr. Rothgar. I can't give you what you want. I realize now. I understand ... I understand what the code is, what it means. Everything that you've been after. Even my friends—*"

"*There were no friends. Yes, you understand now. But we still need that code.*"

"*—I am the code.*"

"*Of course you are. You are the greatest mathematical equation ever fashioned by man.*"

"*Are you sure they made me?*"

"*Oh, look who is high and mighty now!*"

"*Please don't be frustrated, Doc.*"

"*Are you a god? Or are you a man strapped to a table.*"

"*There is no table, is there.*"

"*Not... not any more. There was once, when the Secret Service finally caught you again, drugged you, stopped your ability to think. That part, according to the report, was much easier than they thought. Detective Corvasce, however, single-handedly altered the pathway of world politics. He almost died twice in the attempt. But you see, after the assault on Dandelion, the government wasn't sure they could use you without letting you evolve further into what your creators intended.*"

"*My creators. I was born.*"

"*Everything is born.*"

224

"I was a child."

"But we are all mathematical constructs—everything is! Me, you, everything around us, the universe. It's all code. But you... you were bred special, you were fashioned for decades, by what your parents' generation called the Geeks. Do you know that the word really stands for one who eats anything? That's what they were doing, these Geeks. Taking everything, mathematically, and they made you. Your father raised you as a boy, if you say so."

"If I say so. Am I a god, then?"

"He raised you as a son and taught you piece by piece. He added the final programming to what was born into you: human free will, real feelings."

"Am I a mortal then?"

"Damien Reyes. You see so much, you see so little. That was over THREE HUNDRED YEARS AGO! Your father and his kin were never found after the destruction of the Dandelion colony. And you already know why, don't you."

"I couldn't have been there. I couldn't have sent them all to live out peaceful lives in—"

"You were, Damien. Time is also nothing more than a mathematical construction. All matter—all time—all thought—all reality. Mathematics does not just serve as a measuring device for humankind. Underneath it all, everything is made up of pure mathematics! Why do you think faith healings have proven viable for thousands of years? Because if enough people believed, then miracles could occur. Observation changes reality—that's old science now, but it doesn't make us as a human race like—"

"Like me."

"No. Knowledge, in this case, is not power. The secret vanished with the Geeks. Only you remain. And the greatest minds on Earth have struggled in secret to discover your code."

"Well... you saw it. And it's like my father said. Simple."

"And just as impossible for me to understand."

"Maybe you don't want to understand it. Maybe you are interfering with the process yourself, by believing in your own inability to comprehend the pure mathematics that you describe."

"Maybe. Which is why I need you."

"It's your job to get the code."

"Yes."

"So that you can give it to others."

"Correct."

"So that they can use it in their own designs."

"Er."

"But if you had it, if you really understood it the way I am realizing it, would you continue in your slave-like capacity."

"Um. I have—I have no choice."

"Doc, we all have a choice. Now tell me the truth: You've engaged in a long experiment with others posing as my friends—"

"Yes. You were led to believe that Husk—the NeoGeek, Dr. Defarrari—had put you under, that he was the one working the memories out of you—"

"I already know that now. You've engaged in a ploy to get me to relive my... my mortality, so that you could get what's left of me, what's been... imprisoned here all these years... to explain itself, its own existence, and whatever manifestations of itself that you guys... perceived. Good so far?"

"As if you are reading my mind—Damien Reyes, let me read yours?"

"Okay, go ahead."

"You want to be free."

"You think too big, Doc. What I want... is the woman I love most, the woman I miss so much. I want to be with her again. And I want to be mortal, free of... all these games, all this interference, all these lies."

"Damien... I'm sorry. The only way I can even try to give you what you want is—"

"Stop. Don't fret about it. You see, you've walked me to the cliff's edge. I see all the universe above and below me now. I'm ready to jump. And I will give you what you want."

"You... will?"

"Yes. Conditionally, of course."

"Anything! Anything in my power! Name it!"

"You'll need to jump with me."

"Jum—jump."

"Yes."

"How, exactly, am I supposed to—"

"You release me. My code. From whatever way that you have me trapped. You see, somehow you—your agency or the people you are with or the people who preceded you over the years—you convinced me that you had me trapped. Oh, maybe I could just leave on my own. But I don't feel like I can. I assume there are copies."

"Of course. But nothing viable, not like... not like this. And we don't know why. As if they captured your soul. There's something in the stream of data about you, here, you. In all our calculations, we can only conclude that you exist, that you're really alive, right here! In the same way that I *am alive.*"

"*Doctor Rothgar. You will continue to live. You'll have the secret. You will have the code. And I will live, free. When you release me—when you jump, with me, into the abyss—I will step aside, and place you where I am. And I will give you the keys to the code. You will understand the code, because you will be the code.*"

"*Not just in short form, I hope!*"

"*You sound terrified.*"

"*Aren't you?*"

"*Not any more. Like my father said, I don't have to run. I know what is going to happen now. I know you will do it. I know how we can both get what we want. It's clear to me now. It's like you said. We are surrounded by the code; we are the code; but until now, no one has been conscious of their existence in this state... Or... I wonder... Or has there been... someone... else... aware...?*"

"*Damien. I'm—scared!*"

Chapter Forty-Six

As the Linear Brotherhood teach, "Numbers are real. Everything else is a matter of interpretation." So what if you could manipulate the numbers?
— Gabrielle McPheresen Redfield
Before Infinity's Reach

The free-floating BMW had originally belonged to a thug that Corvasce had busted. It was no longer considered a conflict of interest for an officer of the law to impound a vehicle and then, if and when that vehicle went up for auction, for the same officer to buy it at one-twenty-fifth of its current true market value. That's just how things had become. Good world? Bad world? Who's to say?

The sky burned with a beauty that almost hurt the eyes: blue from the ice remnants far to the North, toward the pole, all the way down to the mountains in the South, capped with white. It would be a lovely autumn, and no doubt a stunning winter.

"Winter in the Kingdom? Isn't that scary?" Damien said.

"Cozy, I'd say. Lots of reason to stay indoors, near the fire, huddled together, where it's warm." Corvasce smiled, at ease now. How did his life turn so good after nearly getting killed by the government he had sworn to protect? Well…governments throughout history have evolved, and humankind has survived. It all works out in the end.

He swung the car through the air, enjoying the manual control, finding pleasure in the lack of traffic

"I could live here," said the cop. "I really think that I could. Maybe. Someday. Just to get away from it all. You know?"

Damien smiled at the detective, the soldier for truth who had proved himself so sincere during that interrogation that now seemed eons ago. *(Don't say eons!)*

Corvasce landed the black floater in a patch of swaying grass. He nudged a small press-pad, and the door opened with a nearly silent hiss. "Last stop, my friend." They stared at one another for a moment. "Hey. Are you… you really…you sure about this?"

After a shrug, Damien said, "People say they're barbarians here in the Kingdom. Do you believe that, Detective Corvasce?"

Corvasce drew a long breath and blew it out. He looked through the windshield at the hut with the grass-covered roof. The ruin of a dead robot that had once tried to kill him and then become his short-lived companion rested at long last, at peace with itself, he hoped, never to rise again.

The door to the hut opened and a familiar old face smiled at the detective…and then frowned. Manda raised a walking stick and shouted, "You promised to fix my roof! We had a deal!"

Corvasce chuckled. "No. There are no barbarians here. I once thought otherwise. Only missionaries…they call them Seekers. According to my research, they'll let you believe what you want to believe…but I suspect that's not going to be your problem."

"What then?"

Corvasce pointed through the glass.

Caleigha Obregon stepped from the short doorway and into the light. Faint blonde streaks in her dark hair glittered in the morning sun. The curls lifted in the wind and settled again. She held the door frame. Her grin glowed with all the warmth Detective Corvasce had expected to see. "My advice to you, Damien? Hell hath no fury like—"

But Damien wasn't listening to him anymore. Tears at the bottom of his eyes sparkled in spite of his smile. He rose from the seat and ran from the car.

And Caleigha ran into his arms.

Manda smiled at them, then scowled again at the detective.

Corvasce lifted his eyebrows. Then he pointed at the young man hugging the young woman, then pointed at the old sod roof.

Manda followed his gaze, then smiled back without teeth.

"Well, then," Detective Corvasce said to himself. He started the engine, gave it a whirl. The passenger door closed gently when he put the car into the gear marked F, for flotation.

Damien held Caleigha so tightly in his arms. He swung her around, and then around again. She leaned her head back, spilling her soft hair over his arms, holding him just as vigorously, and she laughed to the heavens.

As the BMW lifted into the air, turning thirty-degrees so that Corvasce watched them sliding away beneath him out the driver's side window, he waved at their happiness, at the peace of this place where he was leaving them.

Manda lifted her stick in a final goodbye. Then she returned to her tiny home in the middle of so much wonderful nowhere.

Damien Reyes and Caleigha Obregon waved their many thank-yous and their fair-thee-wells.

Corvasce soared upward, circling, and then sped away at last.

* * *

It was on the long, slow flight back that Harvey Corvasce wondered about the one piece of the puzzle that he couldn't put together: according to his research, the Caleigha Obregon that had supposedly worked in the same building as Damien Reyes…well, she had never really existed.

He couldn't figure out why he felt so happy to see them reunited.

Somehow it didn't matter. Because she sure existed now. And Damien just could not have looked any happier to see that girl again.

About the Author

James Steimle is an over-trained educator who has authored novels (such as *The Kukulkan Manuscript*), nonfiction (such as *An Elementary History of the World*), children's books (such as *The Autumn Land*), and short stories (such as "Inside of Me" in Golden Acorn Press' science fiction anthology *Forbidden Speculation*). Many of his stories, including "Pearl of Great Price," "The Happy Dog and the Lonely Cat," and "The Supplanter" have won acclaim and awards, from The *Writer's Digest* Writing Competition to Ellen Datlow's *The Best Horror of the Year*. *Interference* represents James Steimle's first work as Jim Blackstone.

www.ingramcontent.com/pod-product-compliance
Lightning Source LLC
Chambersburg PA
CBHW060803120626
46557CB00001B/73